THE DEADLY DAYLIGHT

AN ALICE ENGLAND MYSTERY

ASH HARRIER

HOLIDAY HOUSE　　NEW YORK

First published in Australia in 2022 by Pantera Press, Neutral Bay, NSW
First published in the United States of America in 2024
by Holiday House Publishing, Inc., New York
Printed and bound in January 2024 at Maple Press, York, PA, USA.
www.holidayhouse.com
First Edition
1 3 5 7 9 10 8 6 4 2

Library of Congress Cataloging-in-Publication Data

Names: Harrier, Ash, author.
Title: The deadly daylight / Ash Harrier.
Description: First edition. | New York : Holiday House, 2024. | Audience:
Ages 9-12. | Audience: Grades 4-6. | Summary: When twelve-year-old
Alice, who receives messages from the dead, discovers a man with a
deadly sunlight allergy was murdered, she and the victim's niece work
together to uncover the truth.
Identifiers: LCCN 2023021114 (print) | LCCN 2023021115 (ebook)
ISBN 9780823455621 (hardcover) | ISBN 9780823457618 (ebook)
Subjects: CYAC: Dead—Fiction. | Ability—Fiction. | Friendship—Fiction.
Mystery and detective stories. | LCGFT: Detective and mystery fiction. | Novels.
Classification: LCC PZ7.1.H3738 De 2024 (print) | LCC PZ7.1.H3738 (ebook)
DDC [Fic]—dc23
LC record available at https://lccn.loc.gov/2023021114
LC ebook record available at https://lccn.loc.gov/2023021115

ISBN: 978-0-8234-5562-1 (hardcover)

Dedicated to the librarians.
You were beacons guiding me to great books
when I was a child, and I'm still grateful today
for the way you bring stories and knowledge to people,
young and old.

one

THE RESONANCE OF TRINKETS

ALICE smoothed down the dead woman's collar. Her dad often missed that detail. He prepared and dressed the bodies, but didn't always notice things like misbuttoned blouses or crooked spectacles.

There were two items for Alice to arrange. They were inside an envelope with the name *Edna Macintosh* handwritten on the front. Alice slipped out a pair of square-cut diamond earrings set in silver, and a photograph of a man dressed in clothing from the 1970s—flared trousers and a shirt with a wide collar—held in a black frame.

She removed a gold stud from Edna's left ear and replaced it with one of the ugly diamonds. But when she came to the right earlobe, there was no earring to replace. Managing the pen awkwardly in her latex gloves, she made a note about it on the envelope. Her dad would need to mention it to Edna's next of kin, as grieving families sometimes made wild accusations when jewelry was misplaced.

Alice tried to insert the diamond earring, but it wouldn't go in. Edna's earring must have been missing for a while, and the pierced skin had grown over before she died. Alice considered her options. She could cut off the earring's stem and use costume glue to stick the diamond to Edna's ear. But that was risky. Occasionally the glue failed. All it would take was a grieving guest to stroke Edna's hair and the earring might fall off. A mishap like that could ruin the funeral.

And what if the relatives changed their minds and asked for the earrings to be returned? Alice didn't want to be responsible for any damage if someone noticed dear Granny's earrings were real diamonds and wanted them back.

Her only option was to re-pierce Edna's earlobe. Piercing an ear was new to Alice, but she didn't want to fetch her dad to do it. He had already spent long hours embalming Edna, then bending her arm into a suitable position to hold the photo frame. It would be silly to call him for such a simple task.

"This shouldn't hurt at all," Alice assured Edna, because you couldn't be too careful.

The earring stem went easily through Edna's earlobe, like pushing a toothpick into an olive. Alice surveyed her work. Not bad. It was slightly off-center compared with the left one, but no one would notice.

Now for the photo. Sometimes dead people's possessions shared stories with Alice. Not always, but every so often an object put a little story into her head. Alice called these items *resonant*—an excellent word she had discovered when she was about nine, meaning anything that gave an ongoing hum. That was what it felt like to Alice—like the item was humming and vibrating with meaning and significance. Sometimes it was just a little sliver of a story; and sometimes it was a full history of the person's life.

This photograph was resonant.

Alice held it, absorbing the story. Edna had been a married woman, and the man in the photo was her husband, Frank. He'd been quite a stern man, although considerate of Edna. He was a soldier in a war somewhere in Asia, and had died of a feverish illness in a canvas field hospital many decades before. He'd tried to write a final letter to Edna before he died, but was too weak even to hold the pencil. Edna had loved this photo of Frank, looking relaxed on his porch, and always kept it on the shelf in the home where she took her last breath just a week earlier.

"How are you getting along?"

When he was in the funeral section of their home, Alice's father, Thaddeus, always moved quietly. It was fitting as an undertaker, he'd told her once. However, Alice was never startled by his sudden arrivals.

"Nearly finished," she replied.

Thaddeus stood by Edna's polished dark-blue shoes. He was tall and slightly hunched at the shoulders. Alice had heard people describe her dad as a haunting figure, and she found that unfair. Yes, his face had a pale, mournful appearance, but couldn't everyone see the twinkle of humor in his eyes? And yes, he did have long, thin fingers, but you needed to have strong hands if you worked with dead bodies—there was a lot of massaging of stiff limbs required. And perhaps he did have a low voice like a ship's distant horn, but that was just right for someone who spoke to bereaved families every day.

Alice maneuvered the photo frame into Edna's hand, sliding it under the woman's wrist. She slotted it into the fingers her father had curled into a gentle gripping position and tilted the frame at a more poignant angle. *Poignant* was another of those wonderful words she had discovered in more recent times. It meant something that was so sad that it almost made you a tiny bit happy. People often used it to describe Alice's arrangement of trinkets with the corpses, which made her proud.

She did a final check of the cuffs, makeup, hair, and position of the wedding band. Then she stepped back and nodded at her father. "All done."

"Lovely." Her father pulled a sheet across the coffin to protect Edna from bugs and dirt. "Dinner's on the stove. Do you have any homework?"

⚜

Alice brushed her burnt-orange hair until it was smooth, and then attempted to put it up into a perfect ponytail. There was always at least one bump, which annoyed her. Some of the girls at school—like Jasmine Pang and Kimberly Larsson—wore perfect, sleek, bump-free ponytails. It wasn't that Alice had to look perfect—it was just that she liked things to be orderly and symmetrical. She suspected Kimberly's and Jasmine's mothers helped them, which made Alice feel a little better that hers had bumps. She had to do it by herself, after all, since she had only one parent, and he was a busy man running a funeral home.

She washed her face and looked at her small ears in the mirror, wondering for a few moments what it would be like to get her ears pierced, like Edna Macintosh. She didn't like pain, but she had seen a girl at school wearing tiny silver dinosaur earrings and thought they were marvelous. Alice was extremely fond of dinosaurs, and her most treasured possession was a ten-centimeter piece of dromaeosaur bone from the Cretaceous period. She'd saved up and bought it from the fossil and gem store at the Quay, and kept it on her bedroom desk where she could look at it every day. Seeing that girl's dinosaur earrings had made her seriously consider piercings for the first time.

Alice picked her way through the organized clutter of her bedroom and collected her school satchel. She had science for a double period today, which made it her favorite day of the week. Her science teacher was a chaotic but interesting person who taught them all kinds of astonishing facts about the natural world, both ancient and modern. Alice couldn't understand why the other kids were so unpleasant about Ms. Littlejohn, calling her "Professor Sprout" and "hedge witch."

She joined her father downstairs. Thaddeus was the only bit of color in the dark kitchen. Most of the rooms in their house were dark, from the mahogany furniture to the aged forest-green wallpaper and stone floors. This was because it was a funeral home built in Victorian times, and everyone knew funeral homes needed to be somber. Alice's bedroom was the exception. Her dad had painted it a sunny yellow when she was a little girl, which she'd liked until very recently. She'd only just started to think she'd prefer a clean, soft gray, the color of the rainy sky over Damocles Cove.

Thaddeus was reading the newspaper, dressed in his rainbow sweater. He wore vivid colors whenever he wasn't working, since he was obliged to wear dull colors the rest of the time. Alice poured herself some cornflakes and milk, then surreptitiously drizzled honey over the top. She wasn't overly keen on honey, but it was better than nothing. Her dad wouldn't have sugar in the house. "More people die from illnesses related to the consumption of sugar than anything else," he often remarked. He was even strict with the amount of honey she used, and she usually had to wait until he was distracted by the newspaper to get the taste of her cereal just right.

Thaddeus sipped his green tea. He drank it with every meal, claiming it was proven to boost digestion and longevity. Alice understood that a man who worked with the dead might value a long life, but she didn't like the taste.

"Could you pass me the *Chronicle*, Dad?"

Thaddeus pulled the *Coastal Chronicle* out from under the *Port Cormorant Mail* he was reading and gave it to Alice. They had two daily newspapers delivered, and he and Alice read them each morning. Her father liked to check the funeral notices, clicking his tongue when he found a mistake in the spelling or details. But he also read the news, and Alice had picked up the habit.

Thaddeus had a cell phone, but he only used it for work calls. He'd read that the radiation from phones caused damage to brain cells, so he used it as little as possible, and wouldn't hear of Alice having one. Alice mentioned this in health class once when they were discussing cyber safety.

Kimberly Larsson had stared. "He won't let you have a phone? How do you survive?"

Alice wasn't sure why she needed a phone to survive, but tried to answer. "I don't go anywhere dangerous. I'm usually at home, or on a walk, or at school."

"But how do you know what's happening?" Kimberly asked.

"I can get my news from the papers."

"Ew, newspapers," Jasmine Pang said. "That black stuff gets on your fingers!"

"Ink?" Alice nodded thoughtfully. "That's true. It washes off easily, though."

"But how do you talk to your friends after school?" Jasmine pressed her.

"What friends?" Kimberly muttered, and a bunch of other kids snickered.

Alice wasn't bothered. She didn't need friends like other kids seemed to. She was perfectly happy on her own at lunchtime, bird-watching on her favorite bench, sitting in the library, or visiting the school laboratories where Ms. Littlejohn let her rummage through trays of natural objects, or clip slides into the microscope to study the organisms.

Alice munched her cereal and read the news. There was a story about a burglary of several bags of sugar from a convenience store, and another about an illegal iguana that had been seized from a pet shop.

She closed the newspaper. "Is it just Edna Macintosh's funeral we've got today?"

"Yes." Her father speared a piece of avocado with his fork—a superfood, he told Alice regularly. "And Miss Laura Timms tomorrow."

She nodded. "Let me know if there's anything that needs to go in with Miss Timms's body after school." She checked the clock. It was eight fifteen. Alice went to brush her teeth, and came back to the kitchen to wish her father goodbye.

Thaddeus got that twinkle in his eyes, which meant he was about to make a pun. Puns were his favorite type of joke, and he was always on the hunt for a new one.

Thaddeus waved his forkful of avocado. "You avo good day, Alice."

She smiled, but it was not a particularly original pun, so she didn't give him any additional congratulations. Alice stepped out the side door of Tranquility Funerals at eight nineteen. She didn't technically need to start the walk to school until eight twenty-two, but she liked to give herself a couple of minutes to work on her long-term project of befriending next door's cat.

She crouched near the fence to check underneath a camellia

bush. There it was—small, smooth, and brindled black and orange. It was sitting completely still, its dark pupils almost filling each amber iris.

"Shh," Alice whispered, extending a hand. "It's all right. You're perfectly safe." The cat flicked its tail.

She waited, squinting at the cat's name tag, but it was impossible to read in the darkness of the shrubbery, and the cat refused to budge. Alice sighed and withdrew. The cat was proving resistant to her efforts. If she ever got within arm's length, it backed out of the bush and dashed through the fence into its own yard. Alice hadn't met their neighbors, who had only moved here a few months ago. They never seemed to be at home.

Her weak leg tended to ache when she crouched down like that. Alice pulled her skirt to the side and rubbed the muscle. It had a mottled color and two dark veins that crossed the surface haphazardly, like rivers on a map. Kimberly Larsson had remarked that Alice's leg was evidence that she was possessed and hadn't seemed interested in Alice's explanation of why her leg was like that.

She smoothed her skirt back down, hitched her satchel onto her shoulder, and commenced the walk to school.

Damocles Cove High School was set on a hill overlooking the water, and had been battered by the ocean winds for over seventy years. The two-story buildings had lost all their paint, and looked somehow bare, as if they'd been stripped of their skin and now only their yellowing bones showed. The roof was orange with rust, and the windows were smeared with a fine layer of sea salt. When Alice was sitting in class, the wind howled and banged at the glass as if it wanted to get in and rush around to tear up books and knock over chairs. The classrooms were always cold, no matter how the sun shone outside.

Alice couldn't help being a little proud to go there, though. Her father had gone to the same school, and his father before him. There were other, newer schools around, but Alice wouldn't hear of going to those. She had a tradition to uphold.

And anyway, Alice had secured, in her opinion, the best spot to sit and eat lunch in the whole school. It was a bench in the courtyard that looked straight into the principal's office window. It was always empty, despite its sheltered position near a flowering shrub favored by native bees and nectar-loving birds. Every day she was surprised by her good luck in finding it vacant. Perhaps everyone knew it was Alice's bench.

At morning recess, she was eating her seaweed rice crackers and watching a brown honeyeater flit from blossom to blossom on the shrub, when the principal strode through the courtyard toward the office door. His name was Mr. Prince, which Alice's father loved to make puns with. ("Mr. Prince is your *pal*.") There were a lot of Princes in Damocles Cove—she'd heard Thaddeus refer to them as a founding family. Mr. Prince was a burly man with vast shoulders. His muscles bulged so much that he looked like he'd been squeezed from a tube into his yellow polo shirt. Mr. Prince had been a soccer player and then a gym teacher before he came to reign over Damocles Cove High School.

One of Alice's favorite things to do was imagine the perfect coffin for people she saw. For Mr. Prince, she pictured an extra-wide mahogany casket with pale-yellow velvet lining. The handles would be pale gold, gleaming and embellished like sports trophies. The flowers on top would be blue and yellow to match his favorite soccer team.

Mr. Prince had Kimberly Larsson at his side, and an unhappy-looking Jasmine Pang trailing behind. "...highly irresponsible," Mr. Prince was saying in his across-the-yard voice. "Reckless and dangerous actions—"

"It's all a mistake, sir," Kimberly interrupted smoothly. She had so much self-assurance. Alice always thought of her as a smaller, meaner adult. "Violet's got it all wrong. It was an accident."

"And I wasn't even there," Jasmine chimed in miserably.

"I'll be calling your parents," Mr. Prince boomed. "There's no place for bullying in Damocles Cove High...."

His voice receded as they rounded a corner, the girls exchanging a vexed look behind his back.

Next came Miss Goodwill, her arm around Violet Devenish as she ushered her toward the nurse's office. Miss Goodwill was the pastoral care coordinator. She had bright-blue eyes, and tortoiseshell glasses that sat on top of her head, holding back a mass of blond curls. Alice thought she was a nice enough woman, but sometimes she interfered too much in the students' personal affairs. For instance, she was continually urging Alice to sit with other kids during breaks.

Alice only knew Violet from a distance. The fair-skinned girl always wore long-sleeved tops and pants, gloves, and long socks, and a hat with a kind of shade-cloth veil covering her face and neck. Alice, who was curious by nature, had been especially curious about why all this was required, but hadn't managed to overhear the reason so far. She assumed it was an allergy—perhaps to bees? It looked like a beekeeper's veil. Violet's nickname was "Violet the Vampire," and she was as friendless as Alice. Violet did have a friend for the first few weeks of high school, but that girl left suddenly and no one knew where she'd gone. Alice had heard kids say that Violet's family of vampires had murdered the friend and drank her blood. She was sure that wasn't true, but she would have liked to know the facts.

"I really think it must have been a misunderstanding," Miss Goodwill was saying.

"She did it on purpose." Violet sounded angry. "She pulled my hat off, pushed me out of the shade, and said, 'Let's see if you turn to dust in daylight, vampire.'"

"Perhaps you misheard her." Miss Goodwill looked even more upset than Violet.

"I didn't," said Violet. "Kimberly's been doing this sort of thing since I started here."

Alice was intrigued. She also thought Violet was probably correct about Kimberly, who had turned harassing Violet into a personal hobby. Kimberly, with her excessive makeup, her blond-pink ombre hair, and her group of terrified friends, loved giving people unpleasant nicknames. She had been calling Alice "Alice in Zombieland" since fifth grade, presumably because she lived in a funeral parlor.

Miss Goodwill caught sight of Alice and pointed her out to Violet. "Look! Alice could use some company. Why don't you two girls sit together at lunch today?"

Both girls were silent, but Alice saw Violet give a slight roll of her eyes. Miss Goodwill turned and fixed Alice with a pleading stare. "You'd like a lunch companion, wouldn't you, Alice?"

Alice shook her head. "No, I'm quite all right on my own, thank you."

But Miss Goodwill was nodding at Alice like one of those figurines that sat on people's dashboards. "Yes, you would. Just for a change, hmm? Give it a try." She squeezed Violet's arm. "What about you, Violet? Come and sit with Alice during lunch today, keep her company." She lowered her voice. "If there's any bullying going on, it certainly won't happen *here*." She gestured toward the principal's window.

Violet looked annoyed, but her shoulders dropped in a kind of silent sigh.

"Fine," she said. "I'll eat lunch with Alice."

TWO
THE QUESTION OF TACT

AT lunch Violet arrived still looking cross. She sat beside Alice on the bench.

"Hello, Violet."

"Hi." Violet dug into her backpack, pulling out a cling-wrapped chicken roll.

Violet held her veil away from her face so she could bring her food to her mouth. At close range, Alice could see she had blond hair and light-blue eyes under the veil—although they could have been green. She was a round, soft-looking girl whose skin had a powdered appearance, almost hairless, and with little natural oil. For Violet, Alice would select a pale casket—possibly ash wood—lined with lilac silk to offset the bluish-white of the girl's skin. Silver embellishments. And a floral arrangement featuring white irises.

Alice got out her own lunch. She always brought sandwiches left over from the previous day's funeral, but was careful not to take the ones that had been offered around the room. Too often she had seen people pick up a sandwich, poke its middle, and return it to the tray. Today's lunch consisted of one triangle of curried egg, two of cucumber, and one of smoked salmon.

They sat in silence for fifteen minutes, eating their lunch and then staring at the concrete path. There were shouts from other parts

of the schoolyard, but kids hardly ever passed through this courtyard so they were undisturbed. The sun was shining, but the cold sea
breeze whistled above them and rattled at the tin roof.

Perhaps Violet would like to have a conversation. Alice tried to
think of something they could talk about—something they had in
common. There was a band sticker on Violet's bag, but Alice wasn't
into pop music. She couldn't see any sign that Violet liked dinosaurs.
The girl's earrings were tiny amethysts. The only thing they seemed
to have in common was being the targets of Kimberly Larsson's
insults. "I'm sorry you had to deal with Kimberly's and Jasmine's
shenanigans before," she said.

"Their what?"

"Shenanigans. Trickery." Violet still looked blank, so Alice
explained. "Their mean prank."

Violet shrugged. "It was nothing new."

"What were they trying to do, specifically?" Alice asked.

"Trying to trigger my allergy, of course."

Alice paused with her sandwich partway to her mouth. "What
allergy is that?"

"Duh. Sunlight."

Alice was startled. "I've never heard of such a thing."

Violet looked bored. "Solar urticaria. I was born with it. My
dad, his brother, and my brother—we've all got it. My grandma had
it too."

Alice was sympathetic, but pleased. This explained so much. "So
that's why they call you vampire," she said. "Because vampires can't
go out in the sun. How much sunlight does it take to trigger the
allergy?"

Violet eyed her. "Why do you want to know that? Did Kimberly
put you up to this?"

"Kimberly doesn't speak to me, except to call me Alice in Zombieland, or imply that my weak leg is possessed by evil spirits."

Violet seemed to relax slightly. "What's wrong with your leg? Did you hurt it?"

"No, I've had it all my life." Alice pulled up her school skirt to show Violet the thin, blotchy limb with its surface veins. "My umbilical cord was wrapped around it in the womb. The circulation to my leg got cut off and it never developed properly. I've had physical therapy, but it's still weak. The doctor calls it muscular atrophy."

Violet blinked a couple of times. "That was pretty unlucky."

"Well, yes, but my twin was even unluckier."

"You have a twin?" Violet glanced around as though she expected Alice's twin to pop out from behind a shrub.

"Yes." Alice showed her the pendant on a chain around her neck. "This is Saint Cosmas. Saint Cosmas and Saint Damian are the patron saints of twins. The Saint Damian one was supposed to be for my sister, but she died. Our umbilical cords were tangled around us both—my leg and Victoria's neck."

Violet's eyes grew round and horrified. "That's terrible. It must have been so sad for your parents."

"Well my mother left when I was an infant," Alice said. "So I don't know how she feels about it. My father has raised me on his own."

They sat in silence for several minutes. Violet bit a nail through her veil and Alice watched the process with interest. There were a number of tiny holes in the veil where Violet had clearly done the same thing before.

"Kimberly pulled my hat off and tried to push me out into the sunlight," Violet blurted at last.

Alice was aghast. "That was very, very wrong of her. You could have died!"

Violet gave another of those casual shrugs, although she looked a little pleased to hear Alice's outrage. "Luckily Miss Goodwill couldn't get hold of my mum, or she would have marched down here and demanded Kimberly get expelled, or something. Not that that would be such a big loss." She paused. "Do you actually live at a funeral place, like everyone says?"

"Yes," said Alice. "Not in the funeral rooms, of course. Our house is in the rear section."

"Still. Dead bodies." Violet grimaced.

Alice wasn't quite sure what Violet was getting at, so she nodded politely.

"Have you always lived there?" Violet asked. "My dad said it used to have a different name."

It was a lovely surprise to find Violet interested in her family business. "Yes, that's true. Tranquility Funerals is Damocles Cove's oldest funeral home. The England family has owned the place for about one hundred and fifty years. Established as England's Funeral Parlor in 1876, it was renamed Tranquility Funerals in the 1990s by Julius England. It is currently owned and run by my father, Thaddeus England, Julius's nephew, member of the National Embalmer's Association."

"You sound like a tour guide," Violet told her.

"I wrote the About Us page of our website," said Alice. "My father didn't agree with Uncle Julius changing the name, but Tranquility Funerals has brand equity now, and we're better off not changing it back."

"What's brand equity?"

"I think it means that local people know Tranquility Funerals is a cheap funeral service, so we should run with it."

"Oh right."

"Uncle Julius lost interest after he renamed it, anyway," Alice added. "He went to live in Germany and left my father in charge. Dad was only twenty-five, but he worked hard and did his best to keep the place running. I'm extremely proud of him. One day, I'll own and run the business."

Violet seemed astonished. "You *want* to run it?"

"Oh yes. Very much."

Violet took a breath, shook her head, and adjusted her glove. She glanced over her shoulder at the principal's office.

"So, my question about your allergy," said Alice.

"Oh yeah, what was it?"

"How much sunlight does it take to start your allergic reaction?"

Violet assumed her bored look again. "I can't have any sun exposure at all. It triggers my allergy immediately, and it won't stop by itself, even when I get out of the light."

"And there's no way to treat it?" Alice asked.

"Well, my uncle George has found this new thing where the doctor exposes your skin to a tiny bit of light every day to build up your resistance. He's thinking about trying it—says my brother and I should too. My mum's totally against it, though. Too dangerous. Even the tiniest bit of sunlight makes me flare up."

"I see. Is it very painful?"

Violet nodded. "But the main problem is Anna Phylaxis."

"Anna who?"

Violet smiled. "*Anaphylaxis*. It's a super-severe allergic reaction. My airway swells, heartbeat goes crazy; I get stomach cramps and a rash. It kills you if you don't have your EpiPen, or call an ambulance, or whatever."

The bell for their next class rang, and Violet was on her feet in an instant. She started walking off, then hesitated and looked back at Alice.

"That was..." She paused and thought about it. "Okay."

"You can join me again sometime, if you need to," Alice offered.

Violet nodded and walked quickly away.

⚜

"Violet Devenish sat with me at lunch today," Alice told her dad as he finished arranging Mrs. Delia Gandour's hair.

He looked up in surprise. "Did she? You've made a friend?"

"No, she just came to sit with me because she was being bullied by Kimberly Larsson again." Alice used a cleansing wipe to remove grime from a fairy ornament that was to go in the casket with Mrs. Gandour. It was not resonant. "Violet has something called solar urticaria. She's allergic to sunlight."

"That's unusual," said Thaddeus. "Is it severe?"

"She could die if the sunlight touches her skin." Alice put the ornament to one side and started on a silver photo frame. Also not resonant. "I hope she sits with me at lunch again because I have so many questions. I'd like to know how she goes to the beach, and what she does in houses with skylights, and if she's ever nearly died, and how often she needs to use her EpiPen, and if her family picnics at indoor play centers instead of parks and—"

"One moment, Alice." Thaddeus had straightened up and was watching her seriously. "This is one of those times when you must show tact."

"Oh," said Alice, disappointed. Tact meant concealing your curiosity. It meant speaking in a hushed voice and quietly assisting when someone at a funeral needed a tissue. It meant not asking the questions she wanted to ask, which meant not getting the answers she wanted to get. Her father was big on tact, especially since Alice had declared she wanted to take over the funeral home one day.

"Imagine if you had a life-threatening allergy," said Thaddeus. "You would feel frightened for your life every time you went out the door, wouldn't you? So, Violet must feel a lot of fear. Would you want to talk much about something that made you feel that bad?"

"Violet seemed fine with talking about it," said Alice. "She made it seem like it was no big deal at all."

"Perhaps it is no big deal to her, then—but pretending it's no big deal is also how some people behave when something *is* a big deal to them."

How inconvenient. Alice was continually frustrated by the way people hid their true thoughts and acted as if they felt one way when they actually felt the opposite. It was exhausting trying to work it out. Why couldn't they all be like Alice and her dad, and just say or act the way they truly felt?

Their assistant, Patty, came in at that moment, hallooing a greeting and clattering a tray of sandwiches into the refrigerator in the funeral parlor's kitchenette. Patty was small, round, and white-haired, with a perpetually cheery face. Her favorite thing in the world was food and she found nothing more rewarding than feeding a group of mourners at one of Tranquility Funeral's services.

"How's everyone?" she said, sticking her head around the door. "Sixty sandwiches in the fridge, Mr. E, and I've restocked the biscuits. You're a bit low on milk—want me to bring a few cartons tomorrow?"

"Yes, please." Thaddeus smiled. "Patty, you're a lifesaver. Mrs. Gandour's family is expecting a midsized service, but you never know."

Patti nodded eagerly. "I have to tell you, Mr. E., I was just at my niece's wedding over the weekend and they had cupcakes spelling out the first initials of the bride and groom. Fancy that, would you! Cupcakes set out in the shape of a letter. What do you say to doing that at a funeral? I could use biscuits or even sandwiches!" She read the name on the envelope of Mrs. Gandour's trinkets. "Delia Gandour. I could spell out *DG* in curried egg sandwiches!" To Alice's surprise, Thaddeus appeared to think about it.

"I don't think—" she began, but her dad spoke over her.

"I'll certainly take that under consideration, Patty," he said. "I'll let you know."

Patty withdrew, beaming. Alice frowned at her father. "Dad, that's a terrible idea."

"Yes, I know," Thaddeus replied.

Alice thought about that. "Is it the case that Patty lacks *tact*, Dad?"

He smiled. "That's exactly right, Alice."

three

AN UNEXPECTED INVITATION

ALICE half expected Violet to join her again at school the next day, but the only time she saw the girl was in math class, and in the distance during the eighth-grade assembly.

However, the day after, she arrived at her favorite bench to find Violet already in place. Her eyes were on the ground and her cheeks seemed a little pink under the veil. "Hi, Violet," said Alice. "It's good to see you. Are you being bothered by Kimberly again?"

"No." Violet tossed her hair as much as possible beneath her restrictive veil. "She got away with it, of course, but she's left me alone for the last couple of days. Waiting for things to die down, I guess."

Alice frowned. "How did she get away with it?"

Violet shrugged. "No one saw it happen except Jasmine Pang, and she's too scared of Kimberly to tell the truth. Kimberly insists she bumped me by accident. She wrote me a babyish little letter saying how terrible she felt about accidentally bumping me into the sunlight and accidentally grabbing my hat to steady herself, almost making it come off." She rolled her eyes.

"That's so wrong!" Alice found the injustice of it highly disturbing. "I'm downgrading her casket immediately."

Violet paused mid-shrug. "What?"

"Oh." Alice wondered if she should explain. Was this tactful?

Probably not. But she'd said it now and Violet wanted an explanation. "Well, I sometimes like to think up coffins that would suit people. The one I had for Kimberly was a polished white casket with fuchsia lining and rose petal decals—you know, because she's so shiny and likes pink. But that's far too good for her. I'm giving her unsanded plywood with squeaky hinges from now on." A smile broke out on Violet's face. "No flowers," Alice added.

"No—just a few prickly weeds." Violet shot her a wicked grin.

Alice nodded, delighted. She'd never suspected anyone else would be interested in her hobby.

"Do you design coffins for all your enemies?" Violet asked.

"They don't have to be enemies. And I don't have enemies, anyway."

Violet raised her eyebrows. "Not even Kimberly? With the name-calling and those looks she gives you?"

"*Enemy*'s a very strong word. I'd call her more of an antagonist."

"Anti-what?"

"Antagonist. It means someone who causes problems for you."

"She's definitely that." Violet took out her lunch—a piece of lasagna—and dug into it. "Are you busy Sunday?" she asked.

"We usually have a funeral on Sundays," said Alice. "Why?"

Violet hesitated. "No reason."

A boy loped into the courtyard. He had on scuffed boots, a long black coat, and wore his hair in a high-gelled, spiky style. Alice remembered him from elementary school and knew he was in the year above them. His name was Calvin Lee, but everyone at school called him Cal. He seemed to arrive at school at odd hours of the day, but he was pleasant enough. He didn't pull his eyes away from Alice like most other kids did. In fact, he usually smiled when he saw her.

"Hey," he said, slowing when he caught sight of Alice and Violet. "You two in trouble?"

Violet glanced at Alice. "No. Why?"

"Oh. I thought this was the bad kid corner. You know. Time-out in front of the principal's office." He gestured at the window.

Alice was about to say that this was possibly the best place to sit in the whole school when it occurred to her that if word got around, she might not have exclusive access to the bench anymore. She remained silent, glad of her presence of mind.

"Why are you here, then?" Violet asked Cal.

He grimaced. "Late to school again. Mr. Prince called me up for a meeting." He glanced at the principal's window again, but it was tinted and they couldn't see in. "Wish me luck." He loped away.

Violet looked at Alice. "What coffin would you give him?"

Alice considered. "A rectangular casket in navy shimmer finish, with black velvet lining. Wrought iron handles and hinges. An arrangement of black orchids and blue roses around a tall, black candle."

Violet was grinning. "That's amazing."

Alice took a bite of her deviled ham triangle, accepting the compliment graciously.

⚜

Thaddeus spooned bean casserole onto Alice's plate. "I have some good news, but I've *bean* keeping it quiet until dinnertime."

He waited until she granted him a smile. "Not bad, Dad."

He nodded modestly. "And the news really is good. I got a call from Luanne Devenish—Violet's mum. You've been invited to Violet's birthday party on Sunday."

Alice was utterly astonished. She hadn't been invited to a birthday party since fourth grade. In fact, she could trace it back to a specific week: the week when Alice did an oral presentation on the process of embalming dead bodies. She'd explained in detail how embalming helped preserve the corpse and, to help her classmates understand, compared it to pickling a snake in a jar. It seemed to fascinate most of them, and they'd asked some good questions about the chemicals and how bodies decayed—but then Jasmine Pang burst into tears and had to go to the school nurse to be calmed down. Since that time, the other kids had drifted away from her. They didn't want to sit next to her anymore, or to be her partner in group work or ball games. Some of the kids even claimed she smelled like dead people, although Alice was certain that wasn't the case. But she hadn't been invited to a birthday party since.

Thaddeus was smiling at her.

Alice seasoned her dinner. Her dad always undersalted his cooking. "Are you coming?"

"No, Violet invited you. I understand it's mostly a family party, with a couple of neighbors, and Luanne said Violet could invite a friend, so she chose you."

Alice ate, thinking. It was pleasant to have been invited somewhere. She wouldn't know anyone except Violet, which wasn't as pleasant. And it sounded like there would be very few other children. In Alice's experience, adults tended to interrogate you about how much you liked school or whether you played sports, which she thought was a dull way to conduct a conversation. But then, there would very likely be cake. Cake was something she didn't get to have often at all.

"I'd like to go," she said. "But won't you need me here for a funeral?"

"I think I can spare you," said Thaddeus. "Patty says Ellen's available to come and help."

"Are you sure?" She reached for the saltshaker again.

Thaddeus raised his eyebrows. "I think your dinner is seasoned enough, Alice."

She withdrew her hand. "I will go to Violet's birthday party."

"Good," said Thaddeus, and he really did seem glad. "What do you think she'd like for her birthday?"

"If it was my birthday, I'd ask for the *Encyclopedia Cretacea*—it's a wonderfully thick book about dinosaurs," she said.

"Yes, but I wonder if Violet is interested in something other than dinosaurs."

Alice thought about Violet. The only thing she knew categorically about Violet was that she had an allergy to sunlight.

"Some new gloves?" she suggested.

Thaddeus twisted his mouth. "Perhaps something more fun? Does she have any interests? Music? Jewelry?"

"Oh, she had amethyst earrings on!" Alice recalled. "I wonder if I could get a matching bracelet or ring at the fossil and gem shop."

"That sounds ideal," said her father. "And I'll keep *Encyclopedia Cretacea* in mind for your birthday next month." Thaddeus's eyes drifted sideways to a photo of him holding Alice and her dead twin, Victoria, on the day of their birth. You couldn't see either baby, really, they were so bundled up in blankets, but her father's face was a peculiar blend of joy and grief. Alice loved the photo, but found it hard to unravel the emotions that swirled in her heart whenever she looked at it.

"I wonder what Victoria would have wanted for her thirteenth birthday," she said.

"I wonder if she would have liked fossils and prehistoric things as much as you," Thaddeus mused.

"Maybe she would have been my complete opposite," said Alice, and the idea startled her. "She might have liked—I don't know. Collecting unicorn figurines. Or fluffy toys."

In the corner of her eye, Alice saw the photo dip to one side, then fall altogether, clattering down onto the cabinet underneath and landing face down. It shocked them both—so much that Alice almost knocked over her water glass. Her father's hand jerked, making him spill bean casserole down his bright aqua-and-purple shirt. He clicked his tongue and cleaned it up with his napkin, then looked at the photograph for a long time.

"That was odd." Alice pushed back her chair and went to pick up the photo. She peered at the tiny dark shadow that was Victoria's face among the layers of blanket. "Did you hear us talking about you?" she inquired. "Were you outraged by the very thought that you would like unicorns or fluffy toys? I suspect you would have liked dinosaurs, too."

She checked the nail in the wall, but it didn't seem loose, so Alice hung the photo back up and returned to her seat. Her father was looking at her with an expression on his face that she had only seen on rare occasions.

"Are you all right, Dad?" she asked.

"Yes." But it was just a breath of a word.

The stain on his shirt looked like it wouldn't be easy to remove. No wonder he was upset.

four
THE BIRTHDAY PARTY

ALICE was successful in finding an amethyst pendant for Violet at a very reasonable price. She was tempted by a silver-capped megafauna tooth for a few minutes, but when she found out it was a reproduction and not genuine she let her dad talk her back into the amethyst.

To get to the Devenish house, Alice had to walk to Wharf Road through the brisk morning breeze. Alice's weak leg twinged as she paced the undulations. *Undulations* was a new word in her vocabulary, discovered the night before in a book about the world's biomes. It meant gentle hills and valleys. Alice said it softly twice, enjoying the way it made gentle hills and valleys of her tongue. At the final summit, Damocles Cove came into view in all its glory. There was the wharf with its row of piers and anchored fishing boats, the catamarans out on the water, the headland with its dirty rocks cutting a jagged outline into the horizon. There was the half-sunk ship moored to a dock, with streaks of rust like bloodstains. Every time she saw the cove, Alice felt like she came alive all over again.

She had plenty of time, so she dawdled along Wharf Road, counting the piers. There were Piers 19, 18, and 17, and for some inexplicable reason, and rather aggravatingly, Alice had always thought, Pier 16 was missing, and it skipped straight to 15. At 15, it was time to turn her back on the sea breeze that was whipping her hair across her cheeks, and walk back up a hill, along Clam Street.

She arrived at Violet's address a few minutes early and surveyed the Devenish dwelling. It wasn't very exciting—not in the least like a vampiric mansion. It certainly didn't have the elegance of Tranquility Funerals, which boasted stained stone walls, a wrought iron gate, and that venerable brass plaque. Violet's house was modern, bland, and fawn in color. The front yard wasn't much more than a circle of pebbles around a birdbath that had no water in it. Alice didn't think birds would visit anyway—not without a nice shrub nearby to hide in. The house felt like it was abandoned or asleep, with its windows covered by white electronic roller shutters—firmly closed. The only thing that made it look vaguely occupied was a car parked in the driveway.

Alice felt suddenly uneasy. The Devenish home wasn't exactly welcoming. But she had Violet's present in her pocket and the promise of cake, so she straightened her shoulders, breathed in some courage, and approached to knock on the door.

The woman who must be Luanne Devenish let her in, welcoming her in a way that Alice found uncomfortable and a little false. Luanne was a tall woman with too many teeth that she revealed in a gritted smile. She ushered Alice through a second front door, which was surprising until Alice realized that this must be a safety measure. Of course—there were three people in the house with a sunlight allergy. A second doorway would protect them from some careless visitor accidentally letting daylight in through the front door.

And it didn't stop there. The Devenish residence was designed with one goal: to keep Violet, her brother, and father completely safe. Bright artificial lighting filled every corner, but there were edge-sealed black curtains on the inside of each window—even with the roller shutters down. All computers, televisions, and devices had special screen covers fitted. Each external door had a tinted screen and several locks, latches, and chain bolts. Alice was impressed by the thoroughness of it.

They found Violet seated at the table. It was the first time Alice had seen her without her hat, veil, and gloves. With her bluish-white skin, Violet looked somehow small and vulnerable, a bit like a hermit crab that had left its shell to find a new one.

"Happy birthday, Violet," Alice said, passing her the present.

Violet looked as if she was so embarrassed it was almost painful. "Thanks."

The awkward silence only lasted a moment longer because two men with the same fair skin as Violet, a woman, and a boy all bundled into the room. The men were so alike that Alice knew at once they were brothers—perhaps even twins. They were laughing about something to do with a Ping-Pong game, swapping affectionate challenges and insults. The round-faced woman was laughing with them. The boy was not laughing. He was thin and pale, with blond hair and thick glasses.

"There's no red soda," he said, his face gloomy. "Dad said you'd get me some." He directed this at Luanne.

"Red soda makes you silly," she answered, her voice sharp. "Everyone, this is Violet's school friend Alice," she added. "Alice, this is Violet's dad, Eric. This is her uncle George and that's her aunty Helen."

The boy looked wounded to have been forgotten. "I'm Lucas," he said.

Violet rolled her eyes. "My brother."

Alice shook hands all around, which caused some smiles from the adults. She knew not to shake hands when she met other kids but working at the funeral home had made it a habit whenever she met a new adult. Eric was smiley, like Luanne—but his smile seemed more natural than his wife's. His brother, George, seemed mainly interested in tasting the food laid out on the table, while his wife, Helen, fussed around with the platters. She was wrestling with the cling wrap over a plate and wondering out loud if her lemon cheesecake had survived the car ride, what with the way George had taken that corner on Wharf Road. Luanne whisked the platter out of Helen's hands, declaring that she would see to it, so Helen sank into a chair. Exchanging a quick look with her husband, she turned her gaze to Alice. "How lovely to meet a friend of Violet's!" she said in a sweet, squeaky voice. "Are you new to the school?"

"No, I've lived in Damocles Cove all my life," said Alice.

"Goodness, so have I—but that's a lot longer than you, dear!" Helen trilled a laugh. "I met George in Port Cormorant and said to him straight up, there's no way I could ever leave Damocles Cove! No, sirree! All my family and friends are here. And my job! I've worked at the bank since I was nineteen, can you believe it? Almost you girls' age."

"I'm only thirteen, Aunty Helen," Violet put in.

"Oh, near enough! Anyway, I made no bones about it. 'George,' I said, 'if you want to be my husband, you'll need to come and live in Damocles Cove.' And he fell for it, hook, line, and sinker! And here we are now today, George working at the wharf and me at the bank, and the Cove's as much George's home as mine. And now we've got Eric and Luanne, Violet, and Lucas living here as well—it's the best thing for all of us, being so close." She smiled around at everyone. Eric smiled back. George wore a thoughtful look. Luanne hacked at the lemon cheesecake with a big silver knife. Lucas spilled the apple juice he was pouring.

Violet unwrapped Alice's present. "Oh wow, that's so cute." She grinned at Alice, holding up the pendant. "Look, Mum—it matches my earrings!"

The doorbell rang, but only Helen and Luanne moved. "I'll get it for you, dear," Helen started, but Luanne practically bumped her out of the way.

"It's my house, my front door," she said in a voice that was somehow lighthearted, but also quite cutting. Helen slunk back into the kitchen and sat in her chair.

"Who's this now?" Eric was asking. "Who else did your mum invite?" he said to Violet.

"Aunty Gina and Lily."

Eric got to his feet. "Another game?" he asked George. His brother followed. "Great idea."

"Oh!" Helen dropped her voice to a whisper and leaned close to Violet. "Your mum invited Gina Prince?"

Violet shrugged. "Yeah. Probably so Lucas can play with Lily. Aunty Gina's not my real aunt," she told Alice. "She's Mum's old friend and lives on our street, so I just call her aunty. She's lives in that gigantic blue house on the corner." Helen glanced at Alice and fidgeted her hands together. "She's George's boss, too. It's a bit funny socializing with George's boss at his niece's birthday party."

"Aunty Gina runs a bunch of the fishing piers," Violet added. "Uncle George works at Pier 19."

"Is she related to our principal?" Alice asked.

"Yeah, she's Mr. Prince's wife—but she's nice. And he never comes over, thankfully."

Luanne ushered a woman and girl into the room. "Come in, come in! Here's Helen—oh, where did Eric and George disappear to? They know we're about to eat. Alice, these are our friends Gina and Lily Prince."

Gina had messy dark curls and a wide, smiling mouth. She wore a purple skirt that swished along the floor, and had a fringed leather bag set with gemstones slung across her shoulder. She mouthed a *Happy birthday* at Violet, who smiled back. Alice wasn't immediately sure what sort of casket Gina should have. Perhaps magenta, with a crushed velvet lining? She would have to give it a bit more thought.

Gina nudged her daughter farther into the room. Lily went to stand beside Lucas's chair, and they regarded each other solemnly for several moments.

"Want to play LEGO?" Lucas asked.

"Okay."

They vanished down the hall. Luanne and Helen started to compete for the prize of loudest and fastest talker, and Alice slipped into a chair next to Violet.

"Thanks for coming," said Violet under the chatter and clinking of teacups. "Sorry it's so boring."

"It's not boring at all, so far," said Alice. "What an interesting family you have. Are your father and uncle twins?"

"Yeah."

"And they both have your allergy?"

"Yep. My grandma had solar urticaria, but she died years ago. It just keeps coming out in every generation of Devenishes. If I have kids, they'll probably get it too."

"Perhaps you're a modern adaptation," Alice mused. "The next stage of evolution. People are going outside less these days. Maybe one day everyone will be allergic to sunlight and we'll all have to live exclusively indoors." Violet half smiled, and Alice remembered that it wasn't *tactful* to discuss her allergy. "Er, are you having a birthday cake?"

Violet laughed. "Yeah, of course. Caramel mud cake."

This was welcome news, since Alice wasn't fond of cheesecake. Gina pushed a large, elaborately wrapped gift under Violet's nose.

"That's from us Princes," she said.

Violet unwrapped a metallic case with a loopy black logo on the top. Her face turned almost purple as she stared at it. Then she came to life suddenly, her breath whooshing out with the words, *"Moon Squad!"* Her eyes shone as she looked up at Gina. "Where did you get this? It must have cost a fortune! Thank you! I love it!"

Gina glowed. It seemed Moon Squad was a band Violet liked very much. She was almost hyperventilating as she opened the case and turned each useless toiletry item over in her hands, squeaking when she saw the band logo printed on its side. Bubble bath, a loofah, body spray. Alice was glad she'd never been given a gift like that. She wasn't sure she could fake gratitude for a pile of scented potions that would molder in a corner of the bathroom. She loathed any form of scented product, other than oatmeal soap.

When the food was all ready, the Devenish brothers came back from their Ping-Pong tournament. Luanne carried hot dogs and sliders around, somehow accidentally forgetting to offer them to her brother-in-law, George, each time. He made a joke about being on the wrong side of the table, but Alice saw him exchange another look with his wife. When it was time for cake, Luanne cut it into eight slices and passed them all out. Once again, George missed out.

"What's happened?" he asked. "Am I on rations, Luanne?"

"Oh dear, what have I done?" she said, frowning around as if she'd forgotten there were nine of them instead of eight. "Oh dear. And I've already taken a bite out of mine—I'm so sorry, George!"

"It's all right," Helen said with a nervous laugh. "I can share with George."

"Mum," Violet said, glaring.

"What? It was an accident!" Luanne declared.

Eric went and murmured to Luanne in a corner of the kitchen, where they appeared to have a low argument. Helen seemed upset, and when she passed her slice of birthday cake to George he was frowning.

"You have it, Cherry-Bomb. I'm quite happy with your cheese-cake, anyway. It's less *bitter.*"

Alice didn't detect any bitterness in the mud cake, but she supposed everyone had different tastes. Her father had advised her to leave within half an hour of the birthday cake. *That's the sign,* he'd told her. *The birthday cake is the sign that the party is coming to an end.* Alice was well and truly ready to go. Meeting all these new people and answering questions about school had worn her out—not to mention the peculiar atmosphere of tension between Luanne and George.

⚜

In the morning, Alice left home at eight nineteen to spend three minutes attempting to coax the neighbor's cat out from under the camellia. It seemed as watchful as ever, and dashed away in terror when Alice accidentally scraped her satchel on the ground.

Violet wasn't at school that day. Alice wondered if she had ended up with a stomachache from all the cakes and treats. Or maybe she'd tried out those smelly Moon Squad potions from Gina Prince and ended up with a skin rash. But when Alice arrived home in the afternoon, her father met her in the kitchen, his face grave.

"I have some sad news relating to the Devenish family," he said, and Alice got a strange, foreboding feeling deep in the pit of her stomach.

"Is Violet all right?" she asked.

"Yes, Violet's fine. But her uncle, George Devenish, was working at the fishing pier early this morning and was exposed to sunlight. He suffered a terrible allergic reaction, and I'm sorry to say he died."

There was a sharp sound nearby that made them both jump. The photograph of baby Alice and baby Victoria had fallen off the wall again.

five

AN UNTIMELY DEMISE

ALICE finished reading an article about George Devenish's death in the *Port Cormorant Mail* and sighed, pushing the newspaper away. It had been a week since the man died. Violet had come back to school mid-week, but she was remote and quiet, and obviously hadn't felt like socializing. Alice had barely seen her. The funeral was scheduled for Sunday.

She looked across the table at her dad. "It was peculiar—the way Mr. Devenish died. Don't you think?"

"A sad accident," said her father.

She nodded. "But it was an odd thing for George to do. To sit on the end of the dock at dawn."

Thaddeus tipped his head. "Well, he was working the night shift at the pier, and he left it too late to run for cover. It's been ruled a 'death by misadventure.'"

"Yes," said Alice. "I know the facts. But why would he sit out there on the end of the dock without any protection when he knew the sun was coming up?"

Thaddeus had no answer.

"His phone was missing, wasn't it?" she added.

"Yes. The police think he must have dropped it into the sea when he started to feel ill."

"Hmm," said Alice. She ate her breakfast meditatively. "I wonder what Violet thinks about her uncle waiting on the end of the dock for the sun to come up."

"Ah, but that would not be a tactful question to ask," Thaddeus said, meeting her eyes.

Alice nodded. *Tact.* What a nuisance.

Alice had always thought that the funeral home foyer was an elegant room. There was a red velvet curtain that stretched all the way across the room, dividing the foyer from the area where services were held. The walls were papered in a pale-gray fleur-de-lis pattern that, when you looked closer, was a little frayed at the joins. But from a distance it looked fine. Big brass floor vases of floral arrangements sat here and there around the room, and there was a polished wooden sideboard for refreshments.

The best thing about the room was a great cast-iron chandelier set with dozens of little yellow bulbs. The wiring in their house was elderly, so the lights often blew, which meant Thaddeus had to fetch their extra-long ladder and change the bulbs at least once a month. Alice had always admired the vast chandelier, even if she never stood under it for fear of it dropping on her head and killing her.

Alice stood with a handful of In Memoriam booklets, watching the mourners mingle. Thaddeus was chatting with Violet's father over by the curtain. Violet and Lucas were standing with their mother, looking pinched and fearful.

People often seemed to look that way at funerals, Alice thought. Helen was being comforted by a friend.

Thaddeus and Eric approached Alice. "Mr. Devenish has brought a small item of significance to place with his brother in the casket," Thaddeus told her. "Will you assist?" Alice placed the booklets on the sideboard and turned expectantly to Eric Devenish. His eyes were red-rimmed beneath his veil, his brow heavy with sadness. He reached into his pocket and pulled out something wrapped in tissue paper. He pressed it into Alice's hand.

"I had the red truck and George had this," said Eric, his voice cracking. He fidgeted with his veil so he could insert a hand and wipe his eyes. "We loved them, as kids. Our favorite things."

"I'll place it with George right away," Alice said, using the sympathetic tone she'd learned from her father.

"Thank you." Eric sniffed wetly.

Her heart squeezed for Eric. She felt an odd sense of connection; she had also lost a twin, even if she'd never had a chance to get to know her. Thaddeus nodded at Alice, and as soon as Eric had released the object into her hand, she moved away, slipping through the curtain into the room where the casket sat. The service was scheduled to commence in just a few minutes, so she had no time to waste.

Alice carefully lifted the large arrangement of lilies and fern fronds off the polished pine casket. They were artificial flowers, reused regularly, because Tranquility Funerals was never extravagant. Reusing flower arrangements was one of the ways they kept their funerals cheap. She unlatched and opened the casket.

George had raised bumps on his face and neck that must have been a severe rash of hives before his death.

They weren't red now, but Alice thought they probably had been. The poor man must have been in terrible pain when he died.

She peeled the tissue paper away from the parcel Eric had given her to reveal a die-cast toy boat in scratched metallic green. It was clearly quite old—and it was resonant.

The little boat held the story of George, a man married to a kind woman who tended to talk too much about small things that had happened during her day. He loved her, but occasionally wished she would shut up. George had always wanted to be a sailor. He adored the creak and pitch of boats, the gentle slap of waves against fiberglass, the rocking motion of the waves, and the blast of sea air against the skin. But his condition stood in the way. He couldn't be trained—who would train a man with a sunlight allergy to drive a boat? Who would employ a sailor who could only work at night?

George got a job as a wharf security officer and took the night watch, listening to the waves against the sides of the boats moored at Pier 19. He directed incoming vessels to vacant moorings, and argued with the captains when they tried to drop anchor in places they were not permitted. He made sure the teenagers who hung around the dock stayed out of mischief. And he always felt a little sorry for the fish gasping their dying breaths when he checked the hauls coming onto the pier.

On the last morning of his life, George stood on the dock, shining his flashlight into the dark water. He was waiting impatiently for a fishing boat. He checked his wristwatch. Soon the sun would rise. He really needed to get back to the manager's hut and get his protective clothing on. There was a ruckus coming from under the dock—music and laughter—and George turned, running his flashlight over the planks, shining it down the gaps. Lights. Purple, red, yellow, purple, green, purple. The boat chugged in toward the dock. Again, the purple light. The story faded as Alice placed the toy boat into the casket. She tucked it under George's hand so that he was almost holding it. The flesh of his hand was covered in the colorless bumps too. She closed the casket lid and re-placed the flowers.

When Alice turned, she caught a twitch in the curtain and the quick withdrawal of a figure. She thought it might have been Violet.

Alice went back to the foyer and resumed handing out booklets.

Her father took his turn to duck into the service room, and a moment later the red curtains opened. That was her signal to start her next tasks: guiding latecomers to their seats, ensuring tissue boxes were available when required, and then waiting at the side of the room with a basket of rosemary cuttings. This could be tiresome because of her bad leg. Her father had told her she was allowed to sit down, but Alice thought it was more respectful to stand.

The service went on much as usual. Thaddeus gave a speech describing George's life, then there were one or two readings, and finally a photographic slideshow. Alice recognized the other Devenishes from the photos and felt a pang of sadness when a picture of George, smiling beneath a ship captain's hat, popped up on the screen. She checked on Violet and Lucas, who were sitting with Luanne, Eric, and Helen in the front row. Luanne was straight-backed, looking blankly at Thaddeus while he spoke. Eric appeared hunched and miserable, Lucas leaned close against him. Violet kept pulling her veil out from her face to wipe tears, and Helen Devenish sobbed openly for her dead husband. Principal and Gina Prince were there, as well—no Lily.

Alice knew people often decided that children shouldn't attend funerals, as if death were something that should only be acknowledged when you reached a certain age. Then you could learn the truth, in the same way you learned what really happened to your baby teeth after they fell out. *Mr. Prince must be wearing a specially made black suit,* she thought. There was no way his muscly arms would squeeze into a normal one. Gina was clutching her husband's hand and holding a tissue to her eyes.

At the end of the service, Alice went along the rows of seats with her rosemary sprigs, offering them to the mourners. Most people took one, then lined up at the casket, murmuring to one another.

Violet had been sitting having a low conversation with her brother, and looked up when Alice arrived in front her, offering the basket.

"I'm sorry for your loss, Violet," said Alice. "Would you like to take a sprig of rosemary to place on the casket? It represents remembrance."

Violet looked around at her mother, who took one herself and nodded encouragingly. Violet chose one and Lucas followed suit.

Alice moved away and watched the mourners in the line. It was the moment of the final farewell—often a time when people sobbed and embraced, knowing the deceased was definitely in the box and really, truly gone. She had sympathy for them, but Alice was accustomed to seeing people grieve, so more than anything she was curious. Who was overcome with sorrow? Who refused to cry? Who looked bored and surreptitiously checked their phone? Who kept one eye on the post-service tea table, determined to get one of the few good chocolate biscuits before they all went?

Violet stood in the line of mourners with Eric, Luanne, and Lucas, shuffling forward whenever someone moved on. When it was her turn, she rested her hand on the pale wooden lid for a moment before placing her sprig of rosemary, then turned and followed her mother. Her face seemed as still and pale as the corpse's.

Thaddeus caught Alice's eye—another signal. She slipped through the curtain into the foyer where Patty had laid out the platters. First, she and Patty stood back and watched as the funeral-goers poured out of the service room for drinks and snacks. After the initial self-serve rush dispersed, Thaddeus drew the big red curtains so that people could try to forget they were in the same room as a corpse, then Alice went to work. She took around plates of biscuits and sandwiches, while Patty refreshed people's tea and coffee from decanters. Lucas claimed four chocolate biscuits before his mother caught him and told him no more.

Alice was too busy to stop and speak to Violet before the family left. There would probably be some kind of party back at Helen's or Luanne's house, although no one ever called it a party, on account of it being for a dead person. But Alice had been to this sort of event, and knew it involved food and drink, people gathering, and lots of chatter, which in her opinion made it a party. She waved at Violet as the family headed out the door, and Violet waved back. She hoped Violet would meet her at the good bench at school tomorrow.

SIX

POSTHUMOUS PONDERINGS

ALICE thought a lot about George Devenish's death that evening, increasingly troubled by what she had learned from his little green boat. Why had he stayed outside when he knew the dawn was coming? There had been at least one boat coming into the dock, as well as noises and colored lights from beneath it, which indicated people were around. Why hadn't anyone tried to help George? And what could possibly distract a man to the extent that he failed to protect himself from the life-threatening rays of the sun?

Alice also had questions about the allergy. She would have thought that only the direct rays of the sun would do any damage—not the soft dawn light. She used her father's old desktop computer to undertake some Internet research, but the information was all about the symptoms and causes of the condition. The amount of light someone with the allergy could stand probably varied from person to person. Her next step was to read every article she could find about George Devenish's death, but she didn't find out anything more than she already knew. The journalists seemed fascinated by the rare allergic condition and went into detail about the symptoms triggered by sunlight, ranging from mild (nausea and an itchy rash) to severe (swollen throat and heart failure). They said nothing about any witnesses. They quoted an allergy doctor who explained that

George had most likely suffered a mild reaction at first, and he sat down on the dock to try to recover. Then he was ravaged with more symptoms as the sun rose, getting worse and worse until his heart stopped beating. This theory matched the evidence of a coworker who found George's body when he arrived to start work.

Alice puzzled over it. What had happened to the people making noise under the dock? And the workers on the boat? Had none of them noticed George was in trouble? George knew he would only get worse sitting out in the sunlight. Why didn't he run for cover or call out for help? At recess, there was no sign of Violet. But at lunchtime, when Alice arrived at her bench, Violet was there, pulling her lunch out of her backpack. "Hey," she greeted Alice.

"Hello, Violet," said Alice. "I'm glad to see you."

Violet went a little pink under her veil and didn't seem to know what to say. She took a bite of her ham roll instead. "May I ask a question about solar urticaria?" said Alice, trying to push as much tact into the question as possible.

Violet assumed her bored look. "Sure."

Alice sat down beside Violet. "Is it only sunlight that triggers a reaction?"

"It's UVB light. That's what makes me react. It's in sunlight, but it can be in other lights too. That's why I have to wear all this gear, even indoors."

"What about at home?" Alice asked.

"We've got safe lighting at home, obviously. If we didn't, we'd have to do everything in the dark."

"I see," said Alice, noting the sardonic tone in Violet's voice. She should probably stop asking questions. Soon. "And was that the same for—" Alice stopped herself, her father's warning about *tact* jumping into her head. "Is it the same for everyone in your family?"

Violet narrowed her eyes and lowered her ham roll. "Are you asking about Uncle George?"

Alice felt awkward, but also a little relieved. Skirting around a subject did not come naturally. "Yes. I'm sorry if that's not tactful."

"Didn't your dad tell you how he died?"

"I read it in the news," Alice said. "But none of the newspapers provided the details."

Violet frowned. "Why do you want details?"

Alice hesitated, not sure how to explain.

"Has Kimberly been asking—"

Alice shook her head. "No, this has nothing to do with Kimberly."

Violet still wore that suspicious gaze. "Alice, at the funeral, what were you doing at the coffin? I saw you open it and do something to Uncle George's body."

Her father might not approve, but an instinct deep inside made Alice speak the truth anyway.

"Your father gave me George's little toy boat to place in the casket—and Violet, I must tell you that I'm not convinced your uncle died a natural death."

Violet stared open-mouthed.

Alice waited for Violet's shock to pass.

After about a minute, Violet released a long breath. Her thumbnail found its way to her mouth and she nibbled it through the veil. "What do you mean it wasn't a natural death? That's crazy."

"I mean there is a possibility there were circumstances or persons that contributed to the untimely death of your uncle."

Violet said nothing.

"I'm sorry," Alice added. "I don't like to be the bearer of bad news."

Violet transferred her gaze to the shrub and continued to say nothing.

"I hope it's not too upsetting to hear this."

Violet gave a short laugh. "No, why would I be upset to hear that my uncle got murdered?"

Alice could see Violet was rattled and put a steadying hand on the girl's arm. "Are you all right?"

Violet shook her off, but didn't cry or walk away like Alice thought she might. She just rewrapped her ham roll and sat in silent thought. Alice wanted to speak but couldn't think of a thing to say. The minutes ticked by and she ate her sandwiches. They were left over from George Devenish's funeral, which made her feel somehow even more apologetic. Not a word passed between them. Violet fiddled with a key ring on her bag that Alice now recognized was the black logo of Moon Squad.

Finally, the bell rang. Violet stood up and shouldered her backpack.

"I'll see you tomorrow," said Alice. Violet only shrugged and hurried away.

⚜

Alice felt uneasy all afternoon. She hoped what she'd said wouldn't upset the Devenish family too much. But that was ridiculous—of course they would be upset. Who wouldn't be upset to hear their loved one had died under suspicious circumstances?

It couldn't be helped. Alice hitched her satchel onto her shoulder and made her way home. Her father was hard at work in the embalming room, so Alice changed out of her school clothes and did her English homework, but she felt restless. She wrote a note saying she had gone for a walk, and left it propped against the kettle for her father to find. Outside, she checked the yard for the orange-and-black cat, but it was nowhere to be seen. Alice started the walk to the wharf.

The wind was as strong as always, blasting fine grit into her eyes.

She walked against it, invigorated. The ocean came into view and Alice paused to glory in the sight. The sky was a pale-gray glare, the ocean a choppy dark blue. The lighthouse at the end of the headland seemed to gaze out over the water, yearning for sunken ships to make it home.

Alice reached the bottom of the hill. Pier 19 sat directly across the road, its gates open. This was where George Devenish had worked—and where he'd died.

She crossed the road and slipped through the gates, taking in the familiar sights. Metal sea containers stacked in towers, graffiti on the manager's hut wall, and fishing boats heaving on the swell. When Alice visited the pier, which she did pretty often, she usually found herself a good vantage point to watch the wharf staff and fishermen at work. They used mechanical arms to swing their daily hauls of crabs, crayfish, and mussels off the vessels. When she'd had enough of that, she would walk along the small beach, or sit and observe the seabirds from a limestone stairway built by convicts more than a hundred years ago.

She stopped at the jetty where George's body had been discovered. It was medium in length—constructed from wood planks that had grown gray and smooth with age. There was nothing special about it. There hadn't been much rain in recent weeks, so seabird droppings decorated every available space. A solitary man was hunched on a small folding stool, holding a fishing line over the edge.

Alice walked out onto the wooden boards. Her heart always jumped when the rocks and sand under the walkway vanished and the dark gleam of water appeared through the cracks beneath her. That moment was pure exhilaration: to be suspended on slivers of wood above the ocean. It was like a cheeky laugh at the wild, devious sea.

She passed the fisherman, but he didn't even look up. Alice checked the bucket at his feet to see if he'd caught anything. There was only a blowfish in there, its dead eye staring up at the sky. She wondered if the man knew blowfish were no good to eat.

She continued walking until she reached the spot where George must have been found. It was a kind of bench, or step, built into the end of the jetty. A teddy bear in a sailor's hat had been tied to the post with a piece of rope, and below it R.I.P. was chalked onto the wood. The teddy had a mournful face, and the way it was tied to the post reminded Alice of a captive. She touched it, just in case it was resonant, but felt nothing but damp, salt-crusted fur on her fingers.

Alice took a seat where George had died and looked around. Directly ahead was the mouth of the cove. A fishing boat was chugging in. At one of the bigger piers, a giant stevedore crane was loading sea containers onto a ship. She could just make out the name painted on the crane's cabin: CARRIE. She stored the pun in her head to tell her father later. To her left was the manager's hut for Pier 19, and beyond that a little beach that ended in a rocky groyne. Alice stood up again and adjusted the teddy, which was hanging at a crooked angle.

"Leave that alone, please," came a voice behind her.

Alice turned. It was a tall man in the blue uniform of pier security—not a young man, but not as old as her father. Alice remembered seeing him at George's funeral. He had a drooping ginger mustache that gave him a slightly morose appearance. In one hand, he held a long black flashlight, although it was still daytime; the other hand rested on his belt.

"It's for George Devenish, I know," she said. "I wasn't going to move it."

He stepped closer, examining Alice. "Are you his…no, you're not his niece," he said, and it sounded like an accusation.

"I wouldn't be able to be out in the sun if I was Violet, but I do go to school with her," she said.

The man practically flinched at her words. He glanced at the teddy bear again.

"Did you know George well?" Alice heard her father's sympathetic tone creep into her voice.

"I worked with him for the last fifteen years."

"I'm sorry for your loss." Alice read the name tag stitched onto the man's uniform. "Mr. Higginson."

He gave her a quick smile. "People call me Higgo." He squinted at her. "You were at George's funeral, weren't you? You a family friend?"

"I work at Tranquility Funerals."

"Oh!" Higgo raised his eyebrows. "You seem a bit young for that."

"My family owns the funeral business."

He covered up a momentary look of horror, but Alice was used to that.

"Are there usually many people around the dock at dawn?" she asked.

"What?"

"People. Around or under the dock at sunrise."

He stared, then ran a hand through his thinning hair. "Look, it's best you come away from the end of the dock, miss."

"Alice."

"What?"

"My name is Alice."

Higgo frowned. "All right, then, Alice. Off you go."

Alice considered arguing. As far as she could see, she had as much right to be there as the fisherman. But Higgo was in charge of security at Pier 19, and if she made a fuss he might see to it that she was not allowed back. She maneuvered around him and headed back along the boardwalk. When she passed the fisherman, there was a second blowfish in the bucket.

Alice went down the limestone steps to the beach and examined a pile of debris for ocean treasures. There were several cuttlefish skeletons, some frayed blue rope, a sponge, and some delicate white filigree weed. She nudged the pile with her shoe and teased out a piece of green glass. Sometimes she found beautiful sea glass, edges worn smooth and round by the ocean. This piece was sharp—a shard of broken bottle, perhaps. Alice kept walking.

Farther along the beach, a group of four teenagers were trudging through the sand toward her. The wind carried most of their words away, and she only caught the odd shout. They kicked rocks along the shore and threatened one another with clumps of rotting seaweed or a discarded fish head.

As they drew closer, their conversation dropped away. A girl in the group fixed her gaze on Alice, staring fiercely. The others looked less hostile, but still sneaked glances at Alice. They were an intriguing group. With their long black coats and angular bodies, they had the appearance of a colony of bats. They slowed down when she reached them, as if they wanted to speak to her.

Alice waited, and when no one spoke, said, "Hello."

"*Hello*," the hostile girl mimicked her. None of the others laughed.

Alice looked at the girl's hair with its dark purple streaks. She had an earring in her eyebrow and two more under the corners of her mouth. The other girl in the group had cherry-colored hair and was riding piggyback on a tall, skinny boy with a multitude of freckles. The other boy she knew—it was Cal, from her school. He looked hastily away when she met his gaze, which told her he had recognized her in return, but didn't want his friends to know that.

The purple-haired girl gave a snort of disdain and pushed deliberately past Alice. Odd, Alice thought, that the girl had decided so instantly to dislike her. The others trailed after their companion.

"Tess, why d'you have to be so mean?" one of them said as they moved away.

Cal glanced back at Alice and gave her a conspiratorial half smile. Alice nodded in reply and continued along the beach.

seven

UNNATURAL CAUSES

ALICE perused the *Port Cormorant Mail* as she ate her corn-flakes. "Plenty of notices for Lionel Mengler," her father murmured, peering down at the obituary column of his own newspaper, the *Coastal Chronicle*. He sipped his wheatgrass blend. "Should be a good turnout for the funeral tomorrow. I'll get Patty to organize extra sandwiches."

Patty could make sandwiches more quickly than anyone in Damocles Cove—she would tell you that herself. Alice doubted Patty's claim from time to time—she had seen the women at the school cafeteria in action.

"Perhaps we could investigate pastries," Alice ventured.

Her father shook his head, smiling a little. "I know you don't think much of our refreshments, Alice. But people don't book funerals at Tranquility for the food. They book us for an affordable service, and if we were to add pastries or cakes to the menu, then we would have to charge more." He raised his eyebrows, and she recognized that a pun had occurred to him. "Things made of *dough* cost a lot of... well, you know what."

Alice sighed. She knew he was right about the cost, but she couldn't help but wonder what their rival, White Dove Cremations, served at their post-service refreshments. She suspected it involved pastries.

"Can you help me with Mr. Mengler this afternoon?" Thaddeus asked. "I need you to take a look at his regalia. I'm concerned it's not quite right."

"Regalia?" she said.

"Uniform, medals and so on."

"Was he a soldier?" she asked.

"A Freemason."

Alice paused with her spoon partway to her mouth. "What's that?"

"It's a traditional club that men can belong to. They support each other in business, have festive meetings, and do charitable works. I understand there are secret ceremonies and handshakes involved."

Alice thought about this. It sounded a little suspicious to her.

"There's a diagram Mr. Mengler's family provided to help us arrange the regalia on his body," Thaddeus added.

"It sounds interesting. I'd be happy to take a look."

She went back to her newspaper. Under an article about the Damocles Cove Sea Dragons swim team, Alice spotted the name Devenish. She read the story with interest.

It was all about a doctor in the nearby city of Port Cormorant who had come up with a way to treat allergies. It wasn't clear what the treatment involved, but Dr. Philip Grampian said it was "perfect for sufferers of solar urticaria." The reporter mentioned George Devenish's death as an example of how dangerous such an allergy could be. Then Luanne Devenish was quoted saying that there was "no way she would allow her children to participate in this dangerous therapy."

This must be the new treatment Violet had mentioned—the one that her mother was so violently against.

"Would you try a new treatment if you had a life-threatening allergy, Dad?"

He looked up. "You mean like Violet's sunlight allergy?"

"Yes. There's a doctor who's trying a new therapy, but her mum won't let them try it. Don't you think it should be Violet's decision, though?"

Thaddeus scratched his chin. "That's a tricky question. Violet and her brother may be a little young to make a decision like that."

Alice nodded thoughtfully. "As an adult, though, would you try it?"

"Probably," he said.

"Me too," she said.

Thaddeus returned to his newspaper.

"I wonder if someone could be murdered with their allergy," Alice added.

Thaddeus looked up again, blinking. "Well, I suppose they could, technically...."

"It would be an excellent way to cover up a murder," she mused. "It would appear to be a natural death. If you did it cleverly enough, no one would ever suspect."

Her father watched her in silence. Alice checked the clock and went to brush her teeth.

The brindled cat was under the camellia bush again. She twitched a twig, trying to ignite its interest. It watched her with those great, dark eyes, and made a movement with its nose that indicated it was sniffing, but stayed otherwise motionless.

Alice went on her way to school.

✤

That week, Violet didn't sit with Alice. Alice realized that she had not been tactful enough and now she was paying the price. She was vexed—another satisfying word she'd discovered in a book about historical kings and queens. It meant cross and frustrated. Alice was vexed because having company at lunchtime had been pleasant, but also because she no longer had someone to ask questions to about the death of George Devenish.

Ms. Goodwill passed by on her way to the office one recess, her blond frizz held off her face by her sunglasses, as always. She smiled brightly, then frowned when she realized Alice was alone.

"Where's Violet today?"

"I don't know, Ms. Goodwill."

She slowed her rapid pace. "You haven't seen her?"

"No," said Alice. "I haven't seen her since Monday. Well, I've seen her in the hallways and in math class, but not here."

"I see."

Ms. Goodwill hovered thoughtfully, then walked on.

Alice saw her again at lunchtime.

"Oh, Alice, just the girl I was looking for," she said, as if she was surprised to find Alice sitting on the bench she always sat on. "I'm starting up a board games club in the library."

"No, thank you," said Alice. "I don't like games."

Ms. Goodwill laughed gaily. "No, darling—I just need someone to pass out some flyers to let everyone know about it." She waved a handful of papers. "I understand you have gym next period and it's long-jump practice, so you won't be participating."

"That's right," said Alice, surprised that Ms. Goodwill knew this. "Because of my leg."

"Excellent. I want to station a couple of pupils in the main walkway, from the end of lunch to the start of fifth period, to hand out the flyers. Practically the whole of middle school passes through there at that time, so it would be the perfect opportunity to advertise the club. What do you say?"

Alice had no objection. It sounded better than raking a sandbox after the other kids landed their spectacular leaps, usually spraying sand into her hair.

"Come with me," said Ms. Goodwill.

Alice followed the teacher, noting the busy yellow-and-red floral pattern on the woman's dress. She pictured a yellow coffin. Yes, bright yellow—with red handles and a great big arrangement of gerberas of all colors: purple, pink, red, orange. And red taffeta lining.

At the corner, Ms. Goodwill turned left instead of right. "It's quicker to get to the main walkway the other way," Alice reminded her.

"Oh yes. Yes. But I just need to check something."

Alice followed, puzzled. Ms. Goodwill seemed to lead her all over the school, peering into the library and around corners and into groups of other students. Finally, she brightened. She charged along a veranda, coming to a stop in front of Violet who was sitting on a step, nibbling at a ham and cheese croissant beneath her veil.

"Violet!" Ms. Goodwill was puffing. "I need another student to help me, and you'll do very nicely. You've got media next, haven't you? Mr. Butters mentioned you'll be working in the studio under bright lighting, and I thought I would rescue you from having to sit out." She explained the flyer-handing-out task, and Violet agreed to help, although Alice thought she seemed reluctant.

Ms. Goodwill set them up on either side of the walkway. Mr. Prince appeared as she was dividing the stack of flyers between the two.

"What's this all about?" he boomed.

Alice resisted the temptation to cover her ears. Mr. Prince was always unnecessarily loud. He read the flyer she passed him and scoffed.

"Board games in the library! What the kids really need is a bit of exercise. When I was a boy, we'd go out onto the playing field or the basketball courts to burn off a bit of energy. *That* was the way to pass the time, I tell you, Ms. Goodman. Less of this…" He mimed scrolling and typing on a phone. "More of this…" He mimed throwing a football.

Ms. Goodwill's smile looked like it was held in place with spray adhesive. "Goodwill."

"That's what I said. Board games! They need to get outside and move."

"We need to have activities for all types of students," she said, still smiling. "Not everyone's as athletic as you, Mr. Prince."

"They should be, Ms. Goodwin. They should be." He cracked his knuckles. "A bit of air and a bit of sweat—that's what kids need. There wouldn't be half the problems in the world today if everyone did a bit of a sport."

"What about kids like Violet and me?" said Alice. "It's difficult for us to do a sport. And to be honest, I don't enjoy competitive activities."

He stared as though she'd confessed she didn't like ice cream. "I'm sure you would if you got involved," he said, then strode off, muttering that no one had ever worked up a healthy sweat from a board game.

"He obviously hasn't seen my year nine boys doing RPGs," Ms. Goodwill told Alice and Violet with a wink. "Okay, you two. Start handing out flyers when the bell rings. When everyone's gotten to class, you may sit and chat throughout period five, then you can catch everyone again as they go to their next classes. That should be enough to get the flyers to as many people as possible. Afterward, you can go to period six as normal. You girls are complete gems! Have fun!" She trotted away.

Alice regarded Violet across the hall. Kimberly Larsson came along the walkway with Jasmine Pang. Alice held out two flyers, which they pointedly ignored. Kimberly stopped to examine Violet.

"I hear the vampire slayers got to your uncle," she said sweetly. "Maybe you're next, Violet."

Jasmine tittered nervously.

This was not only tactless, but extremely rude. Alice gave Kimberly a stern look. "I've been to Violet's house and I can assure you her family are *not* vampires. There wasn't a fang in sight."

Kimberly rolled her eyes, flicked her hair, and walked on. "She's been downgraded again," Alice told Violet. "Cardboard box coffin, slightly battered."

Violet gave her a wan smile. Their next customer was a younger boy on his way to the bathroom. Alice handed him a flyer. He looked at her like she had an unexpected number of heads, then at the flyer as if she'd passed him his own execution order.

"Freaks," he said, including Violet in the insult.

Violet made a face at his back and sighed. "This sucks," she muttered.

"How is your family doing?" Alice asked. "I hope your dad isn't too prostrated with grief."

"Huh?'

"Prostrated. It means you are lying upon your front, unable to get up or function. But I don't think it's meant literally. Prostrated with grief means you can't think or do anything because you're so sad."

"Oh."

Violet watched as Alice passed another flyer to a girl who

technically should have been Violet's customer. She was walking closer to Violet's side, but Violet didn't look like she was going to give her one.

"Dad's okay," she said when the girl was gone. "He went back to work on Monday."

"I'm glad to hear it. And yourself?"

"Huh?"

"How are you coping?" Alice's sympathetic tone crept back in.

"I'm fine," said Violet, but she didn't meet Alice's eyes.

The bell rang at that moment and within seconds there was a roar. An avalanche of middle school students filled the hallway, pushing and dodging in both directions. Alice and Violet handed out flyers as best they could, with some students ignoring them and others causing traffic jams when they swung back to grab one. Then as fast as it had begun, it was over, except for Cal Lee, who was late as always, running along the hallway with his coat flapping. "Thanks!" he panted, snatching the flyer Alice held out as he raced past.

Alice took a seat on the closest bench and Violet sat on the one opposite. She pulled a manga book out of her bag, opened it, and appeared to be immersed in the story for most of period five, although Alice thought she'd spent an extremely long time on one page. Around thirty-five minutes, to be exact. She wondered if Violet had reading difficulties.

At last Violet closed the book and looked up. "I was thinking about what you said about Uncle George."

Alice sat up straight, relieved Violet had brought it up. "Yes?"

"He died of an allergic reaction, you know that, don't you?"

Alice nodded. "Yes. But I do have a feeling there was something underhanded going on."

"What-handed?"

"Underhanded. Suspicious."

Violet put her book away and pulled a cupcake in a little plastic container out of her bag. It had pink icing and sprinkles, and looked delicious. Violet took an aloof bite, and Alice tried to focus on more important matters.

"I saw a newspaper piece on Monday about an allergy doctor in Port Cormorant," she said. "It mentioned your uncle."

"Yeah, Uncle George found that doctor about a year ago. The reporter who wrote the article called Mum to get a quote from her, too."

"Your mother sounded like she didn't think much of this doctor."

"Uncle George tried to talk Mum and Dad into using the therapy on me and Lucas, but Mum said absolutely not."

"What did your father think?"

Violet hesitated. "Dad wasn't as freaked out about it as Mum, but he agreed with her in the end. He usually does. Mum was really mad at Uncle George over the whole thing."

This explained the tension at Violet's birthday party. "I'm sure your uncle was just trying to help," said Alice. Violet picked some of the icing off her cupcake—wastefully, Alice thought.

"Uncle George took my little brother to see the doctor without telling Mum. When she found out, she didn't speak to him for ages."

"Ah. I can see why that upset your mother," Alice said slowly.

Violet bit her nail. "What's with you thinking Uncle George's death wasn't natural, anyway? You can't go around saying stuff like that without a reason."

"I wouldn't do that." How could she explain her ability to read the resonance of dead people's belongings? She had never told anybody about the stories she heard from the items belonging to corpses that came through the funeral home—not even her father.

It probably wasn't normal to know unknowable things by touching everyday items, and Violet might find it alarming. She brought her eyes back to Violet's face, which was tight with worry. "I get feelings sometimes. I have a feeling now."

"A feeling?" Violet exclaimed the word. "A *feeling*?"

"A strong feeling," Alice said firmly. "I suppose you could call it an intuition. It happens sometimes with the bodies." Violet fell silent and Alice waited apprehensively. Would she think her mad? Or would she find Alice too creepy to be around? Kimberly Larsson had once theorized that Alice was actually one of the dead bodies from Tranquility Funerals, brought back to life by Thaddeus England. Ever since then, Jasmine Pang had looked at Alice with terror in her eyes.

"Want to go to the Quay together tomorrow night?" Violet asked, surprising Alice greatly.

"Friday night? I think that should be all right," said Alice. "I'll have to ask Dad, but I don't think he'll object. Do you like the Quay?"

Violet shrugged. "Yeah. Mum would rather me go out at night-time than daytime, and the Quay's open at night. We can get fish and chips or whatever."

"I like chips!" said Alice.

Violet nodded. "And we can talk more about Uncle George."

The late Mr. Lionel Mengler's regalia was truly beautiful. The apron and gauntlets were sewn from splendid turquoise fabric, decorated with rhodium chains and pins. The chart that his family had supplied to show how to arrange the regalia was also a work of art. Alice studied it. Sure enough, Patty and her father had gotten it wrong. Alice gently unpinned things and adjusted them, using tiny invisible stitches to hold the tassels in place.

The final pin, known as a collar jewel, was in the shape of a bird of some kind—a pheasant, perhaps, or maybe a phoenix. It was resonant. As she pinned it, Alice learned the story of Mr. Mengler, who had arrived in the country from Germany as a young man, and found a brotherhood with the Freemasons when it seemed no one else would accept him. He treasured his Masonic friendships and gave excellent discounts when they needed boots repaired, keys cut, or batteries replaced in watches. He was a big fan of the regular Freemason feasts, and had introduced his new friends to the joy of pork schnitzel.

His wife was occasionally annoyed with his dedication to his order. It took up a lot of his time, and he fussed so much over the correct cleaning and placement of his collaret and pins. But she secretly thought he looked very handsome in his lodge officer uniform, and she didn't mind the ladies' nights they occasionally put on. And she always got a very good price at the dog groomer, who was a Freemason as well.

Alice was a little disappointed that she would miss Lionel Mengler's funeral because of school. She would have liked to see the Freemasons forming a guard of honor in their delightful turquoise uniforms, and the wife with her immaculately groomed dog.

Her father arrived just as she finished.

She stood back. "Doesn't he look marvelous?"

Thaddeus came to stand beside her, and they both gazed down at Mr. Mengler. "Oh, Alice, you've done a wonderful job. What a noble appearance he has."

Alice glowed, admiring her handiwork. "I like the gauntlets. He looks a bit like a knight."

"Yes, very medieval."

Alice pulled off her latex gloves. "Dad, Violet's invited me to go to the Quay with her tomorrow night." She refrained from mentioning the fish and chips. Her father was opposed to fried foods. "We thought we might eat while we're there. Can I go?"

"Just the two of you?"

"Yes."

Thaddeus scratched his chin. "I'm meeting a client in the afternoon, so I can't take you. But it's quite a family-friendly place, so I don't think you'll be in any danger. And if you leave before sunset, you won't be walking in the dark. I can pick you up afterward."

"That sounds perfect," said Alice.

Her father admired the corpse for a few more moments, then pulled up the sheet. "What shall we have for dinner tonight?"

"I was thinking about pork schnitzel."

"Hm, we do have some pork," said Thaddeus. "But fried schnitzel is not terribly healthy. We could have lean pork steaks with a side salad, perhaps."

Alice sighed. "All right."

eight
CREATURES OF THE NIGHT

ALICE walked to the Quay on Friday evening and waited at the fish and chips shop door. The sun had only just fallen below the horizon, and Violet was a little late. Alice didn't blame her. If she had a condition like Violet's, she would wait until after sunset to make any excursions too.

Violet arrived in her mother's car, dropped off directly outside the fish and chips shop. Mrs. Devenish took a moment to wave and peer intently at Alice before she drove away. Violet adjusted her glove and joined Alice.

"The gem shop's already closed?" Violet looked disappointed.

Alice was pleased to hear Violet also liked that shop. "Hello, Violet. Yes, unfortunately it is. You still have your veil on, even at night?"

"Yeah, I can't guarantee the lights here are safe for me." She glanced around the lit-up row of shops. "Ultraviolet light, remember?"

"Of course," said Alice.

"Should we have a walk around before we get some chips?" Violet asked.

"Yes, all right." Alice fell into step beside her. "You know, Ultraviolet would be a wonderful nickname for you. Much better than Violet the Vampire. Ultraviolet almost sounds like a superhero."

Violet gave her a startled half smile.

"Is candlelight safe?" asked Alice.

"Yeah, of course."

"And firelight?"

Violet nodded.

"What about fairy lights? Or colored Christmas lights?"

"They're all fine—I think, anyway. Mum's the one who works out whether a light is safe." Violet slowed at an accessories store window. It was closed, but there was a display of tiaras and bangles. "That one's nice," she said, pointing.

Alice barely glanced at the jewelry. She wasn't at all interested in fashion accessories. "Is there anywhere at all where you're safe?"

Violet gave one of her shrugs. "Not really, but you get used to it. I'm safe at home—we've got the right kind of lights with no UVB."

"I'm glad there's somewhere you can take all that gear off," Alice told her earnestly. "It must be such a nuisance."

"Like I said, I'm used to it."

"Well," said Alice. "I'm impressed with the way you've adapted to the requirements of your allergy."

Violet glanced at her. "You talk strange."

Alice was taken aback. "Do I?"

"Yeah. You're really formal, like you're being interviewed for a private school, or something."

"Oh."

They walked on, passing an ice-cream shop and a surf clothing outlet. Alice looked down at the dark glimmer of water in the gaps between the boardwalk timbers. They were over the water.

"Your uncle wanted to be a sailor, didn't he?" she said to Violet.

"Huh?"

"Your father said so at the funeral."

"Did he?" Violet made a bemused face. "I didn't know that. I guess he couldn't, because of—you know..." She waved her gloved hand.

"But there must be a great number of career opportunities available to people with a sunlight allergy," said Alice. "Your uncle worked night shift. You could follow almost any career path you wanted and simply do the work at night."

Violet laughed. "Uh-huh. Like midnight surf lifeguard? After-dark gardener? Night vet?"

"Well, I suppose not *every* career path would be suitable for night work," Alice conceded. "Although I believe some of those things have potential. Night gardening might appeal to some customers. It would be good for pest control—imagine the snails you could eradicate. And late-night vets charge extra, so you would make a lot of money. But there are plenty of other jobs. Fashion designer—no one cares what time of day they work. Artist—you could paint all night long and have exhibitions in the evenings. A manager of a twenty-four-hour convenience store. You could work from sundown to dawn and use hired staff for daylight hours."

Violet was shaking her head with a smile. "You're so weird, Alice."

There was a ruckus ahead of them and both girls looked up. The kids Alice had seen at the beach earlier in the week were milling around, including Cal. They ranged in age from about thirteen to fifteen. They were swearing, shoving one another, and being generally objectionable, causing frowns from the adults in passing families. The girl with purple streaks of hair caught sight of Alice and Violet. "Look." She nudged one of her friends, pointing at Alice and Violet. "Check out those two."

Violet started to turn around to walk back the other way.

"Wait," said Alice. "That's Cal, and these kids hang around the pier where your uncle worked."

"So? Let's go."

"Hey," the purple-haired girl called to Violet. "What's with the gloves? Are you, like, a magician or something?"

Cal pushed her arm. "Tess, shut up."

She shoved him back and grinned at Alice and Violet. "What are your names?"

"I'm Alice," she said readily. "This is Violet."

"Let's go," Violet mumbled.

Tess approached, staring unabashedly at Violet. "So, what's with the gloves—and the shade-cloth thing for your face?"

Violet didn't speak, and Alice didn't think she had the right to explain Violet's allergy on her behalf. However, she felt compelled to say something, so she addressed Tess.

"Your name is Tess, is it? I've seen you at Pier 19."

That got Tess's attention. "Who even *are* you?" she demanded, as though Alice hadn't just introduced herself moments before. The two lip piercings gave Tess's mouth a permanently downturned, sullen look.

"I'm *Alice*," she said again. "I'm in year eight at Damocles Cove High."

Tess snorted. "They're from your school, Cal. Friends of yours?"

"Leave them alone," Cal urged. "Come on, let's go to the arcade."

She completely ignored him. "Why's your friend dressed like that?" she asked Alice.

"That's her business." Alice kept her voice pleasant but firm. Tess clearly hadn't been taught good manners.

"I'm only asking."

"Yes, but Violet wouldn't ask you about your purple hair or your piercings, would she?"

Tess's group of friends all burst into laughter. Tess acted as if she couldn't hear them but her gaze hardened on Alice's face. "How about you let her speak for herself?"

"I don't believe she wishes to speak to you."

Violet's gloved hand had crept around Alice's wrist and was tugging her away. Alice gave her a reassuring glance. "It's all right," she said.

Cal had come to stand at Tess's side and was telling her to back off in a low tone. "She's got allergies, that's all," he said. "And they're only year eights."

"Aw, you being a hero, Cal?"

He sighed. "Leave it, Tess. Go on. Go home, or something."

She bristled and let loose with a string of foul words. Thankfully, one of the other kids took Tess's arm and they dragged her away, shoving and stumbling along together until she was laughing and seemed to go willingly. Cal remained.

"Sorry about Tess," he said. "She's..." He grimaced. "Nasty, sometimes."

"I'm fine," Alice assured him, then glanced at Violet who seemed even paler than usual. "Are you all right, Violet?"

"Yeah," Violet said faintly.

Alice thought she could do with some comfort. Hot food and a rest, perhaps.

"Come on," she said. "Let's go and get our chips now."

"You're getting chips?" Cal said. "I'll come."

⚜

Cal was good company, without his friends. He was chatty, laughed a lot, and didn't say anything at all to Violet about her protective clothing, which seemed to cheer her up considerably. Alice asked if he wanted to join them for a meal, but he said he was running short of cash, so she bought extra chips so he could share. She usually had money, because her father paid her a small wage for her work at the funeral home, and she had very little to spend it on.

The three sat on the white sand under the floodlights that shone on the little beach and unwrapped their meal. Cal ate chips two or three at a time, as if he was in a great hurry. Violet still had her veil in place.

"These lights are as bright as daylight," Alice said to Violet. "I think they must contain UVB."

"No, that's not how it works," Violet told her. "Some lights might not look that bright, but they've still got UVB. You can't tell by looking."

Cal wanted to know what they were talking about, so Violet explained her allergy. "I've seen you wearing the hat and stuff at school but didn't know the facts," he said.

"Let me guess," Violet said flatly. "You've heard I'm a vampire?"

He gave a lopsided shrug. "Nah. Dunno."

"They call me Alice in Zombieland," Alice added in. "Zombies and vampires. It's almost as if we belong together."

Violet chuckled, her eyes bright beneath her veil.

"Why do they call you Alice in Zombieland?" Cal wanted to know.

Alice was obliged to explain that she had been raised in a funeral parlor and worked there as a part-time job and would one day inherit the business. Cal was so surprised he forgot to devour squid ring and chips for a few moments.

"Wait, you work there?" he said. "Is that legal?"

"If it's a family business, then yes, it's legal for a child to work there," Alice said.

"Yeah, but—a kid, working in a morgue?"

"It's not a morgue," she said. "We don't do autopsies. We receive the bodies from the morgue and prepare them for burial. And host the funeral service, of course."

"Yeah, but…" Cal shook his head. "It's a weird after-school job. I mean, dead bodies. Am I right?" He appealed to Violet, who shrugged. "How often do you do funerals?" he asked Alice.

"We run about eight to ten services per week," she said.

"And you've been working there how long?" he asked.

"Dad let me start helping when I was about ten years old."

"So you've been to about ten funerals a week since you were *ten*?"

"No, of course not. I can't attend the ones Dad does while I'm at school, so I only go to three or four a week—on the weekends, or during school breaks."

"Okay, let's say you've got funerals happening about fifty weeks a year, and you're going to three a week, that's…" Cal tried to work it out.

"About a hundred and fifty a year," Violet supplied.

Cal shook his head, shoving in more chips. "That's a lot of death for a thirteen-year-old to be seeing."

"I'm not thirteen yet, but my age is irrelevant. Everyone sees lots of what they have in their life."

His eyebrows knitted. "Huh?"

"Well, if someone has a business selling hardware," said Alice, "they would see a lot of hammers and nails."

Violet grinned and Cal gazed at Alice, his chips momentarily forgotten. "You've got an interesting brain, Zombie Queen."

Alice liked this new nickname.

"I'm a creature of the night, too," Cal added. "I stay up till three or four a.m., most nights."

"Why?"

"I'm a gamer. Most of my gaming buddies are in the northern hemisphere and it only gets interesting after midnight."

"What about school?" Violet asked. "You must be wrecked in the mornings."

Cal gave a crooked shrug. "I'm usually late." He ate four chips in one go and shot them a sheepish smile.

Alice saw an opportunity to expand her inquiries about George Devenish. "Cal, I saw you and your friends at Pier 19 the other day. Do you go there much? At night, maybe?"

Cal brushed squid ring crumbs off his T-shirt. "Why?"

"Well, Violet's uncle died there a couple of weeks ago."

He looked sharply at Violet. "That guy was your uncle?"

She nodded.

"Wow. Sorry to hear that. He had a stroke or something, right?"

"No, he had an allergic reaction," she said. "He had the same sunlight allergy as me."

Cal's eyes widened, and for a moment he looked so struck with horror that Alice thought he might be choking silently on a chip. Then he dropped his gaze.

"Were you and your friends at Pier 19 anytime that night?" Alice asked. "Maybe you saw George there?"

Cal kept his eyes down. "We weren't there." He didn't eat any more chips.

"Are you sure?" she asked. "It was on—what date was it, Violet?"

"The sixth," she said. "The day after my birthday."

"So you weren't there on the night of the fifth or the very early morning of the sixth?" Alice asked Cal.

He shook his head, still staring at the sand. Alice and Violet exchanged a look.

At last Cal glanced up. "Well, I'd better go see where my friends have gotten to. Thanks for the chips." He loped away.

Violet held her veil out so she could wipe her mouth with a napkin. "Cal's hiding something."

"Yes." Alice drew patterns in the sand with her finger. She uncovered a fine scalloped shell, bright pink in color. She brushed the sand off, and found a tissue to wrap it in so it wouldn't get crushed in her pocket.

Violet was staring at the black water with its light-flecked ripples. "You reckon Cal and his friends were there when Uncle George died?"

"There were people around, although I don't know who," Alice said. "That's why I think it's peculiar that no one witnessed George being taken ill." She thought about the voices under the dock and those colored lights George saw on his last morning. "Who else worked at the pier with your uncle? Do you know any of them?"

Violet chewed her thumbnail through the veil. "There's another security guy—Higgo."

"Yes, I've met him."

"And there's Aunty Gina—she manages the pier. Collects the rent from the boat owners and pays the workers and stuff. And I've seen another guy working there, but I can't remember his name."

The information about George's death was starting to build up. Alice decided she would think it through carefully when she got home. Perhaps there was a clue among these facts—something that would explain what she'd seen through George's toy boat.

"What time is your dad picking you up?" Violet asked. Alice checked her watch and saw it was 7:45.

"Nine p.m., he said."

"My mum's coming at eight thirty." Violet scrunched their fish and chips paper and stood up. "Should we get ice cream and go to Time Warp?"

Alice liked the idea of ice cream, but she wasn't sure about the arcade. It was a loud place, with the pings and trills of electronic games, and lights flashing from every direction. She could give it a chance, she supposed. She got to her feet and walked up the beach with Violet.

"I think I might visit Pier 19 again this weekend," she said.

Violet shoved the chip paper into a trash can as they passed. "What for?"

"I'd like to speak to the people who worked with your uncle."

They walked along and Violet said nothing for a while, but when they had almost reached the ice-cream shop, she turned to face Alice.

"Look, if you're going to go around asking questions about Uncle George because you think someone saw him and didn't help him or whatever, then I think I should be there too. I mean, he was *my* uncle. I'll come to Pier 19 with you this weekend."

"But your allergy…," said Alice.

"What about it?" Violet retorted. "I've got protective clothing."

"Will your parents allow it?"

"Probably." Violet paused. "I might have to be creative about how I explain it to them. Mum's a worrier."

Alice couldn't think of any further objections and had to agree that it was Violet's right to be involved. "Well then, I propose we go on Sunday."

"Yep, that works for me." Violet turned away and studied the board listing sixty-seven flavors of ice cream and thirty-six toppings. "What are you getting?"

"Vanilla," Alice said firmly.

NINE

PRIVATE INVESTIGATIONS

WHAT sort of investigating would the police have done on George Devenish's death?" Alice asked Thaddeus.

It was Sunday morning, and there were no funerals scheduled for the day. Her father was seated across the kitchen table, wearing his bright-yellow bananas shirt to celebrate. He'd been clicking his tongue over a misspelled name in the *Coastal Chronicle* obituaries, but now he put down the newspaper and spread tahini on his grain-and-seed toast, considering Alice's question.

"I suppose they would have asked to speak to any witnesses or persons in the area," he said. "They would have reviewed any CCTV footage and spoken to his wife and the other staff members. And they would have read the reports from the autopsy."

"What about searches?" said Alice. "Would they have searched the area in and around the dock? Underneath? Or any boats that came in to the pier around the time he died?"

"I expect so," said Thaddeus. "It depends if they thought there was anything suspicious afoot."

Alice frowned. "A foot?"

"It means *going on.*"

"I see." Alice drizzled honey over her cornflakes. "Do you need help with any bodies today?" she said. "Violet and I were planning to go for a walk."

"No—there's nothing that can't wait until you get back." Thaddeus gave her a searching look. "Seeing Violet again already?"

Alice moved the newspaper closer and scanned the front page. "I'm interested in her uncle and the condition that caused his death."

"You are being tactful about that, aren't you Alice?"

"I believe so," she said.

"Are you becoming friends with Violet?" Thaddeus asked. He sounded hopeful.

"Perhaps," she said absently. She was reading a story about a theft of patient files from a doctor's office, which was between the one about the endangered leafy sea dragon endemic to Damocles Cove, and another about some teenagers who had harassed shop owners at the Quay.

"That would be nice for you—to have a friend to see on weekends and so forth." Thaddeus took a drink of his green tea.

Alice got her father to message Violet's mother, and it was agreed that Violet would be dropped off at Tranquility Funerals at ten. Thaddeus went to the embalming room to work on a body, so Alice got herself ready, then went outside to work on her relationship with next door's cat. It was there today, crouched on the low wooden fence between their yard and the neighbor's.

"Good morning," Alice said in a soft voice.

The cat regarded her with large eyes, as wary as ever. Alice took a slow step closer, and very, very gradually extended her hand. The cat sat up and Alice paused, catching her breath, but it didn't run away. It simply sat and looked at her. Her hand was just centimeters from its black nose, which twitched.

"I've heard it might rain later today," Alice said in the same low, comforting tone her father used when he was explaining the cost of a casket to a client. "I hope you have somewhere to take shelter."

She inched ever so slightly closer and the cat suddenly withdrew, turning and dropping down off the fence in a single fluid movement. It vanished around the side of the neighbor's house in a flash of black and orange.

Alice sat down to wait for Violet, and before long the Devenish car rolled up. Alice expected that Violet would be dropped off, but her mother parked the car and got out. She strode up the steps toward Alice and stared at the old brass plaque beside the door that read ENGLAND'S FUNERAL PARLOR.

"Good morning," said Alice. She followed Luanne's gaze to the plaque. "That's what our family business used to be called. This was once the front door, you see. Now we use it as our private entrance. The Tranquility Funerals sign is around the corner—as you know."

Luanne blinked. "Is your father available?" she asked.

"He's at work in the embalming room," said Alice.

"Oh!" Luanne looked aghast. "How—how…"

"Interesting?" suggested Alice.

"Yes. Interesting," Luanne said faintly. She put an arm around Violet. "Well, I'll show you how to use Violet's EpiPen in case of an allergic reaction."

Violet rolled her eyes and looked embarrassed, but Alice listened avidly as Luanne talked her through how to remove the protective cap and inject the EpiPen into Violet's leg.

"If I had a reaction, I could do it myself," Violet assured Alice.

Her mother inhaled sharply. "Violet, you know you might pass out if you have a reaction. Then who's going to use the EpiPen on you, *hmm*?"

"I promise I will swoop into action, seize the EpiPen, and stab Violet in the thigh with it just as you showed me," Alice told Luanne solemnly.

Violet's mother stared so hard at Alice's face, she thought for a moment she'd said something wrong. Then she nodded once, shortly, and went back to the car.

"Your father will pick you up at three sharp," she called to Violet, who waved.

"Let's get a snack and walk straight down to the pier," said Alice.

She led the way inside and fetched cheese sticks and rye crackers for them to eat. She held out some for Violet, who just gazed at it.

"Don't you eat cheese?" asked Alice. "Or perhaps you don't like rye? I wouldn't blame you."

"I'm not hungry."

A thought hit Alice. "We don't keep the dead bodies near our food, if that's what you're concerned about."

Violet spluttered and coughed. "No! I didn't think that!" But she did sound slightly relieved. "Cheese is fine," she said, taking it. "I'll skip the crackers."

"Let's go."

Alice led Violet through the gate and out onto the sidewalk. They walked toward the pier in silence for a few minutes, nibbling their snacks.

"Do you see them?" Violet asked, startling her.

Alice looked around. "See who?"

"No, I mean, does your dad let you see them? The dead people you do funerals for?"

"Of course. I arrange their keepsakes and jewelry, check that their clothing is neat and tidy—that sort of thing. My father is a talented embalmer and arranges the corpses beautifully, but he always makes sure I check his work. It's for the best. We wouldn't want to upset the families by missing some little detail."

Violet didn't answer. She stared at the remainder of her cheese stick, and when they passed a house with a garbage can out front for collection, she dropped it swiftly in.

They reached the crest of the hill and the cove came into view, sparkling under the blue morning sky. Alice paused to enjoy the sight for a moment, then pushed on with renewed energy. At the bottom of the hill, they crossed Wharf Road and went through the gates into Pier 19. A metallic clang sounded at intervals so regular, it sounded like the tolling of a bell.

"I see Higgo down there," Violet said.

Alice followed her finger, pointing to the dock. The tall man she'd spoken to last time was standing slouched against a post beside a fisherman. They appeared to be chatting.

"Come on," she said. "Let's go and talk to him."

Violet hung back as if she were shy. Alice gave her arm an encouraging squeeze.

"Don't worry, I'll do the talking."

Higgo didn't see them coming, so they caught the last part of his conversation as they approached.

"Trouble is, our hands are tied," he was saying. "Can't touch them, can't force them to do anything. The uniform doesn't scare them. All we can do is call the cops and hope they don't have anything better to do than clear out a few underage troublemakers."

Alice thought that an extra-long coffin would be required for Higgo, on account of his height. He was red-haired—a lighter red than her own, almost sandy—and heavily freckled. A nice cedar casket with silver satin lining would suit him, and an arrangement of tiger lilies for the top.

At that moment, Higgo glanced around and saw Violet and Alice. He straightened immediately, pushing himself up off the post. The fisherman looked up and observed them, then tucked his grizzled gray beard back down into his jacket collar.

"Violet!" Higgo sounded almost distressed. "What are you doing here?"

"Um," said Violet.

Higgo's gaze fell on Alice. "And you. I told you to clear out."

"We came to pay our respects to Violet's uncle George."

Silence followed her statement. Higgo's eyes became a little shiny, and when Alice glanced at Violet she also looked as if she might cry. Higgo turned his head to where the teddy bear in a sailor's hat was still strapped to the post at the end of the dock. Violet and Alice followed his gaze.

"Did you put it there?" Alice asked him.

Higgo gave an awkward nod. "Come on, let's get you two off the dock and leave Ernie to fish in peace."

He led them back along the jetty, their shoes making low clonking noises on the old wood.

"How's your dad?" he asked Violet. "Is he holding up okay?"

She mumbled something in reply.

"We were wondering about the night George died," Alice said, increasing her pace to keep up with Higgo. "Were you working that night?"

He glanced back at Alice. "What did you say your name was?"

"She's my friend—Alice," Violet supplied. "I hope it's okay to ask you about Uncle George," she added.

Alice recalled that she needed to use *tact*. "Yes, we're very sorry for the loss of your friend. It's clear you were fond of him—from the memento you've left on the dock."

Higgo was silent for a few paces. "George was a good man. He was my little boy's godfather."

Violet glanced at Alice, who nodded encouragingly. "So, were you here that night?" Violet asked.

Higgo shook his head. "There's only one security officer on at a time. I was sick for my shift that night."

"Oh, so you were supposed to work?" Alice asked.

"But Uncle George covered for you?" Violet added.

"Yeah. I got a stomach bug from Harry—my little boy. I could barely move." He gave a grimace. "At least it was over quickly. I was fine by the next day."

"What time were you supposed to be working?" Alice asked.

"The graveyard shift."

"The *graveyard* shift?" Alice repeated wonderingly.

"Two a.m. till nine a.m."

"I see," said Alice. "But you called in sick, so Gina had to get George to take your shift?"

Higgo half nodded. "Something like that."

Violet frowned, puzzled, but Alice came straight out and asked. "*Something like that?* So it didn't happen quite like that?"

He sighed. "Gina didn't organize it. We're not supposed to swap shifts without the manager's permission, but I was out like a light. My wife was worried there'd be no one to watch the pier, so she took matters into her own hands and called George." Higgo kept his eyes on the ground while he spoke, and Alice thought she knew why: he felt responsible for George's presence here on the morning he died.

"That was an unlucky chain of events," Alice said. "But completely out of your control."

His eyes came up to her face. She couldn't tell if he was grateful or affronted. They had reached the end of the jetty, but Higgo kept walking, heading toward the gates as if he wanted to see them off the property altogether.

"So, Uncle George was supposed to do your shift, two till nine," Violet said. "He must have known he'd need his protective gear for when the sun rose." She looked quite disturbed by this.

"Can *you* think of any reason why George wouldn't have noticed the sun was about to rise?" Alice asked Higgo. "Perhaps something was going on that caught his attention—distracted him? Some people around, or something like that?" She waited hopefully, but Higgo's mouth was closed in a grim line. "It's such a pity there was no one here to assist him." She waited again.

No reply. The wharf workers resumed clanging.

"Did you get in trouble with your manager for swapping shifts with George?" she asked. "You said it's not allowed, normally."

Higgo stopped abruptly and turned around to face her, which made the two girls stumble to a halt.

"Under the circumstances, people have been pretty understanding," he said, his voice tight. "My wife made a mistake. She didn't know the rules and was just trying to help. Gina's been good about it."

Alice nodded. "I'd like to speak to Gina."

Higgo looked taken aback.

"To, um, say thanks for the flowers she sent for Uncle George's funeral," Violet put in.

"Oh. Right." He glanced at the manager's hut. "She's not here today. But there's no need to go see her, anyway—the flowers were the least the company could do." He shifted his feet and shot a look at the workers farther along the wharf. "Look, you two should really get going. It's not a place for kids."

"Yes, you said that last time," Alice said, seizing on his words. "What do you do when you see kids down here? I know that teenagers like to hang around on the beach or under the dock sometimes."

Higgo gave her a long stare. "Are you one of *those* kids?"

"No."

He didn't move his gaze. "You sure?"

"Yes, quite sure."

"Because we told them to stay away from here. It's a dangerous place."

"Why is it dangerous?" Alice asked.

He gestured. "Isn't it obvious? Boats, workers, heavy machinery, deep water. Lots of opportunities for someone to get injured."

"I see." Alice perceived that Violet was shuffling her feet as though keen to leave. "Well, thank you for talking to us, Higgo."

He nodded, staring at Alice. Violet headed for the gate, and Higgo turned toward the manager's hut.

"Let's not go home right away," Alice said to Violet. "I thought we could take a walk along the shore."

"Why? It looks gross down there. There's loads of seaweed and garbage."

"I want to look under the dock. Maybe there were kids down there on the night of George's death."

Violet seemed as if she absolutely did not want to go down and look under the dock, but she twisted her mouth, hesitating. "It was kind of weird, how Higgo spoke to you when he thought you were one of the kids who hang under the dock."

"Exactly. Come on. There's a set of steps down to the beach just over there." Alice pointed to the stone stairs.

Violet still hovered. "Okay, but if we see anyone down there, we're *not* going under the dock, Alice."

"Why not?"

Violet rolled her eyes. "Because it's sketchy!"

Alice considered this. "Yes, perhaps you're right. I agree to your terms."

ten
SOME FINAL WORDS

I OFTEN find beautiful treasures here," Alice said to Violet as they arrived on the shore. "Shells, driftwood—"

"Oh, that is seriously disgusting." Violet was staring at a rotting fish head on the sand.

"Yes. There are some unpleasant surprises, too."

Alice led the way under the dock. It was abandoned: dank and shadowed. Violet slunk along behind her, looking around herself fearfully.

"You're probably safer under here than you are out in the sun," Alice pointed out.

"I'd rather risk the sunlight, thanks," Violet said. "This place is so creepy. I bet criminals and gangs hang out down here."

"Or possibly teenagers who want a secret place for a party," Alice answered. She examined the underside of the jetty, peering through the cracks. "If someone was standing up top, you'd be able to see who it was, don't you think?"

"Probably."

Alice scanned the mussel-crusted posts and damp limestone rocks, and the sea beyond. "I wonder if the police checked down here for witnesses—or evidence of witnesses."

"They did." Violet was holding a gloved hand to her nose as if she didn't like the smell. "Dad told us about it when he got home from the station after identifying Uncle George. He said they did an investigation to rule out all the other possibilities. They searched the whole pier, and some of the other nearby piers, too—18 and 20."

Alice was a little disappointed. If anything had been found, she was unlikely ever to know about it. "I guess the tide would have washed away anything left behind by now."

"Anything the tide could reach." Violet nudged the damp sand on the waterline with one shoe.

Alice read some of the graffiti on the underside of the jetty. She saw the name TESS and pointed it out to Violet.

"Looks like Cal's friends do come here sometimes," Violet said. "Although that doesn't mean they were here that morning."

"And it doesn't mean they *weren't* here that morning," Alice said mildly.

She continued scouting around, but all she found was a sand-filled chips packet and some strands of black caught on a splinter.

"Is that hair?" Violet asked, coming closer.

"I think they're threads from a piece of fabric."

"Oh. Maybe from someone's scarf. Or beach towel."

Alice raised an eyebrow. "Or perhaps a long black coat—like the ones Cal and his friends wear."

Violet's eyes widened. "Oh! You're good at this, Alice."

Alice nodded her thanks. "Would you wait here a minute, Violet? I'd like to do an experiment. I'll go up on the dock and check what I can see of you when I look down. And you check what you can see of *me* when you look up."

Panic leaped into Violet's face. "Higgo said we weren't allowed on the dock."

Alice was unfazed. "No, he said the pier wasn't a place for kids and it was dangerous. In fact, it's a public location and I am quite entitled to be there. However, I won't make a nuisance of myself—it's just a brief experiment."

Seeing Alice's determination, Violet sighed. "Fine, but *I'll* go up onto the dock. You're not leaving me alone down here."

While she waited for Violet to climb back up the stone stairs and step out onto the jetty, Alice sat on a ledge of concrete surrounding one of the damp wood posts. She scuffed at the sand with her shoe, wondering if anything important was buried underneath—any further evidence of a witness to George Devenish's death. After a minute, Violet's footsteps came scurrying along the dock. Alice could see her quite clearly from underneath. Violet came to a halt, nervously casting her gaze around the dock before crouching down to peer through the cracks between the timbers.

"I see you very well," Alice called, standing up. "Do you see me?"

"Sort of," Violet called back. "I can tell there's someone down there but I can't really make out your face. It's too dark." She stiffened suddenly and peered through a gap with one eye, then the other. "Hey, I see something."

Alice looked around the sand at her feet. "Where?"

"There's sort of a ledge up at the top of the post here." Violet stuck her fingers through a gap between the boards. "There's something sitting on the ledge, something silver."

Alice climbed up onto the concrete ledge to get closer to Violet. It was difficult because of her weak leg, but she managed it by using the good one to hoist the rest of her up, hanging on to the damp post with her hands. She found her balance and let one hand go, reaching up to feel around. "Careful," said Violet. "That's it. You've almost got it! A bit to the left."

Alice's hand closed on something smooth and cool. She brought it down off the top of the post and lowered herself awkwardly back onto the sand, examining the small silver cylinder.

"What on earth is it?" she asked.

⚜

Alice studied their find as she wandered along the beach with Violet. "You're quite certain it's a portable phone charger?"

"How can you honestly not know what it is?" Violet shook her head. "Loads of people have them."

"I haven't seen one up close before. I don't have a phone." Alice inspected the plug end and Violet peered at it over her shoulder.

"It's got a USB connection. You could use it to charge a phone, camera, Bluetooth speaker, stuff like that." Violet drew a sharp breath. "Oh no. Alice, look."

Alice looked up and saw Cal and his group of friends walking toward them along the shoreline. Tess was there.

"Let's go," said Violet, doing a hasty about-face.

"Wait, Violet, I want to speak to them."

"What? No way! Let's *go*."

"Cal's with them. He's nice."

"I don't care!"

Alice pushed the portable charger into her pocket and took Violet's arm to give her confidence. Tess spotted them and shouted, "Alice in Zombieland! Violet the Vampire!" and waved.

They met the group over a big pile of seaweed. "Hey, Alice. Hey, Violet," Cal said, smiling.

"Hello," said Alice, and Violet echoed the greeting miserably.

"What are you freaks doing down here?" Tess asked. Alice was slightly taken aback, but decided this was just Tess's way.

"I often come down to walk at the pier or on the beach."

Tess raised her pierced eyebrow and snorted a laugh as though Alice had said something ridiculous. Cal introduced them to the other kids this time. There was Amy, a girl with hair so unnaturally red it was almost crimson. She appeared to be in a relationship with a tall, skinny boy named Gav.

Tess clearly wanted to be the center of attention. She addressed Violet, nodding toward the pier. "Hey, Cal said that's where your uncle died."

Violet nodded, looking small and shocked. Even Alice knew Tess had been extraordinarily tactless, but she seized the opportunity to talk about George Devenish.

"We were just speaking to George's coworker, the security officer, Higgo," she said, watching carefully to see how this statement would affect them.

Sure enough, there were some shifty glances exchanged. "What for?" Tess wanted to know.

"To find out why he wasn't at work on the morning George died—why George had to take his place."

"He *was* there, wasn't he?" Gav came into the conversation late.

Amy elbowed him and he made a noise of protest. "Higgo was here?" Alice asked. "What time?"

But Gav had clammed up, perhaps realizing he shouldn't have spoken.

"No, that was a different morning." Tess said this so casually that Alice couldn't be sure if it was true or not. "They all blur together when you party late."

"Do you come here at night?" Alice asked. "To hang around under the dock?"

"We had all-night parties here sometimes," Amy conceded. "Not anymore, though."

"Why not?" asked Alice.

"They cleared us out," said Tess. "Said it wasn't safe for *kids*." She rolled her eyes.

"When did that happen?" Alice said, watching Cal carefully. He seemed to be looking at the water.

"Couple of weeks back," said Amy.

"Hey, do you guys wanna come to the skate park with us?" Gav asked Alice and Violet.

"We have to go," Violet mumbled to Alice. "Dad's picking me up at three."

"Thank you," Alice said to Gav. "But we have to get going."

"Aw, they gotta get home to their mummies and daddies," Tess lisped.

Alice regarded her, wondering if she was being deliberately irritating. Violet fidgeted at her side. Alice turned to depart, then recalled the portable charger in her pocket and spent a few moments weighing up her options.

"You coming, Alice?" Violet hissed.

"Yes. Just a moment. We found something under the dock and I was wondering if it belonged to any of you." She drew the silver charger from her pocket and held it up, taking a good look around the entire group as she did so.

There was a pause—a couple of glances at Cal.

Gav, who'd been distracted by a dead jellyfish, looked across. "Hey, that's your charger, Cal!"

"Nah," said Cal.

"Yeah, it is."

"Nah, look, I've got my charger right here." Cal put his hand into the pocket of his long black coat and pulled out a tangle of cables, earbuds, gum wrappers, and finally a blue portable charger.

"Oh." Gav shrugged. "I thought yours was silver." Amy elbowed him again.

Cal pushed his gear back into his pocket and offered Alice a crooked smile.

"I'll take it." Tess pushed past Cal to hold out her hand for the silver charger.

Alice hesitated.

"You *found* it, didn't you?" Tess added, staring hard at Alice's face. "If you don't want it, I'll take it."

Alice was unable to think of a good reason to keep the charger and handed it over. Tess examined it, shot a fleeting glance at Cal, and shoved it into her jacket pocket. Alice and Violet turned to go.

"See you guys later, okay?" came Cal's voice.

Alice nodded. "Goodbye."

⚜

"We're going to be late." Violet was walking fast. Alice struggled to keep up.

"Will your dad be angry?" she asked, puffing.

"Mum will. I didn't realize how long we were walking on the beach."

Alice's leg was becoming painful. "I don't think I can go any faster."

Violet didn't slow her pace. "Mum's overprotective. She messages and phones if Lucas or I are just a couple of minutes late."

Alice concentrated on trying to keep up, but by the time Tranquility Funerals came into view, her leg felt heavy and shaky. Violet slowed abruptly, exhaling with relief.

"It's okay, he's not here yet. We've still got a couple of minutes." She noticed Alice's limping and her face creased with worry. "Ugh, sorry. Are you okay?"

"I'll be fine," said Alice, although it really did ache. She let herself through the gate and held it open for Violet. "Do you want to come inside?"

"I'd better wait out here. Dad'll be here any minute."

"I'll wait with you." Alice seated herself on the step with relief.

Violet stared absently at the mailbox. "Maybe you're right about Uncle George's death, I mean. It's strange, how suspicious people are acting. Higgo. Cal and his friends."

Alice was pleased to hear this. She was confident in her belief that George had died under peculiar circumstances, but it was good to know Violet was willing to entertain the idea.

"So you're all right with me investigating it?"

"*Us*, Alice. We'll investigate together. Just do *not* tell any of our parents, okay? They'll think we're being silly or having a mental breakdown from the grief, or something. I know what my mum's like. She'll just send me for counseling or whatever, and say I'm having—what d'you call it? Delusions."

"Wouldn't she want to know if something suspicious had happened to her husband's twin brother?" Alice asked in some surprise.

"Probably not, if I'm honest." A car slowed on the road in front of the house. "Here's Dad."

Eric Devenish wound down the window and stared at the house through his veil. Violet let herself out of the gate and opened the car door, but turned back to Alice before she climbed in.

"Thanks. That was..." She trailed off, then grinned unexpectedly. "Fun."

"Come on, Violet," said her father. "Your mother's expecting us."

Violet slipped into the car. "See you tomorrow," she called to Alice.

Alice watched them drive away, Eric Devenish glancing back at her more than once. Alice waved and went inside to see if her father needed help with his corpse.

❧

"Violet's mother seems very overprotective of Violet," Alice remarked to her father over dinner, adding cheese to her spaghetti Bolognese.

It wasn't actually spaghetti; her father preferred the health benefits of zucchini noodles. Alice did not, but so far, she had not been able to persuade him of her point of view.

He made a noise of agreement.

"There's a doctor in Port Cormorant who treats serious allergies, but Luanne won't let the children see him. In fact, she seemed quite angry at George for trying to get her to let them see the doctor."

"Yes, that was mentioned during the planning of the funeral," said Thaddeus. "George had become friendly with Dr. Grampian and he was supposed to come to the service, but Luanne didn't want him there. But it wasn't up to her—George's wife, Helen, had the final say, and ultimately nothing was done to stop Dr. Grampian from coming."

Alice looked at him. "So the doctor *was* at the funeral?"

"No, he didn't come in the end. Perhaps he knew it would stir up unpleasantness. He sent a floral arrangement with a card instead."

Alice sat up sharply when she heard this. The family of the deceased often left it up to the funeral home to dispose of floral tributes and cards. "Is it still here?" she asked.

"The flower arrangement? No, it was donated to the assisted living home with all the others. The cards are still here. Helen Devenish said she would drop in and pick them up, but she hasn't done so yet. I've packed them up to send to her."

"I can put them in the mail tomorrow, if you like?" Alice offered. "I pass a mailbox on my way to school."

"Thank you, Alice, that would be helpful."

"I'll fetch the package after dinner, so I don't forget in the morning."

"It's on my desk, in the office," said Thaddeus.

When they had finished the meal and cleaned up the kitchen, her father went to watch his favorite television program. It was about wealthy British people who were trying to find homes in expensive parts of Europe, but rarely seemed to like anything they found, and often ended up staying in Britain.

Alice went into the funeral section of their home. It was dark because the light switch was on the other side of the room, but Alice knew her way. She crossed the foyer and slipped through the great red curtain. In the moonlight coming through a window, Alice could see a casket, its lid closed ready for tomorrow morning's funeral. It contained Professor Joan Kostakidis. Alice had arranged a necklace and ring—a matching set of silver asps—on the professor before dinner.

The ring was resonant with details about Joan. She had been fascinated by snakes since childhood, when she had secretly kept a green tree snake she'd found as a pet. As a young woman, she became a medical doctor at her parents' urging. But after years of postgraduate study on toxicology, Joan eventually found her way back to her beloved snakes. She had been doing groundbreaking research on antivenoms, but unfortunately died after being bitten during a fang-milking session in her laboratory. Alice couldn't think of a more fitting death.

She accidentally bumped the professor's casket in the dim light. "Excuse me," she said.

Professor Kostakidis did not respond.

On the far side of the service room was a door marked NO ENTRY. It led to their office and embalming room. Once she was in the office, Alice flicked on the light. The faint, familiar scent of embalming chemicals and death seeped under the door from the next room. She located a couple of large envelopes on her father's desk, one of which looked promising. It was stuffed full. She turned it over and found the name Helen Devenish and a local address written in her father's looping hand.

It had not yet been sealed, so Alice drew out the stack of cards from within and flicked through, checking the scrawled names and messages. In the middle of the pile, she found the one she was looking for.

To Mrs. Helen Devenish,
My sincere sympathy for your loss.
George was an optimistic and courageous man,
and I shall certainly miss him.
Dr. Philip Grampian

Alice reread the card, committing it to memory. It was disappointingly ordinary—much like the other condolence cards she saw every week of her life. She shuffled through the remaining cards, identifying one from Higgo, signed *Leonard, Petra, and Harry Higginson*; and one from George's manager, signed *Gina, Chad, and Lily Prince*. And right at the bottom of the stack, a grubby-looking card that had almost escaped her notice.

George, I'm sorry.

It was signed with a single letter, scrawled so untidily that it could be a *G*, a *C*, or perhaps even an *L*.

Alice packed all the cards back into the envelope and sealed the end. She switched off the office light and carried the envelope past Professor Kostakidis in her handsome oak casket. Back in the house, she could hear the television in the living room, and her father's gentle snore from the sofa.

Alice went to the refrigerator and poured herself a glass of milk. She sat at the table to drink it, reflecting that in all her years at the funeral home, she had never once seen a condolence card that contained an apology to the corpse.

eleven

A CONTROVERSIAL THEORY

VIOLET joined Alice at the beautifully situated bench the next day. She sat down and held her veil out to maneuver a corn chip into her mouth.

"Yesterday was weird," she said. "What was the story with that charger, d'you think?"

"It almost certainly belonged to Cal." Alice ate a carrot stick meditatively. "But I suppose we might never know for sure."

"I don't like Tess. She's horrible." Violet turned to Alice, her eyes twinkling under the veil. "What coffin would you give her?"

"Deep, dark teak with gothic embellishments and a dramatic bloodred rosebud arrangement," Alice said promptly.

Violet wrinkled her nose. "Too nice for her."

Alice disagreed. "Tess seems spiky all over, but I suspect she is rather soft and vulnerable inside. Like an echinoderm."

Violet snorted, but she appeared to be thinking about Alice's words. A bird landed in the bush near the bench and poked its long beak into a loopy red blossom.

"I hope you and your father got home on time last night," Alice said.

Violet shrugged. "Mum went a bit crazy at us, as usual. She argues with Dad about it all the time. She's over-the-top. It gets boring." Violet chewed her lip. "Dad had a bit of skin damage on his wrist and she went crazy about that, too."

Alice was immediately interested. "Was he a little lax with his personal safety?" Violet looked blank. Alice reworded. "I mean, was he careless about his allergy?"

"You can't be careless, or you end up in pain."

Alice was picturing the rash she'd seen on George Devenish's hands and face. "What did your father do to damage his skin, then?"

"Don't know. That's why Mum was mad, I suppose. Dad said he didn't know how it happened, and Mum said…" Violet trailed off and looked down at her packet of corn chips. "She's got this crazy idea that he's been seeing Uncle George's doctor—you know, that specialist Uncle George took Lucas to see without telling anyone?"

Alice drew a quick breath. "Dr. Philip Grampian?"

"Yeah."

"What did Dr. Grampian actually do with your brother? Did he expose him to light?"

"No." Violet sounded quite certain. "Lucas is a whiner. He would have screamed bloody murder. He said the doctor just looked at his skin and sat down to talk to Uncle George for a while. That was it."

"But your mother was upset?"

Violet raised her eyebrows. "Understatement. And now she's accusing Dad of getting the treatment himself. Dad says he's not, but Mum's really suss."

"Was your uncle being treated by Dr. Grampian?"

"No, but Uncle George was interested in getting treated." Violet eyed her.

"They were acquainted, I think—George and Dr. Grampian. I understand there was some argument over whether or not the doctor would be allowed to come to the funeral."

"Oh, you mean Mum's letter?" Violet rolled her eyes. "Mum sent your dad a letter to say not to let Dr. Grampian come."

"Yes," said Alice. "But your aunt Helen wanted the doctor there."

"Aunty Helen said anyone who wanted to come should be allowed," said Violet. "Normally Aunty Helen buckles as soon as Mum tries to boss her around, but this time she just kept saying the funeral wasn't about anyone except Uncle George. Dad told Mum to stop going on about it, thankfully. It was getting embarrassing."

Cal came around the corner and raised a hand in greeting. "Hey, night creatures." He paused at their bench.

"Hi, Cal," said Alice. "Have you been called up to Mr. Prince's office again?"

He reddened and laughed. "Maybe. But I couldn't help it. Epic battle went down at two a.m. I was needed."

When Alice stared, Violet laughed. "He's talking about a computer game, Alice."

That made sense. "Have you considered finding an antipodean gaming community? The hours might be more suitable."

"Anti-what? Is that a new game?"

"No, antipodean players. It means people living in the southern hemisphere."

Cal and Violet exchanged a look. "She knows all sorts of bizarre words," Violet told him.

"Calvin Lee!" Mr. Prince's voice boomed through the window and Cal gave a start. He hurried toward the office door.

"Poor Cal," said Violet. "Always getting into trouble."

Alice disagreed. "There are many things he could do to change his tardy habits," she said. "Give himself a strict deadline to finish gaming for the night, for instance. Or set an alarm to remind him to go to bed."

Violet was grinning. "*Really?* Are you even a teenager, Alice?"

"Not yet," said Alice. "My birthday's next month."

Violet shook her head. "You're so weird."

Alice decided not to be offended. It sounded, if anything, quite affectionate—and anyway, being weird wasn't a bad thing, in Alice's opinion.

⚜

"I thought you might like to see this," Thaddeus said to Alice, passing the newspaper across the breakfast table.

In between articles about an amateur dramatic production of *Romeo and Juliet* and the discovery of a strange species of frog in Damocles Cove, there was a story about a seminar on allergies. It was to be hosted by Dr. Philip Grampian on the topic of his new treatment, and it was scheduled to take place in Damocles Cove over the coming weekend.

"That sounds intriguing!" she said, looking at her father. "It's free, too. Do you mind if I attend?"

"I don't see any harm in your going along, if you have an interest in the topic," he said. "What time is it?"

"Saturday morning. Do we have a funeral?"

Thaddeus leaned over to check his schedule book, which was currently on the kitchen bench. "Miss Pooney at ten a.m. It's going to be a very small service. I think Patty and I can spare you."

"Thanks, Dad. Why do you think Miss Pooney will have a small service?"

"It's a government-funded funeral, so I expect we will only get a few volunteers from the local church attending. She had no friends or family—no one to organize the service for her."

Alice nodded. "How sad not to have anyone to attend your funeral." She wondered for a moment whether she would have anyone at her own funeral, were she to get struck by lightning or fall into a ravine. Her father, obviously. But would anyone else come? It was an unpleasant thought. Some of her teachers might decide to go along from a sense of duty. Perhaps Violet would come, she thought, brightening—or even Cal. They weren't friends, but they were definitely acquaintances.

"Very sad." Thaddeus crunched his ancient grain toast spread with tahini. "Poor Miss Pooney."

At school, Alice told Violet about Dr. Grampian's seminar and invited her to come along.

Violet stared. "Are you insane? My mum would kill me!"

"Oh." Alice considered that. "Do you mean because she disapproves of the doctor's methods?"

"Duh," said Violet. "She literally *hates* the guy."

"That's a shame. I thought you might be interested in finding out more about the treatment."

"I am, kind of. But there's no way Mum would let me go." Violet chewed her lip for a few moments. "Unless I don't tell her."

Alice raised her eyebrows. "Do you mean you will sneak out? That's not a good idea, Violet. In fact, I probably shouldn't have even invited you, but I didn't think about the fact that your mother would object."

But Violet had set her jaw. Her eyes gleamed beneath the veil. "You know what? She's always trying to control what me and Lucas do—and even Dad. I'm over it. This Grampian guy could be a mad scientist or maybe he's got some good ideas. I should be allowed to judge for myself. I should at least be able to find out more about something that could potentially let me live an easier life."

Alice was increasingly uneasy. "But, Violet, even if Dr. Grampian isn't a mad scientist, you know you couldn't start any kind of treatment program without your mum's permission—don't you?"

"Well, obviously." Violet shot Alice a quick smile. "But if I think it's worth a try, I can at least start deploying the nag factor."

"The nag factor?"

"You know, when you keep on at your mum or dad about something until they can't take it anymore and agree to do what you want. That was how I got my phone."

Alice was bemused. "I'm not sure I fully agree with your decision to defy your mother, but I can't fault your determination."

Violet shrugged, but Alice thought she seemed a little pleased at the thought of being a rebel.

twelve
THE CORPOREAL BEQUEST

ON Saturday morning, Alice waited for Violet, growing more and more agitated. They had planned to meet at nine, but Violet was almost ten minutes late. Alice checked the window and paced the house, then when it got even later, she went out the front to wait in the yard. At last Eric Devenish dropped Violet off. Alice met her at the gate.

"We need to leave right away to catch the bus," Alice told her. "Otherwise we might not get to the town hall in time."

"I'm ready."

They walked as briskly as Alice's leg would allow, and arrived at the stop just moments before the bus. All this left Alice feeling quite discombobulated. She had to take some calming breaths and sip from her water bottle when they were seated. She wondered about Violet, who surely understood the discomfort of being late, what with her strict mother. But perhaps it had been beyond Violet's control. Perhaps Eric Devenish was the unpunctual one.

The trip to the town hall was only fifteen minutes by bus. They disembarked and joined the small crowd of people lining up at the registration table. Alice gazed around with interest at the other people who had chosen to come and hear Dr. Grampian. Some of them appeared to be medical people. They had intelligent faces and expensive clothing. Others looked like parents—less formally dressed and somehow more rumpled in appearance, as though they'd rushed out of the house after ensuring their highly allergic children had eaten a wheat- or nut-safe breakfast. There also appeared to be grandparents in attendance—neat, elderly, and rather less desperate—or perhaps these were simply people with spare time on their hands who liked to keep their minds active by attending public lectures.

Alice and Violet took brochures and provided their names at the registration table. They went inside, and Violet chose seats in a hidden back corner of the auditorium.

"We'll be able to see better if we sit closer to the front," Alice pointed out.

Violet stayed where she was. "I don't want the doctor to notice me."

"Does he know you?"

"No. But if he sees my veil and gloves, he might realize who I am." She glanced around herself. "Alice, back when Dr. Grampian saw Lucas with Uncle George, Mum phoned his office and blasted him. She said she could report him because he saw Lucas without her permission. She was going to do it, too, except Dad talked her out of it. Dad said it was probably a misunderstanding—maybe the doctor thought Lucas was Uncle George's son."

Alice looked at the stage area with its lectern and projector screen. "Do you think Dr. Grampian might have ill feelings toward your family because of your mother's phone call?"

Violet gave her head a little shake. "You talk so weird, Alice."

The doctor came in at that moment and started arranging the lectern and clicking through his slideshow to test that the projector worked properly. He was black-haired, with thick glasses and slightly pointed ears that gave him an otherworldly look. The lights were still up in the auditorium, and Violet ducked down in her seat, pulling the hood of her jacket over her hat and veil. Alice sat down, sitting forward on the edge of her seat, and slightly sideways to block Violet from the doctor's view.

He looked up and scanned the crowd. It was hard to tell because of the thickness of his glasses, but he seemed to pause on Violet and Alice. Violet made a frightened gasping noise, and Alice leaned even farther left to conceal her. It felt like the room froze.

Then Dr. Grampian looked down at his microphone and reclipped it at a more secure angle. Alice heard Violet start breathing again.

Soon the lights in the auditorium dimmed and there were enough people in the seats in front of them that Alice whispered to Violet that she was safe. Violet dared to sit up a little. The doctor was introduced by a woman who ran a support group for parents of allergic children. She was so excited to welcome Dr. Grampian that she'd gone pink in the cheeks. She might almost have been introducing a celebrity.

Dr. Grampian had a habit of shuffling his notes every couple of minutes. Alice found it annoying. However, he didn't even seem to need the notes; once he warmed up to his audience, he spoke with great energy and passion, the light glinting off his glasses. Alice thought he would be suited to a high-gloss mahogany casket with maroon satin lining, understated chrome fittings in a modern style, and a display of proteas for the top.

Some of Dr. Grampian's talk was complex science that bewildered Alice. Violet seemed to follow it better, perhaps because she knew more about allergies. In fact, she was so fascinated, she forgot she was hiding from the presenter. The doctor concluded his seminar by asking for questions, and Violet's hand shot into the air.

"You don't mind him seeing you now?" whispered Alice.

"Oh!" Violet pulled her hand back down.

Luckily, dozens of other hands had gone up as well. The question session went on almost as long as the talk itself. At last the doctor said the session was over and invited people to contact him for an appointment if they had more questions. He left the stage to a standing ovation.

Alice and Violet stood up. "Wow." Violet's eyes were shining behind her veil. "Imagine if it worked. I could cure my allergy. I could be a real person."

Alice was about to say that Violet was quite real, cured or not, but she was interrupted by a squeak of shock. She followed Violet's gaze and saw, getting out of his own chair across the auditorium, a familiar man in a veil just like Violet's.

Violet grabbed Alice's arm and tugged her toward the exit. "That's my dad!"

At that moment, Eric Devenish glanced across the room and caught sight of his daughter. His eyes widened in astonishment.

Violet started to run, but Alice wasn't having that nonsense. She unclamped Violet's hand from her arm and pulled her back.

"Come on," she said. "There's no point trying to hide now. Let's go and find out what your dad's doing here."

They wove toward Eric, and he dodged people in order to reach them somewhere in the middle. He looked outraged to see Violet, but instead of confronting her right there, Eric steered the girls out of the town hall. He ushered them down the road and into a coffee shop.

"Do you want a drink?" he asked, glancing distractedly around the shop. "A cake?"

"No, Dad!" said Violet to Alice's disappointment. Cake had sounded delightful. "What were you doing there?"

"Me?" Eric twitched his hat and veil back a few inches so he could shoot his daughter a glare. "What were *you* doing there?"

Violet grew flustered. "I was—I..." She looked at Alice.

"I invited her," said Alice. "I was interested in knowing more about Dr. Grampian's work and I asked Violet to come with me."

Eric shot Alice a hard look, then sank into a chair and brought a hand up under his veil to rub his face.

"Dad?" said Violet.

"You mustn't tell your mother about this," he said. Violet's eyebrows rose.

"Violet? I want your word that you won't tell her."

"Well, then," she said evenly. "Tell me why you were there."

Eric groaned, but before he could answer a waiter appeared. "Can I get you folks something?"

"Coffee," said Eric.

"A vanilla milkshake, please," said Alice.

Violet was far too fixated on learning the truth from her father to order a drink. The waiter melted away and Violet seized Eric's hand.

"Dad. Please."

He sighed. "To tell you the truth, Vi, I was curious. Your uncle put a lot of faith in this Grampian fella and I wanted to know more. But your mum's dead against it. She's convinced he's a quack. I didn't feel right about making an appointment to see him, just in case she found out. So I decided I would just slip into his lecture while she thought I was at my weekly bowling league, to—you know—find out a bit more, see if this guy can help us." He seemed to recall that Alice was there as well, and tried to explain. "Luanne's got a good heart, but she's been caring for us all for so many years now, she thinks she always knows best. Sometimes it's like there's no room for new ideas."

Alice nodded. "It's probably very frightening for her. She might think you'd be in terrible danger if you tried a new treatment."

"Or she might not know what to do with herself if we could manage on our own," Violet muttered darkly.

Eric opened his mouth as if he might argue, then closed it again and gave a tiny shake of his head.

"So, how did you like Dr. Grampian's talk?" Alice asked.

Eric seemed taken aback. "Oh. Pretty good. Interesting."

"It sounds amazing," Violet broke in. "Was Uncle George actually planning to start treatment, Dad? Do you know?"

He twisted his mouth, hesitating, then blurted an answer. "He was already being treated. He told me in confidence that he'd been seeing Grampian for a year."

"A year!" Violet practically choked. "Why didn't he tell us? Does Aunty Helen know?"

"Yes, Helen knows. They never talked about it in front of your mother, though. They knew how she would react."

"Only because Uncle George took Lucas to Dr. Grampian without permission," said Violet. "Maybe Mum wouldn't have been so freaked out about the treatment if he hadn't done that."

Her father's eyes dropped to the table and he wrung his hands.

"You knew about that?" Alice said. "You were involved, perhaps?"

Eric cast an imploring look at Violet. "It was me who asked George to take Lucas—just to get an opinion. I couldn't stand watching you kids go through what your Uncle George and I went through, without any hope of a treatment."

Violet's mouth hung open. "Dad! You got him to take Lucas to the doctor and then blamed Uncle George for it? That's—that's horrible!"

Eric's eyes were glistening with grief. "It wasn't like that. I asked

George to get the doctor's opinion on you kids trying the treatment. Grampian said he would need to see one of you to make any kind of recommendation. Lucas's class was going to the swimming pool for end-of-year celebrations, so he had the day off from school, but Luanne needed to go Christmas shopping, so she arranged to leave him with George and Helen." He took a breath. "I suggested George take Lucas to see Dr. Grampian. I told Lucas not to tell your mum, but he let slip that they went for ice cream in Port Cormorant. Then your mum wouldn't rest until she knew exactly where he'd been and why."

"Ugh, Dad," said Violet.

"I know," he said dolefully. "It was a big old mess. Your mum called Uncle George and said he'd endangered Lucas's life. I was at work, so I didn't even know what was going on. The first I knew of it was when George called me to say he would take the blame. He didn't want to get me into trouble with your mum."

Violet's shoulders slumped. "Poor Uncle George. All those horrible things Mum said to him about putting Lucas in danger. And the whole time, *you* were the one who organized it."

Eric's face was wretched. "Your uncle never stopped looking for a solution to our allergy. He wanted an easier life for all of us. He was a brave man."

The coffee and milkshake arrived, and Violet decided she did want something after all, so a soda was duly ordered and the three had their drinks. Eric wiped his eyes and sipped his coffee, gradually recovering his equilibrium. Before long, Violet and her father were enthusiastically discussing Dr. Grampian's methods, which left Alice to contemplate the thought of George Devenish secretly participating in the treatment.

"Did George tell you anything about the treatment itself?" she interjected during a pause in the conversation.

Eric nodded. "It involved shining a filtered light onto the skin and making the light stronger over time. George used a special lamp on his skin at home every day. The doctor tested his reaction and adjusted the light level each month, then George would start on a higher dose."

"Was it working?" Violet sounded almost breathless.

"It was too early to tell," said Eric. "The doctor had never worked with a sunlight allergy before—only nuts and eggs, beestings, that sort of thing. But Dr. Grampian seemed to think George was doing well. He wasn't having any serious allergic reactions to the filtered light."

Alice thought about the rash marks on the dead man's face and neck. "Is it possible the treatment might have led to his death?" she asked.

Eric's jaw sagged. "What?"

"I'm asking if Dr. Grampian's treatment may have contributed to your brother's death."

Eric rubbed his forehead again. "You don't pull any punches, do you, young lady?" He gave an uneasy laugh. "No, it had nothing to do with it. They would have found it in the autopsy. And he was only getting a tiny little bit of exposure."

"Did the police know George was being treated for the allergy?" Alice asked.

Eric shrugged. "Helen would've told them, I'd say. I'm sure the treatment had nothing to do with his death. I mean, he was having treatment at home every day at breakfast time, or in Dr. Grampian's clinic—not down at the pier in the early hours."

This was undeniable. Alice sipped her milkshake. "We'd better get going, Vi," Eric said to his daughter. "Mum will be expecting us."

Violet nodded. "Can we give Alice a lift home?"

"Of course." Eric observed Alice for a few moments. "How about you come back to our place for lunch, Alice? I'll phone ahead to Luanne, but I think she'd be happy to have you over."

"Thank you," said Alice. "If I can just borrow a phone to call my dad first—but I don't imagine he will object."

Violet passed her phone to Alice.

"Just don't let on to Luanne about this Dr. Grampian business," Eric added. "I've got a bit of thinking to do before I speak to her about it all."

Alice considered this condition for a few moments, then nodded her acceptance. Under the circumstances, she felt it was reasonable for Violet and her father to keep their interest in Dr. Grampian's treatment a secret from Luanne Devenish—at least for now. And it wasn't her secret to tell.

⚜

Luanne Devenish seemed delighted to host Alice for lunch. She prepared savory baked pastries—something Alice rarely got at home and loved. Violet's brother, Lucas, sitting at the table in shorts and a T-shirt, only spoke to ask if he could watch his favorite anime show while he ate. Luanne said no because they had a guest. He slumped back in his chair, his thin legs milky-white under the table, and stared at Alice when she asked for the ketchup. She found it rude, but tried to ignore him.

Halfway through their meal, there was a knock at the front door. No one moved except Luanne. She returned with Helen Devenish. Helen talked ceaselessly all the way. She looked much better than when Alice had last seen her at the funeral; her eyes were bright and her face expressive. Alice thought that a warm, polished pine casket would suit the woman—pewter handles and forest-green velvet lining. Daisies and pink roses for the top.

When she saw them all sitting around the table, Helen exclaimed. "Oh no, I've interrupted your lunch—I'll come back later."

"Don't be ridiculous, Helen." Luanne pushed her firmly into a chair. "Have you eaten? There's plenty to go around, help yourself."

"No, honestly, Luanne—I can't impose like this, let me come back later, won't you? Oh no, for heaven's sake—don't go to any trouble. Oh, if I must stay, I'll just sit here and join in the conversation—no, I don't need any food—no, no, don't get me a plate. Oh my goodness. No, I'm definitely not eating. Well, I haven't eaten yet as it happens, but I don't need anything. No, don't serve me any! Oh my goodness, you're not giving me a choice, are you? Just one, then—no, just one, Luanne! Yes, the pastie, please. No more. Oh, all right, one of the spinach ones. Absolutely no more, though. Just a beef pie. Thank you. This is too much—too much. Hello again, dear." This last part was directed at Alice.

"You remember Violet's friend Alice from her birthday party?" said Luanne, reclaiming her seat.

"Of course." Helen squinted at Alice. "Have I met you somewhere else, as well?"

"You may remember me from the funeral home that hosted the service for your husband," said Alice, smiling in polite greeting as her father had taught her to do.

Helen was silent for a full ten seconds, her mouth agape. Eric coughed. "Alice's father runs the funeral home," he said to his sister-in-law. "Alice helps out at the funerals, don't you?"

"Yes. And I assist with aesthetic services."

"What's *ez-theddick*?" asked Lucas.

"Aesthetic. The beautification of the corpse," Alice told him. "Makeup, dressing, hairstyling, accessorizing and, on some occasions, placing wadding inside the cheeks, wiring the jaw, and stitching the lips to prevent mouth sagging. I don't do those last things, though—not yet."

Lucas's eyes had grown enormous.

Eric coughed again. "Helen, how's your week been? We haven't seen you for a few days. Have you started feeling a bit more like yourself?"

"Oh, you know." Helen sighed and took a bite of a pastry. "Every day's a struggle. But I got back to work with Helping Communities yesterday. I went and saw the old dears at Our Lady Assisted Living Home; took them some brownies and a jigsaw puzzle. Dear Albert can hardly see these days, but he still has a go at the puzzles we bring! It drives poor old Maisie mad." Helen chuckled.

"That's good, Helen," Luanne said, nodding encouragingly. "It's wonderful to see you getting out of the house. It's so important when you're coming to terms with a life change like yours."

"What life change?" asked Lucas.

Violet rolled her eyes. "Uncle George dying, dummy."

"Kids," Eric admonished. "Have a bit of sensitivity."

Violet looked awkward. "Sorry, Aunty Helen."

"It's fine, sweetie. Don't you worry about me. You know me, I just get on with things."

"Did you have to sew up Uncle George's mouth?" Lucas asked Alice.

"Lucas!" Luanne hissed.

Helen held a napkin to her eyes for a moment, then smiled bravely around at them all, although Alice noticed she skipped over Lucas. "It's quite all right. I don't want to act as if nothing's changed. I can't just pretend George wasn't one day the biggest part of my life and the next, gone." She glanced at Alice. "It's even nice to see *you* again, dear. I don't want to forget a single thing—not the funeral service, nothing. It was a lovely service, didn't you think, Luanne? Eric? Lovely. I was very happy with Tranquility Funerals—and they were affordable, too."

"Yes, they did a good job," Eric agreed. "George would have liked it."

"It was respectful," Luanne said with a nod. "Being respectful to one who has passed is so important. More important than some realize."

She said this with an air of double meaning that made Alice wonder what Luanne was trying to say. Helen's eyes had dropped to her plate, but Lucas stared openly at his mother.

"How do you be *not respectful* to a dead person?" he asked.

Luanne mumbled something about doctors with disgusting morals.

"Luanne," Eric said quietly.

"I'm sorry," she said. "I'm sorry, Helen. It's just, I'll never forgive him."

"Who?" Lucas was mystified. "Uncle George?"

"Of course not!" his mother snapped. "That awful doctor, wanting poor George's remains for his irresponsible research!"

"Ohhh, Dr. Grumpy-Man," said Lucas.

Eric murmured his wife's name again. Helen truly seemed to have lost her appetite now. She gazed down at her plate, her lips trembling.

"Is that true?" Violet asked softly. "Dr. Grampian wanted Uncle George's body for research?"

Luanne confirmed it with a single impressive nod. "He tried to talk your poor aunt into it before the funeral—can you believe it? He pressured her until she almost gave in! The insensitivity. The nerve!" She forked a piece of sausage roll savagely into her mouth.

Eric cleared his throat. "I don't think this is fair on Helen at all. It's not the time *or* the place for this conversation," he added when Lucas opened his mouth to ask another question.

Alice was watching Helen. Her color had all drained from her cheeks, and she was only able to steady the trembling of her hand by clutching it around her water glass. She flicked a frightened glance at her sister-in-law and gave an audible swallow.

If Alice didn't know better, she would have thought the woman had something to hide.

thirteen
AN UNSATISFACTORY ANSWER

ON Tuesday, there was an athletics carnival and Thaddeus gave Alice the day off from school. He was always supportive when it came to Alice's weak leg, and he seemed glad of the extra help in the funeral home when she had to miss these sorts of events. Today Alice found her assistance was especially welcome.

The body Thaddeus and Patty were working on for the afternoon's funeral belonged to a former punk rocker, who had left instructions to be buried in a full costume. There was quite a bit of jewelry to arrange—spikes and rings. But the dead man had requested a mohawk, and neither Thaddeus nor Patty could make it look shocking or anarchic, no matter how much hairspray they used.

"It just keeps flopping over." Patty sounded angry and dug into her pocket for a breath mint—a sure sign that she was on her way to a bad mood. She always sucked breath mints when she was in a bad mood—it stopped her from swearing.

Alice sent her to have a cup of tea and found their strongest hair paste. She sculpted a style that would have made a cockatoo proud, and used spray acrylic to fix it in place. Then she helped Thaddeus buckle spiky leather cuffs onto the man's wrists and decorate the body's ripped vest with safety pins.

The body was finished in good time, and the funeral party,

many of whom had also worn their old punk outfits in honor of their friend, were duly impressed. When the service was over, Alice helped Patty vacuum the carpet and wash the dishes. Thaddeus gave Patty half the leftover sandwiches to feed her husband and son. He and Alice sat down to eat the remaining sandwiches for a late lunch.

"Punks have such an interesting way of dressing," Alice commented. "I've never seen so many spikes."

"Yes—I would say the corpse looked very *sharp*." Thaddeus grinned triumphantly.

"A passable pun," she allowed, checking the contents of her sandwich. Mortadella. "I've been thinking about George Devenish."

"Again?"

"Did you know George and Eric Devenish were twins?"

"Yes, Eric mentioned it."

"Identical twins?" she said.

"Yes. But Eric said they were quite different people," said Thaddeus. "He said George was a dreamer—he longed to explore and have adventures, but was stopped by the allergy, whereas Eric was more content to live a quiet life in safety."

"How enlightening," said Alice.

"Oh, bravo, Alice," said her father. "Nice pun."

Alice took no notice. "I found out over the weekend that George was getting treatment for his skin allergy with Dr. Grampian."

"Really?"

"Yes, and now Luanne Devenish suspects Eric is doing the same."

Her father raised his eyebrows but didn't reply. He ate an avocado triangle and Alice ate a curried egg triangle, both thinking.

"I wonder if Victoria would have been like me," Alice said after a while. "Would she have been contented and cheerful like me, or would she have longed for more—like George Devenish?"

Thaddeus stopped eating for so long that Alice looked up at his face. There was sadness there.

"Have the Devenish twins got you thinking about your own twin?" he asked.

She nodded.

"Well," he said. "I like to think Victoria would have been a cheerful child, but no one can be expected to be happy all the time."

Alice wondered if he was speaking from experience. "Was my mother a happy person?"

"Not as such," her father admitted. "I mean, we couldn't expect her to be bright or cheery, in the face of your sister's passing. But then, your mother naturally needed plenty of buoying up. She tended to the melancholy."

"Melon…"

"*Melancholy*," he said more slowly. "It means faintly sad."

"Ah." Alice selected her final triangle: a cream cheese. "Do you think she regrets running off?"

Thaddeus rubbed his chin. "I don't know what she feels about that, but I'm certain she thinks about you and Victoria every single day. It was her nature to think long and hard about anything she cared about."

Alice liked that. "Do *you* think Victoria and I would have been similar?"

"You weren't identical, as you know." He gazed at the photo on the wall. "Victoria had black hair, while yours was red, even from birth. I wish I knew what she would have been like as a person."

"Was Victoria ever alive?" she asked. "Or did she die before she was born?"

"Victoria was born dead," her father said. "The doctors detected that she had died before she was born—in fact, the doctors were worried you were both dead, so it was a wonderful joy when you turned up still alive. You were both so little. I held you both while your mother and I cried, my little dark-haired, still Victoria in one arm, and my little squirming, red-faced Alice in the other."

Alice looked at the grief lines in her father's face. People tended to think her father was unshockable. She had seen it when people planned their loved one's funerals. They assumed he couldn't be touched by sadness or death, since he'd seen so much of both. No one thought about what it had been like for Thaddeus to arrange his own baby's funeral, abandoned by his wife, and caring for the demanding, living daughter with her floppy leg.

After lunch, she told Thaddeus that she was going for a walk.

"Take care, Alice," he said.

"Of course, Dad."

Outside the front door, the cat was under the camellia bush again, peering at Alice with its big, dark eyes. She could have touched it—she just had to stretch right in. Alice did not do that. If she made a grab at it, the cat would never learn to trust her. She extended her hand slowly, a centimeter at a time. With its head up like that, she could almost read the name tag on its collar. Alice squinted, tipping her head. It appeared to start with *M* and end with *A*.

"Good afternoon," she whispered. "How are you today?"

The cat watched her.

"Would you like a pat?"

The whiskers on the left side of its face twitched. It resettled on its front paws just slightly.

"I'm your neighbor. You're very welcome in our yard." Alice shuffled forward a little to give the cat easier access to rub itself on her fingers. It inched backward.

Alice withdrew. *M* and *A. Mina? Medusa? Macadamia? Mozzarella?*

She set off on her walk to the pier. It was a shame Violet was stuck in the library at school. Conditions were perfect for investigating.

When she reached the gates of Pier 19, she stood and surveyed the scene for a few moments. A fishing boat had just docked, and workers were unloading a crateful of crayfish using the mechanical arm. Higgo was supervising, chatting with a crew member. At the top of the stone steps, a small figure in black sat watching. She recognized him.

"Cal!" she called out.

He saw her and got to his feet, hurrying over. "Hey, Alice! What are you doing here?"

"I came for a walk. I'm off school today because of the athletics carnival."

He smiled. "Me too."

She glanced at his legs, wondering if he had a medical issue like hers, but just in time, remembered it might not be tactful to ask. She noticed his long black coat had a pull around the hem and remembered the black threads she'd seen caught on a splinter under the jetty. Interesting.

"I was playing online with some guys in the States, but Mum had a go at me." Cal grimaced. "I went out to get her off my back."

"Do you live with your mum and dad?"

Cal fastened his top button against the sharp breeze. "Just Mum. Dad's got a place in Port Cormorant with his partner."

"Do you have any siblings?" Alice asked.

"A younger brother. He lives with Dad, though."

In the distance, a white car turned in through the pier gates and came to a stop outside the manager's hut. As Alice watched, a curly-haired woman got out of the driver's seat. She turned back to the car and said something to someone inside, then shut the door and went to the hut, unlocking the door, and letting herself in.

"Was that Gina?" said Alice. "The manager of Pier 19?"

"Yeah, that's her," Cal said.

Alice looked at Cal. "You know her?"

"I've seen her around. She's married to Mr. Prince; did you know that?"

"Yes." Alice started walking toward the hut.

Cal scrambled after her. "Where're you going?"

"I'd like to speak to Gina," she said.

"What? Why?"

Alice paused and thought about her answer. She didn't particularly want to reveal what she knew about George's death, especially since Cal and his friends were among those who may have been present. But she quite liked Cal. She honored him for standing up to his friends when they had been unpleasant to her and Violet.

"It's interesting to meet the people who knew our funeral home's clients," she said, which was true, if not a true answer to his question.

Cal stared at her. "You're weird, Zombie Queen."

Alice smiled. She was growing quite fond of that nickname.

"I'll come, too," he added.

They made their way along the pier to the manager's hut and knocked on the door. Alice tried to see who was in the car while they waited, but all that was visible was the top of a head. Whoever it was had to be short—perhaps a child—or someone hunched down to hide from view.

When she opened the door, Gina looked at Cal for several moments, then transferred her gaze to Alice for an equally long examination. She had beautiful eyes, like a horse or a fawn—so dark the iris and pupil were almost one. Beyond her, Alice spied a whiteboard mounted on the hut wall with the roster of security officers' shifts. HIGGO was written at regular intervals down the board: Monday, Wednesday, Thursday, Friday, and Saturday. Someone had tried to rub out the name *George*, but it must have been there a long time, and the text marks persisted. The name ASHOK had been penned over the top.

"I'm sorry to interrupt your work," said Alice.

"Alice?" She flicked her gaze between Alice and Cal again. "What do you kids need?"

"I apologize for turning up unannounced," said Alice. "I'd like to speak to you about your former employee George Devenish."

"Would you, now?" Gina said in surprise.

"Alice is friends with Violet," Cal put in. "George's niece."

Gina frowned. "I know who Violet is."

"Gina is a friend of Violet's mother," Alice told Cal.

"If Violet wants to speak to me about her Uncle George, she can. The pier isn't really a place for kids."

Alice was becoming a little tired of hearing that. "Violet can't be here today."

"She's at school, I imagine—where you two should be."

Cal looked away.

"I have a medical excuse," Alice told Gina. "It's been cleared with your husband. I don't mean to take up your time, but I just wanted to ask about George's shifts. I understand he wasn't meant to work that night, but Higgo's wife called George and asked him to come in. Is that right?"

Gina's eyebrows rose. "What's this about? I don't see how it's your business."

Alice was intrigued. "Is it private information?"

Gina was stiff for a moment longer, then sighed and seemed to relent. She chuckled slightly. "I suppose there's no harm in talking about it." She opened the door a little wider and leaned against the frame, glancing across the pier where the cray fishermen were shouting instructions back and forth. "Yes, poor George wasn't supposed to be working. That's what made it so awful. If proper procedure had been followed, he wouldn't even have been here. I have other security officers I would have called before I called him."

"Because of his allergy?" Alice asked.

Gina nodded. "He usually only worked the seven p.m. to two a.m. shifts. With George's allergy, there's no way I would have asked him to cover a two-to-nine shift." She gazed at the ground and shook her head.

Alice waited a respectful moment. "Why do you think he came in to do the shift?" she asked. "Knowing that it would take him into the dawn light, I mean."

"We don't know for sure," said Gina. "I guess he was trying to help. He probably thought he could cover just a few hours until we figured out someone else who could come in. But no one could get hold of me. My daughter had been playing with my phone and she'd set the ringtone to silent, so I didn't hear any of the phone calls. I feel terrible about it." She stared out at the water, biting her lip. "George and I understood each other. We shared a love of the sea."

Alice was relieved to understand a little more about George's final night. "So, George came in to cover for Higgo for a few hours, but no one else came to take over, so he stayed."

Gina was nodding. "The sunrise caught him by surprise."

Cal looked puzzled. "But he would have known what time sunrise was, right?" he put in. "Like, he would've had his phone, or a watch."

"The police didn't find George's phone," Alice recalled. "They think he dropped it into the sea."

"He wouldn't have been able to get himself to safety once he started having a reaction," said Gina. Tears came to her eyes and she wiped them with an impatient hand. "It incapacitated him."

Cal seemed uncomfortable and dropped his gaze, but Alice patted the woman's arm. "I'm sorry for your loss."

Gina couldn't help a small smile through her tears. "You're very mature for such a young person."

"Well, I am twelve," Alice said.

"Extraordinary."

Alice took advantage of Gina's warm words. "Can you think of any reason why someone might want to apologize to George after he died?"

Gina's eyes widened. *"Apologize?"*

"Do you know anyone who would want to say sorry to him?" asked Alice. She felt Cal staring at her.

Gina seemed confused. "I—I'm not sure. I suppose *I* wanted to. I mean, I was sorry I missed those phone calls. If I could apologize to George, I would." Her eyes were wet again.

There was an especially loud shout from the dock, and Gina glanced down there before looking back at them, her expression serious.

"My pier's a busy place, boats coming and going, machinery running back and forth across the pier, and workers everywhere. It's not a good place to hang around or meet your friends." She smiled at Alice, then Cal. "There's another big haul due to dock sometime soon and we can't have people putting themselves in danger. There have been too many kids getting themselves into trouble down here."

"Do you have a lot of kids hanging around?" Alice asked with interest.

"Not anymore," Gina said. "We try to clear them out as soon

as we spot them. And on that note…" She raised her eyebrows and nodded toward the gate.

"Thank you for speaking to us," Alice said, and turned to leave.

"Hang on," said Gina, and she dug into the handbag she'd placed on the desk. She pulled out a couple of chocolate bars and pressed them into their hands, trying not to smile. "Here you go, you rascals. Stay out of trouble, okay?"

Alice accepted with surprise and Cal mumbled a thanks. As they went back past Gina's car, Alice detected movement and a small face appeared at the window—a little dark-haired girl. Lily Prince. She grinned at them and held something up, as if to show them.

"What is that?" Alice asked. Whatever the girl was holding was alive and squirming.

"A kitten?" Cal laughed. "Who takes a kitten for a drive in a car?"

"That's Gina's daughter," said Alice.

The girl had lowered her kitten now. Alice waved at her and she waved back, looking delighted.

"May I ask you a question you might not wish to answer, Cal?" Alice asked as they reached the gate.

Cal shot her a startled look. "Okay. What?"

"Were you and your friends at Pier 19 on the morning George died?"

Cal's cheeks went pink, but he kept his gaze on the ground and shook his head. "Nah."

"You're sure?"

"Yeah."

It was unsatisfying, but Alice was obliged to accept his answer and walk on.

In her bedroom that night, while she was getting into her pajamas, Alice wondered if she was being a little overimaginative. Was it wrong of her to investigate George's death? There didn't seem to be anyone who would have wished him dead. And she hadn't been able to find evidence that others had been around on the morning he died—unless you counted the portable charger. And that could have belonged to anyone or been left there at any time. Perhaps she should let George Devenish rest in peace.

When she shoved her stiff dresser drawer closed, Alice bumped a small wooden box off the top. Somehow, in the fall, it came open, and its contents bounced and slid under the dresser. Alice got down on the floor and fished underneath until she felt what she was looking for: a small, coin-like object. Her dead twin's Saint Damian pendant.

Her father had given it to her when she turned ten. She opened it on each birthday to wish her sister many happy returns and commemorate the anniversary of Victoria's passing. Alice looked at the pendant for a few moments.

She felt suddenly sorrowful for Eric Devenish, having lost his twin after so many years of having a brother. They'd been through so much together, especially sharing their allergy. It must be an infinitely deeper pain than hers, to have known and loved a twin before losing him. Alice touched the Saint Cosmas pendant at her neck. If it was her twin who had died at the pier, she would want to know the whole truth.

She *would* keep investigating. Perhaps George's death had been a sad accident, but there were signs that something deeper had been going on. She owed it to Eric to uncover the truth. And Violet.

And Victoria.

Alice put the Saint Damian pendant back where it belonged and closed the box.

fourteen
THE CASE FILE

VIOLET now joined Alice on the best bench near the principal's office each recess and lunchtime. Alice tried to use the time to discuss what they knew about George and his death, his work at the pier, his treatment with Dr. Grampian, and anything else that might be relevant, but Violet didn't always want to talk about her uncle. Sometimes she wanted to talk about the Korean band she liked. She also liked to yearn for a pair of shoes she wanted and a vacation camp she would have liked to go on, but her mother had refused both.

Alice was surprised by the sociable natter. She tried to bring the conversation back to the more pressing issue of George Devenish, but Violet rolled her eyes.

"Do you ever think about anything else?"

"Of course," Alice said, bemused.

"So why don't you talk about anything else?"

"I do. But I talk about George's death with you because it's what we have in common."

"Maybe we have other things in common too," Violet said.

"I suppose it's possible." Alice doubted it. She had little in common with anyone else, especially in her own age group.

"What music do you like?" Violet pressed her.

"I don't listen to music, although the classical music Dad plays at funeral services is quite good."

Violet blinked a couple of times. "Well, which YouTubers do you watch?"

"I don't have a phone," Alice reminded her. "Dad lets me use the computer for research purposes when I'm doing a school project."

Violet filled her cheeks with air and blew it out slowly. "Okay, what television shows do you like?"

"Documentaries on archaeological finds," Alice answered readily. "Particularly Middle Ages archaeology. I'm very interested in the history of village life, peasants, the plague, and witchcraft. Fascinating."

Violet's frown was deepening. "Hmm," she said. "Do you like K-drama?"

"Do I like what?"

"Never mind. What about shopping. Do you like shopping?"

"For what, specifically? I don't mind grocery shopping, as long as the store isn't too crowded. I like the fossil and gemstone shop at the Quay."

"Oh, I love that shop!" said Violet, her face lighting up. "They have the cutest pendants."

"I like the volcano stone and petrified wood," said Alice.

"Hey, I know," said Violet. "Why don't we go to the gemstone shop together this weekend? You could even sleep over, if you want?" She examined her sneaker as if it were deeply interesting.

Alice couldn't see anything unusual about Violet's shoe, so she considered the offer. The thought of Violet's tense mother and staring younger brother made her hesitate. "I'll come to the gem shop but I'm not sure about sleeping over."

"Don't you like sleepovers?" Violet asked.

"I've never had one before."

"Oh, right." Violet mulled it over. "Would you rather I stay over at yours, then?"

Alice did prefer that idea. "Yes, that should be all right. I'll need to check with my father, although I don't think he'll mind. I'll still need to help with any funerals, but if the service times fit, you can certainly stay over." Alice regarded Violet. "Are you sure your mother will permit it?"

"I can talk her into it," Violet said airily. "I'll use the nag factor. She'll want to meet with your dad beforehand, to go through what to do if I have an allergic reaction and stuff, but I think she'll let me stay. She's always at me to make more friends." Violet rolled her eyes again.

Alice thought that sounded like an interfering and obnoxious thing to be bothering your child about, but she tactfully said nothing. Violet seemed pleased with the prospect of the weekend shopping outing and sleepover. She wore a small smile as she pulled out her phone and sent a text message. Alice could see her typing to her mother, saying she had been invited to stay at Alice's place—which wasn't strictly true, since Violet had asked to sleep over, but Alice didn't like to be overly pedantic.

"It will give us a good block of time to go over what we've learned about your uncle's death," Alice said, folding the piece of foil in which her sandwiches had been wrapped.

Violet gave a shrug and bit into her banana.

⚜

Alice had two funeral services to attend on the weekend. They organized for Violet to sleep over on Saturday night, then they could visit the Quay on Sunday morning.

Saturday's deceased was Mr. Colin Craddock, bachelor. He was to be buried wearing a Port Bank long-service pin, which was resonant. While positioning the pin on the body's lapel, Alice learned that Mr. Craddock had led a solitary existence. His sole joy was the bank position he held for his entire working life. He wasn't ambitious enough to rise above head teller, but he loved his job anyway. Mr. Craddock had recently retired. He'd found his life utterly meaningless without his beloved job, and promptly died. His loyal, bossy housekeeper had supplied Tranquility Funerals with the long-service pin.

Alice finished her work at Saturday's funeral, then spent a couple of hours preparing the house for Violet's visit. At around four in the afternoon, the private doorbell rang. Alice and Thaddeus went to answer it.

Violet hadn't been exaggerating about her mother's need to give full instructions on how to manage Violet's allergy. "It's not just sunlight," she told Thaddeus on the doorstep. "Any UV light could trigger a reaction. The main thing is not to assume Violet's safe once she's inside, even after dark. She'll need to keep her sleeping veil and gloves on through the night, just in case some light comes through a window or skylight in the morning, or if someone switches on an overhead light."

Violet stood next to her mother, looking bored and a little embarrassed. Then she had to wait through another speech, this time directed at Violet herself, and occasionally Alice, about the dangers of staying in unfamiliar environments.

At last Violet groaned and pushed past Luanne, stepping inside. "Enough, Mum! I'll be fine. I know how to look after myself. Come on, Alice, show me your room."

"I'll pick you up at the Quay tomorrow morning, eleven sharp!" Luanne called after her.

But Violet slowed down as she walked through the kitchen and into the living room. "What's going on in here?" she said, turning to Alice with her eyes wide.

"I thought you might like to go without your protective gear, so I've arranged things to make you completely safe," said Alice.

Violet stared around at the tea lights burning on every table and bench. Alice had raided the funeral home's candle supply, then stuck the curtains to the door and window frames with strong tape. She had even placed duct tape over light switches in the off position to prevent accidental switching on. The external doors bore reminder notes—*Do not open until you have checked Violet is not nearby.* Finally, she showed Violet her bedroom, which was similarly taped up and candlelit.

Violet wore a strange look on her face. "You did all this so I could stay here?"

"Oh no—I knew you could stay here regardless. But I thought you might like to feel more comfortable for the night."

Violet put down her bag and looked around Alice's room. After a few moments, she pulled back the Velcro strap on one glove and removed it, then the other. She shrugged off her jacket and kicked off her shoes and the long socks. Last came the hat with the tinted veil. Violet blinked around the room, her lips curving into a smile. Her eyes came to rest on Alice.

"Cool room," she said. "How long have you been collecting beach stuff?"

Alice was puzzled. "I don't collect beach stuff."

Violet laughed. "Alice. Look around you."

Alice followed Violet's gaze and realized what she meant. Everything, from the wooden floor to her white headboard, was covered in things Alice had found at the beach. There were pieces of old fishing nets, seashells, items preserved in jars, sun-bleached driftwood, sections of rusted chain and anchors, dried seahorses, chunks of coral, and sea urchins.

"It's not a collection," she said. "I occasionally pick up interesting things."

"That you find at the beach? That's called having a beach collection."

Alice frowned at her bedroom. Violet laughed again and Alice gave up on the argument.

"My father is making a stir-fry for dinner," she told Violet. "I hope that's something you don't mind eating."

"Yeah, that sounds okay." Violet turned to rummage in her backpack and whipped out a paper bag. "I brought some chips and chocolate for later."

"You did?" Alice was delighted. "How wonderful! But my father won't approve," she recalled with a pang of disappointment. "He's very health-conscious."

"Don't worry, I won't tell him." Violet pushed the contraband back into her bag. "What do you want to do? I brought my Bluetooth speaker. We could listen to music. Or I saved watching AlistairXOX's newest video so we could watch it together."

"That sounds enjoyable." Alice found a notebook and pen. "But first, let's collate all our facts."

"Facts?"

"About your uncle George."

Violet groaned and flopped onto Alice's bed. "Do we have to?"

"Yes, we do. We won't get to the truth if we don't take the project seriously. We've discovered all sorts of things that indicate strange goings-on surrounding your uncle and his place of employment. Even if I'm wrong, something is afoot and I'd like to understand it."

Violet hesitated. "Something is a foot?"

"I mean, something odd is going on."

"Oh. What, though?"

Alice seized the opportunity and opened the notebook, writing the number 1. "Firstly, your uncle was secretly receiving treatment from this doctor. Second, unbeknownst to your mother, your father asked George to take Lucas for a consultation."

Violet shuffled forward to see the notebook, becoming interested in spite of herself. "And Aunty Helen was involved."

Alice wrote that down as point 3. "Fourth, Dr. Grampian wanted to take possession of your uncle's body for scientific study."

"Yeah, and he put pressure on Aunty Helen to let him do it," Violet added.

"Then there was the anonymous card."

"What card?"

Alice recollected that she hadn't told Violet about the strange card. "There was a note addressed to your uncle among the condolence cards. It only said, 'I'm sorry,' and was signed with a single initial."

Violet went still. "It said 'sorry'?"

"Yes. Nothing else. Just 'George, I'm sorry.'"

"And what was the initial?" Violet breathed.

Alice gave her an apologetic look. "It could have been a *G*, or a *C*, or an *L*. I couldn't quite be sure."

"That's *super* weird," said Violet, staring abstractedly at Alice's duvet cover.

"I thought so too." Alice wrote about the card in her notebook. "Why would someone be sorry?"

"Can I see it?"

"We had to post the cards off to Helen, I'm afraid."

"Maybe it was my dad," said Violet. "Could it have been an *E*?"

Alice thought back to the card. "I don't think so, but I suppose it's possible."

"Who do we know who starts with those letters?" asked Violet. "*G* could be Grampian!"

Alice wrote that down. "Or Gina Prince. *L* could be Leonard—that's Higgo's first name. Or Luanne, your mother—or Lucas, your brother."

"It's not Lucas," Violet said, waving a dismissive hand. "And why would Mum say sorry?"

"Because of their argument, maybe?" Violet seemed doubtful. "What about *C*?"

They both thought for a minute. "Cal," Alice suggested at last. "Calvin Lee."

"Cal?" Violet's nose scrunched. *"Really?"*

"I'll get to Cal and his friends in a minute," said Alice. "Let's stick with your uncle and his work for now. I want to make a few notes about the circumstances of your uncle taking the dawn shift. When I spoke to Gina, she said she never assigned George daylight shifts at all."

"I'm still annoyed you went and spoke to Aunty Gina on Tuesday." Violet had her eyebrows up. "I really think I should be with you whenever you're investigating. He was *my* uncle."

"Yes, but you weren't available on Tuesday." Alice had already explained this to Violet once. "Gina said she wouldn't have called George in to replace Higgo." She noted this down. "But her daughter had set her phone to silent, so she didn't hear it when Higgo's wife called to report him sick."

"So Higgo's wife just called Uncle George instead."

Alice noted that down as well, then thought it over. "It could all be a tragic chain of events, I suppose."

"It does seem like a *lot* of stuff had to go wrong," said Violet. "Like, if Higgo hadn't got sick, they wouldn't have needed to replace him. If Aunty Gina's phone volume hadn't been turned down, she would have called in one of the other security guys. If Higgo's wife hadn't called Uncle George, he wouldn't have gone in to work."

"And if something hadn't happened to distract him, he wouldn't have been out when the sun rose," Alice finished.

Violet nodded. "After Dad told me Uncle George had been getting treated by Dr. Grampian, I wondered if maybe Uncle George messed up. Maybe he thought his treatment had made him so much less allergic, he could handle being exposed to sunlight."

"That's an interesting thought," said Alice, noting it down. "Perhaps your uncle had false confidence in his body's ability to withstand morning light? He wasn't wearing protective gear at all, despite the risk of UVB light." Alice was growing excited. "Perhaps he thought his body was already at the stage where he could take some risks."

"No, Uncle George never wore his protective gear at night. He thought that was over-the-top. He and Mum argued about that, too. Uncle George said Mum was paranoid, making us wear our gear at night as well as day."

"Oh!" Alice regarded Violet. "So not everyone with your condition wears protective gear all the time?"

Violet shrugged, looking uncomfortable. "I'm on an allergy forum with some other teenagers. There's a girl in Sweden who's got the same thing as me. She says she only wears protective gear outside in the sunlight, not inside or at nighttime."

"Do you *ever* take it off under indoor lighting?" Alice asked. "Outside of home, I mean?"

"Mum won't let me," Violet admitted. "I got burned once when

I was a toddler. It was at a playgroup. She says she took off my veil when we got inside because there were no windows in the hall, but the indoor UV lights burned my skin, and ever since then she's only let me take the gear off at home."

Alice added: *George did not wear protective gear on his night shifts* as another point in her notebook. She privately wondered if Violet's mother was putting unnecessary restrictions on Violet and Lucas.

She showed Violet the list. "So, in addition to the twelve points I've written down already, there are Cal and Tess and their friends. I still suspect they may have been under the dock that night."

"The portable charger," Violet said. "The way they acted when you showed it to them was so sketchy. I think it was definitely Cal's."

"I agree." Alice added the point to her notebook. "I felt that they were all covering for Cal when he denied the charger belonged to him, which would have put them—or at least Cal—at the scene. They didn't want us to know he'd been there."

"Didn't they *admit* they were there, though?" Violet screwed up her face with the effort of remembering. "Cal's friend said they saw Higgo there that morning, right?"

"Yes," said Alice. "You're right. The tall boy, Gav, said Higgo was there. But Tess said it was a different morning."

"Yet Higgo wasn't supposed to be at work. He was sick. Write that down," Violet instructed. "Why would Cal and his friends lie about being there that morning? Do you think they're worried they'll get in trouble?" She seized Alice's arm, her eyes opening wide. "Do you think they *saw* Uncle George having an allergic reaction and didn't help him?"

Alice unclasped Violet's hand from her arm and considered the idea. "Cal's friends aren't particularly polite people, but I don't think they would ignore a dying man. However, they certainly know something they aren't telling us."

Violet sat, apparently deep in thought, while Alice finished making her notes. "You know, I'd love to get a look at Uncle George's records," she said at last. "His autopsy report, the police file, stuff like that." Her eyes landed on Alice. "I don't suppose the funeral home gets sent anything like that?"

"I don't believe so," said Alice. "I could ask my father…"

"No, that's fine," Violet said quickly, then added, "But, like, where would those sorts of records be kept if the funeral home *did* get copies?"

"In our client files, I suppose," said Alice.

"In your…office?" Violet asked.

"Yes. We have filing cabinets for client records."

"Do you think we could take a look?" Violet said.

Alice thought about it. "My father might let us. I can ask him at dinner."

Violet flashed Alice a smile. "No, don't worry about it. I doubt there'd be anything useful there."

fifteen
NOCTURNAL PURSUITS

AFTER their candlelit dinner, Alice remembered to be a good host and let Violet choose some of the activities. She watched the AlistairXOX video—which made little sense and certainly didn't make her laugh like it made Violet laugh—then listened patiently to Moon Squad songs for what seemed like a very long time. At nine, Thaddeus put his head around the door, wished them good night and told them not to stay up too late. Alice unrolled the spare mattress and made up Violet's bed on the floor. The two got into their pajamas.

"Listen." Violet sat on the bed in front of Alice, her hair amber in the candlelight. "I've got an idea. But first, chocolate."

Alice ate a row of honeycomb-chip chocolate—extremely delicious—and listened to Violet's idea.

"You and I know that something about Uncle George's death is a bit weird, right? But the cops and doctors, my dad, and Aunty Helen—none of them know. That means his death wasn't properly investigated. But no one is going to listen to us, are they? We're thirteen years old—"

"I'm twelve," Alice corrected her.

"Twelve, thirteen, whatever. The point is, no one would believe us if we tried to tell them something weird happened to Uncle George. So, *we* need to do the investigating, right?"

"That's what we're doing," Alice said, breaking off another row of the excellent chocolate.

"Yes! That's right. And to do it properly, we need facts. You wrote down all those facts before—"

"Almost twenty of them," Alice agreed.

"Yeah, but we need more. And I'm his niece, so I think I've got a right to the information."

"What information?" asked Alice.

"Anything that might have been sent to the funeral home." Violet stopped and watched Alice, her eyes shining bright.

"I very much doubt there was anything relevant sent to us."

"But what if there was? Can we at least check?"

"You want to check?" Alice popped the last square into her mouth and ate it pensively. "My father's already gone to bed," she said.

"But we can just go and take a quick look without disturbing him," said Violet.

Alice examined the idea from every angle. It sounded reasonable and logical, and yet, something about it made her feel ever-so-slightly uneasy.

"Why don't we wait until morning, so Dad can help?" she said.

"Nooo," moaned Violet. She wrapped up the remaining chocolate, to Alice's regret, and jumped off the bed, pulling Alice up by the hand. "Bring your notebook, and we'll see if we can add more facts. Then when we get back, we'll finish the chocolate. Yeah?" She lifted her bare foot. "What's that?"

Alice spied something coin-like on the floor. "Oh!" She retrieved it and stared at the closed wooden box on her dresser. "How did that get there?" She opened the box and placed Victoria's Saint Damian pendant back inside, closing the lid firmly.

"Come on," said Violet. "Let's go take a quick look at this file—and then more chocolate."

They took a candle each and padded down the hall. Thaddeus had extinguished all the candles in the living area, leaving the house pitch-dark. Alice opened the door to the funeral home foyer, and paused.

"I didn't tape any of the lights in here," she said. "We must remember not to switch them on. Perhaps we should go back and get your protective gear."

"No, we're here now. Let's just get on with it." Violet's voice sounded thinner now, and less confident. She was looking nervously at the corners of the shadowy foyer.

Alice led the way to the great red curtain and, because it was so dark, took a few moments to find the opening. When they were through, Violet made a funny squeaking noise.

"Are you all right?" asked Alice.

Violet pointed. "Is—is there someone in that?"

Alice looked at the object of Violet's distress: a coffin visible in the moonlight coming through the funeral room's high window. "Yes. That's the casket of Mrs. Bridie Tierney."

Violet seemed to have frozen on the spot. Alice tried to reassure her.

"Don't worry. She's dead."

A moment's silence, then Violet burst into hysterical giggles. She clapped a hand over her mouth to muffle the noise. Alice wasn't sure exactly what had amused Violet, but she led the way to the office and located the key beneath a copper vase of artificial lilies sitting on a low shelf. Alice unlocked the office door and again had that sense of misgiving.

"I wonder if we should have asked Dad before we did this," she said, glancing back toward the foyer.

"Seriously, Alice," Violet said through her giggles. "It's fine. Remember, he was *my* uncle."

"Yes, I suppose." Alice raised her candle and nodded toward the filing cabinet.

Violet looked over her shoulder, gave that strained giggle again, and crossed the office, placing her candle on top of the cabinet. "Is it locked?"

"No. We only lock the office door. The top drawer is *A* through *H*."

"Huh?"

"It's in alphabetical order," Alice explained. "George Devenish's file will be in the top drawer."

"Oh, right. Gotcha." Another giggle escaped. Alice thought it must be a nervous giggle.

Violet rumbled open the top drawer and attempted to flick through the hanging folders with her trembling fingers. Alice moved in to help. She quickly located the *D* section and drew out the folder for *Devenish, G.* Violet took it over to the desk and Alice set down her candle beside it.

The first page was an itemization of costs for the funeral. The next was a set of papers covered in Thaddeus's handwriting—notes from his meeting with Helen to plan the service. It contained bulleted details about George's life and family for the eulogy, and a couple of song titles Helen had selected for her husband's send-off. The next item was a printed email.

Dear Mr. England,

I'm writing to advise that Dr. Philip Grampian must be kept OUT of the funeral proceedings for my brother-in-law, George Devenish. Grampian is an unscrupulous, irresponsible man who bullied my brother-in-law into bringing my child—my YOUNG child—in for an unapproved consultation. He is now attempting to push George's wife, Helen, into donating George's body for research. This is a horrible position to put poor Helen in. I have reason to believe this man will stop at nothing to get what he wants, and I want to make it very clear that the Devenish family does not want him involved in the funeral at all.

Regards,
Luanne Devenish

"Mum's letter," Violet whispered. "She only told Dad after she'd sent it. He said she shouldn't have done it because it's Helen's business, not ours."

"I don't believe my father would have done anything about it, anyway. He has a policy of not getting involved in personal disputes. He always tells the families they have to sort out their own arguments about who attends the services and who doesn't. Dad believes there's too much *he-said-she-said* in those arguments, and it's not up to him to decide who's right or wrong."

"Dr. Grampian didn't come, though," said Violet.

"Perhaps your mum warned him directly, as well."

"I wouldn't put it past her." Violet turned to the next page. "What's this?" she said, pulling out a stapled document.

"Those are the receipts for transport of the body," said Alice. "This one's for the transport from the mortuary to our funeral home. And this one is…" She paused, reading the receipt.

"Alice?"

"It's a little unusual," she said. "Normally the transport is to a crematorium or cemetery, but this is an address in Port Cormorant. I don't recognize it. Do you know where he was cremated?"

"No. Write down the address," said Violet, passing her a pad of sticky notes. "We can look it up on my phone."

Alice did so. The next page in the file was a list of items supplied by Helen for dressing George's remains. The next sheet after that was a legal-looking document on quality paper, with a Port Cormorant University seal on it.

"What's that?" Violet whispered.

"I'm not sure. I haven't seen anything like it before." Alice brought the candle closer and read the letter aloud.

> ATTN: Thaddeus England, Funeral Director Re: Donation of remains
>
> Dear Mr. England,
>
> I am writing to request the release of the body of George Albert Devenish into the university's possession.
>
> Mr. Devenish's legal spouse, Helen Amelia Devenish, has provided approval for the donation of his body to the Port Cormorant University Center for Allergy Studies, specifically for use within the micro-exposure program led by Dr. Philip Grampian.
>
> Ms. Devenish has signed a declaration (enclosed) that during his lifetime, Mr. Devenish expressed a wish to donate his remains to further the Center's work on treatments for life-threatening allergies. Acting on his wishes, Ms. Devenish has fully authorized us to collect her husband's remains from your place of business after the deceased's funeral service on the 16th of this month.
>
> We have engaged a local transport business to manage the removal of the body and trust that the enclosed papers

and signed documentation lay out full instructions for a smooth handover.

If you have any questions relating to this matter, please contact us on the details below.

Yours sincerely, Lisa Headingly

Dean of Medical Sciences, Port Cormorant University

Violet's eyes were wide in the candlelight. "Aunty Helen really did come close to donating Uncle George's body," she said. "They must have sent this before she changed her mind."

Alice picked up the corpse transport receipt and held it next to the university letter. The addresses matched. "No, Violet. This receipt says the body was definitely taken to Port Cormorant University. I don't think your aunt changed her mind about donating his body at all."

⚜

Back in Alice's room, they got through all the chocolate and chips, their discussion going on late into the night. Alice and Violet woke after eight on Sunday morning and ate breakfast by candlelight. They dressed for their shopping trip at the Quay, although neither of them was as interested in the outing anymore.

"I can't really ask Aunty Helen about donating the body," Violet said when they were walking to the Quay. "No one's supposed to know."

"That's true," said Alice. "And anyway, it's your aunt's right. Your mother might not like it, but donation of a body concerns no one except the deceased and their next of kin." She glanced at Violet's tight mouth. "It might cause conflict in your family, if you tell the truth."

"Yeah," was all Violet said in response.

They trudged the rest of the way to the Quay in silence. Alice's suggestion that they get churros seemed to lighten Violet's mood a little, and the two spent quite a long time looking at the items for sale in the gemstones shop, and nibbling their deep-fried treats.

"Rose quartz," Violet murmured, pulling an elastic bracelet of the pink stones over her gloved wrist. "I like these best."

Alice was surprised by Violet's preference. The pale stones were bland and uninteresting, in Alice's view. She showed Violet a piece of obsidian.

"Obsidian is an igneous rock formed by the rapid cooling of viscous lava from volcanoes," she said. "It can be millions of years old. Isn't that amazing?"

"Yeah, but the rose quartz is really pretty," said Violet.

Violet bought the bracelet. Alice bought a little piece of autunite in a Perspex case after reading a description of the lurid green crystal that said it would fluoresce under ultraviolet light.

"It's like you," she said to Violet when she'd finished explaining this unusual property. "It reacts to UV light."

Violet gave her a half smile. "Another freak, huh?"

"You are not a freak, Violet," Alice said, extremely serious. "You're unique and interesting."

"Hey, Zombie Queen! Ultraviolet!"

The two looked up and saw Cal loping toward them, grinning. His hair was gelled up high and his long black coat flapped in the breeze.

"Hello, Cal," Alice greeted him.

"How're you doing?" he said, and Violet murmured a hello.

"We're very well, thank you, Cal," said Alice.

For some reason this amused him "You kill me, Zombie Queen."

He looked at the paper cup in her hand that contained the one-and-a-half churros she hadn't been able to finish.

"Would you like one?" she offered. "I'm finished."

Cal accepted readily, devouring both the full and half churros in moments. He dropped the cup into a trash can. "What are you up to?" he asked. "Just hanging out here for the day?"

"No, we're nearly done," said Violet. "My mum'll be here in fifteen minutes."

"And I'll need to go home, too," Alice said. "I'm helping with a service this afternoon."

Cal's shoulders dropped. "Bummer."

"Aren't your friends coming down?" Violet asked.

He shook his head. "Nah. Everyone's busy. I'm so bored."

"You don't feel like playing your computer games?" asked Alice.

"There's no one interesting online at the moment." He sighed.

Alice felt sorry for him. "And you don't have any homework?"

He laughed but reddened. "Probably."

They strolled toward the main entrance of the Quay, Alice observing the emerald glimmer of water through the jetty planks beneath their feet. While they waited for Luanne to arrive, Violet and Cal conversed at a rapid pace. It seemed Cal was also a fan of AlistairXOX, and he and Violet laughed together about something hilarious the YouTuber had done. Alice noticed a dried-mud bird's nest tucked into a beam above the swimwear shop. The parent birds brought food at regular intervals. She thought they might be welcome swallows but would need to check her father's bird book later.

"There's Mum," said Violet, hitching her backpack higher on her back. To Alice's great surprise, she leaned in for a brief hug.

"Goodbye," said Alice. "I'll see you at school tomorrow."

"See ya." Violet crossed the parking lot, slipped into her mother's car, and was gone.

"Are you going home right away?" Cal asked.

"I can stay a little longer."

"Cool. Wanna go for a walk on the beach?"

"Yes, that would be nice," said Alice.

They walked down the little beach, which was busy with young families under sun shelters and children digging in the sand.

"Have you seen your friends this weekend?" Alice asked.

"Yeah. I caught up with them last night. We hung out under the dock and played some music."

"At Pier 19?" Alice asked.

Cal looked away. "Nah. Pier 20. It's quieter there. No one's using it, so they don't have security officers wandering around or anything."

"But Pier 19 is busy, isn't it?" said Alice, watching him carefully. "There's always at least one security person walking around. Boats coming and going day and night. Wharf workers and fishermen."

Cal shrugged and stared at the sand beneath his black boots.

"You must have noticed how busy it is," she pressed him. "You and your friends used to go there, didn't you?"

Again, he didn't answer.

"Cal, I've been wanting to ask you something. You'd know where the security cameras are around Pier 19—do they cover the dock?"

"How would I know?" he mumbled.

"Cal," she said patiently. "I know you and your friends used to hang out there. It's all right. You can tell me."

He was silent for a while longer before sneaking her a sideways glance. He sighed and shoved his hands into his coat pockets.

"Fine. We *used* to go there."

"And the cameras?" Alice asked again.

"Gav noticed them. He and Tess wanted to make sure we didn't get caught on CCTV, because we always get blamed when anything happens. There's one camera on the manager's hut roof. It points at the pier, where the forklifts and stuff are. There's another one in the parking lot, and there's one on the dock. It points along the jetty, but it wouldn't pick up anyone under the dock, I don't think."

"Thank you," she said. "I'm glad I know that."

"Why are you so obsessed with George Devenish?" Cal asked.

"Obsessed?" Alice frowned. "I wouldn't say that. I'm interested."

"It's sort of weird."

"I don't mind being weird," she assured him.

Cal laughed at that. "I like how weird you are." Then he went quiet again.

Alice saw something on the beach that made her stop and stare. "Look," she said. "What is *that*?"

Cal looked and gave a gasp. "That's an iguana! Oh wow. It's beautiful. Look at the color. It's on a little harness!" He chuckled.

The young boy who owned the iguana was parading it along the shore on a leash, his face the picture of pride. A gaggle of smaller children trailed behind him, asking questions, and trying to get close enough to touch the iguana's tail.

"Surely they're not supposed to be kept as pets," Alice said.

"Yeah, they can be!" They watched the animal raising its little legs one after the other as it marched along, like a flexible soldier. Cal's face was avid. "They cost a fortune, though. He's amazing—look at him. Wow!"

"You like iguanas?" she asked.

"Reptiles. All reptiles. I love them—they're, like, my thing. I'm dying to get a pet snake or a bearded dragon."

They watched as the boy and his iguana went along the beach. Alice turned toward the Quay. "I'd better start heading back. I don't want to be late for work."

Cal fell into step with her. "Who's on the slab today?"

"That's disrespectful," she scolded him.

"Sorry. Whose funeral, I mean?"

"Today we have the service for Bridie Tierney, aged eighty-nine. She led quite an interesting life. She became a nun when she was a young lady, but met a man in the hospital while she was visiting the sick. He had a serious illness. She found herself developing feelings for this man, and eventually couldn't bear to think of being without him. He recovered from the illness and asked her to marry him, so she left the convent and gave up being a nun. It was a very difficult decision for her, and her family found it painful, too, especially since they didn't much like her husband. He was a man with no faith, and they were a devout family. He did love Mrs. Tierney very much, though."

"Whoa." Cal was gazing at Alice with rapt attention, so she continued.

"Mrs. Tierney's sister is angry at their brother because he refuses to pay for a full Catholic funeral. He says Bridie gave up her right to that when she quit being a nun. It's unfair because he knows that's not true. The truth is, he doesn't want to pay the extra cost. Her sister sent us all the items she kept from when Bridie was a nun: her rosary and her watch pin with her saint name engraved on the back—a gift from their parents. She wants to bury them with Mrs. Tierney, but she asked us to conceal them in the casket. They have antique value and her brother might ask for them back. I don't know, though. I suspect that's her anger talking. I doubt the brother would stoop so low."

Cal's mouth was hanging slightly open. "What exactly is your job at the funeral home, Alice?"

"I arrange the mementos on the bodies and help out at the funeral services."

"How come you know so much about the people? I thought you must be writing the speeches or something. Does your dad tell you everything about them?"

Alice gave an uneasy shrug, thinking of Mrs. Tierney's resonant watch pin. "I notice things."

"You've gotta be the most observant person ever," Cal told her. "You should be, like, a detective or something."

Alice imagined herself a detective for a moment, collecting evidence. Or a forensic scientist testing that evidence in a laboratory. Those were interesting thoughts. "I'm going to run Tranquility Funerals when I grow up," she said, but she filed the thoughts away for later.

They arrived back at the Quay. "Thank you for the walk, Cal. Goodbye." Alice started to walk toward the Quay exit.

"Wait, Alice." She turned to him and Cal came closer. He rubbed his mouth as if he were suddenly uncertain. "Do you—you and Ultra—want to come to a party? We're hanging out on Friday night, down at Pier 20."

"What sort of a party?" she asked.

"Just music, talking, that sort of thing. It'll be pretty chill."

"I don't think my father or Violet's mother would let us attend a party at the pier at night," she said.

"Oh, right. Fair enough." He seemed crestfallen.

"Doesn't *your* mum mind?" she asked.

"Nah. She doesn't care what I do."

Alice found this very sad. She gave him an encouraging smile.

"I'm sure she does. Perhaps she doesn't realize you'd *like* her to worry about you."

He snorted a laugh. "I don't want her to worry! She might try to stop me."

Alice doubted this was the case, but said nothing.

"Hey," he added. "We're not scary, or anything. We usually just get a couple of pizzas and hang out. Why don't you come down in the afternoon if you're not allowed out after dark? You can just check out the party, and if you don't like it, you can leave. We'll probably stay and party late, but you could go home at sundown if that makes it easier."

Alice considered the invitation. "Do you need an RSVP right now?"

He stared. "Nah."

"Well, I will speak to Violet and give you our response as soon as possible. How can I contact you?"

Cal said he would give her his phone number and was puzzled when she pulled out a paper and pen to write it down. She explained that she didn't own a phone, which seemed to shock him.

"Not even an old data-less flip phone?"

She shook her head. "You can call the funeral home landline if you wish to speak to me. The number's on our website."

Cal gave his head a tiny shake. "Okay. Talk to you soon, Zombie Queen."

sixteen

A DIFFICULT DECISION

THADDEUS sat down beside Alice and poured hot water through a strainer of ginger tea. "Alice, did you happen to go into the office? I found my desk in slight disarray."

Alice looked up from the article she had been reading in the *Coastal Chronicle*. It was about an elderly local woman who claimed to have spotted a small monkey in her shrubbery. The woman had explained how the creature had scampered up a tree and vanished from view. The reporter had also interviewed someone from the Department of Parks and Wildlife, who gave a scathing response, declaring that the old woman's claims were "ludicrous."

"What does *ludicrous* mean?" she asked Thaddeus.

"Ridiculous or unbelievable."

"Ah. Thank you. Yes," she added. "Violet and I went into the office on Saturday night to take a look at her uncle's file. We learned some surprising things."

Thaddeus nodded. "I should have talked to you about this earlier, but it didn't occur to me that it would be a problem." He proceeded to explain privacy laws and the necessity of protecting personal client information.

Alice crunched her cornflakes, nodding intermittently. "How

interesting," she said when he was finished. "It makes perfect sense. I wish I had known this before Saturday."

"Well, it's done now, and we can only hope there are no negative consequences. If Violet mentions something she saw in the files to her family and they ask where she found the information, they may decide to make a complaint against me. I'll deal with that if it occurs. In the meantime, I'm going to start locking the filing cabinet."

"Oh, but I won't go into the cabinet without permission again," said Alice.

Thaddeus smiled and took a spoonful of oats. "I trust you won't be a *cereal* offender."

Alice gave him a tolerant smile.

"But if you're having friends to stay the night," he went on. "I really should put extra security in place. You never know when someone might become curious."

"That's true," Alice said. "Although it's only Violet—I don't suddenly have dozens of people visiting."

"It's something I should have done long ago," he said.

Alice sipped her own tea—subtly sweetened with a little honey. "On the subject of socializing, I've been invited to a party on Friday."

Her father blinked at her two or three times.

"It's under the dock at Pier 20. It's an evening party, but I know you probably wouldn't want me out at night, so I thought I might go just for the afternoon, if you approve."

He studied her. "Do you *want* to go?"

Alice considered the question. "I think so. I like the person who invited me. He seems nice and I feel sorry for him."

"Why?"

"He has only one parent, like me; but I don't think his parent is very caring, like you."

Thaddeus broke into a smile. "What a lovely thing to say, Alice."

Alice was still thinking about Cal. "I suspect they don't have a lot of money. He always seems hungry. And he misses a lot of school and stays up late playing computer games, and he hangs around with people who can be quite offensive. I think he needs more supervision and support. But for all that, he's a nice boy."

"And these are the people who are having this soiree?" asked Thaddeus.

"That sounds French," said Alice.

"Yes, it means a small evening party."

"Lovely. Yes, Cal invited me and Violet to the *soiree*, and I presume his friends will be there, too. He said they listen to music and talk and eat pizza."

"Pizza," he said. "Hmm. You can have a healthy dinner later at home, I think. But if you do want to go, I trust you not to place yourself in danger. I like your idea of leaving before it gets dark—you are only twelve, after all; even if it's just for another month. I can pick you up from Pier 20 at sundown."

"Yes, that sounds suitable." Alice folded the newspaper and took her bowl to the sink. "Although this all depends on Violet wanting to go along, too."

"Of course."

She went to brush her teeth and kissed her father goodbye. The neighbor's cat was in the Englands' front yard again, hunched between two lavender bushes. Alice tried a different approach this time. She didn't go any closer, but stopped in the middle of the path and addressed the cat from a distance.

"Good morning, cat. Mustafa? Manzanilla?" It didn't respond to either of these guesses, so she held out a hand and softly snapped her fingers. "Would you like a scratch around the ears?"

The cat was distracted momentarily by a bee. Alice considered this progress: it had never taken its eyes off her before. Maybe it was getting used to her.

"Well, I need to get to school now. I hope to see you in the afternoon."

The cat winked, which made Alice smile. It had looked so intentional. She walked to school with a jaunty air, feeling optimistic. She hoped Violet would be permitted to attend Cal's Friday afternoon *soiree*. It sounded like it might be an interesting experience.

⚜

Violet did not share Alice's enthusiasm for the soiree.

"A party, under the dock, with Cal's friends?" Violet said when they were sitting on the bench near the principal's office, eating their morning snack. She had a chocolate muffin. Alice had vegetable crudités and hummus, and couldn't repress a twinge of envy.

"Yes, that's right," she said.

"Not a *chance*," said Violet.

"Why not?" Alice asked.

"Because they're a sketchy crowd, probably doing illegal things. I thought you were suspicious of them, anyway?"

"Well, yes, I do suspect they were under the dock at Pier 19 on the night George died, but just because they were there doesn't mean they were actually involved in his death."

"Make up your mind." Violet sounded impatient—even irritated.

Alice studied Violet, trying to work out what was bothering her. "I assure you, I never suspected Cal and his friends were implicated in your uncle's death. I simply thought they could have been present in the area and may have seen something of interest. I don't think a group of schoolchildren would go around injuring people or failing to help someone who had taken ill."

Violet heaved a sigh. "That's *exactly* what they would do. And they're not schoolchildren."

"They're children and they attend school," Alice pointed out.

"Do you consider *yourself* a child?" Violet challenged her.

"Of course."

Violet rolled her eyes. "We're teenagers, not children."

"Teenagers up to eighteen are children, and I'm not even a teenager yet," Alice reminded her. "Whatever the case, do you honestly consider Cal and his friends dangerous?"

"Yes. Yes, I do." Violet squished the remainder of her muffin in its paper wrapper and tossed it at the trash can. It missed. She dragged herself up and retrieved it, dumping it into the can with a *thunk*.

"Is that why you don't want to go to the party on Friday?" Alice asked.

Violet shrugged. "I don't want to hang out with them. They pick on us."

"Cal doesn't," said Alice. "In fact, he asked his friends to be nice to us."

"They're probably setting us up, Alice."

Alice was baffled. "Setting us up?"

"You know, tricking us into going down to the dock so they can hide and watch, then laugh at us."

"Why would they laugh at us?"

"Because we thought anyone would actually invite *us* to a party."

Alice was shocked. "You really think they would do that?"

"Yeah, I do. You can't trust people."

Alice had always found most people fairly trustworthy and was obliged to sit and think about Violet's words in silence for some time. Violet scuffed her shoes and stared at the opposite office wall.

"I don't believe Cal would do that," Alice decided at last. "It would be extraordinarily cruel and not at all funny. Cal doesn't strike me as that kind of boy in the least."

Violet peered at her. "Do you like him, or something?"

"Yes. Don't you?"

Violet went pink beneath her veil. "He *seems* okay. I don't like his friends."

"Perhaps you're right." Alice didn't believe Violet was right, but preferred not to upset her. "Why don't we treat this Friday as an opportunity to find out what they're like? My father said he can pick us up. If they do try to maltreat us, my father will put a stop to it."

Despite her sour mood, Violet couldn't help a laugh. "You talk *so* weird." She took one of Alice's carrot sticks and crunched it down. "My parents probably won't let me go, anyway. But I'll think about it."

❧

By Wednesday, Violet had made up her mind not to go to the party, and no amount of logical argument would convince her otherwise. Alice was disappointed, but accepted Violet's decision.

She didn't like making phone calls, but steeled herself and called Cal after school. He didn't pick up. However, later in the evening, the phone rang. Thaddeus took the call and passed it on to Alice.

"A boy, for you," he said.

As suspected, it was Cal. "Hey, Zombie Queen. I saw a missed call from a landline and knew it must've been you."

She was impressed by his deductive abilities. "Thank you for calling me back. I just wanted to give you our apologies. Unfortunately, Violet and I must decline your invitation."

It seemed to take him a few moments to work out what she meant. "Aw, you're not coming to the party? Why not? You working?"

"No, we don't hold funerals on Friday evenings. Or any evenings, in fact. Violet—" Alice realized just in time that telling him Violet thought she would be bullied by Cal's friends might not be tactful. "Violet can't go," she finished awkwardly.

"You can still come on your own, though, right?" he said.

"Without Violet?" she asked, a little taken aback.

"Yeah! You don't need to be shy. We wouldn't leave you out in the cold with nobody to talk to."

Alice puzzled over this new option for a moment, then made a decision. "Thank you, but I think not. I can't leave Violet out. Perhaps when she knows you a little better, she will feel more comfortable about attending parties with you and your friends."

"So Violet thinks we're losers, does she?"

Alice could have kicked herself. "Not losers," she said quickly. "She's a little intimidated by some of your group, that's all."

He gave what sounded like a soft sigh. "Oh well. Whatever. You could still come, if you wanted to, you know. *You* don't think we're losers, do you?"

"Not at all."

"Cool. Well, it's your choice, but it'd be good if you came." There was a noise in the background of his call. "Ugh, gotta go. My mum's nagging me to take the trash out. Might see you Friday. Ciao, Zombie Queen."

❧

To Alice's bemusement, Violet became quiet and serious when she relayed the phone conversation the next day.

"He actually said that?" she asked, her pale eyebrows knitting. "He was worried I think he's a loser?"

"He thought you believed he and his friends were 'losers,'" Alice corrected her. "But I told him that wasn't the case. He encouraged me to come without you, but of course I told him no."

Violet's eyes landed on Alice. "Why not?"

"Well, because he invited *us*." Alice's reasoning was becoming blurry. "It didn't feel right. One of *us* can't go, so neither of us ought to."

Violet's expression changed. "So you said no, even though you wanted to go?"

"Yes. It would have been a good chance to interrogate them—tactfully—about their presence at Pier 19 that night." Alice said this with a slight shrug, then she was surprised at herself. She wasn't a shrugger—never had been—and often thought it was a poor form of communication chronically overused by her classmates. Perhaps the habit was rubbing off from the time spent with Violet and Cal.

Violet kept watching her with that peculiar expression. She got up and paced around the courtyard, past the principal's window, and the flowering bush with all its bees, and the garbage, and the blank office wall, and finally back to the bench, where she stood in front of Alice with her hands on her hips.

"Fine," she said. "We'll go."

Alice was so surprised she didn't speak.

Violet sat down and picked up her sandwich. "Just for the afternoon, though. And if anything seems sketchy, we're leaving."

"But…"

Violet held up her hand. "It's done. We're going."

Alice had little choice but to be satisfied with this mystifying change of heart.

seventeen

THE SOIREE

FRIDAY was cooler than it had been over the past few weeks, and Violet had brought a hooded jacket to Alice's place. It had a veil stitched into the hood and, when Violet put it on and surveyed herself in the bedroom mirror, Alice complimented her on the ingenious design.

"Does it look okay?" Violet asked, maneuvering her hands into the hood so she could change her earrings.

"Yes, your jacket looks very warm and comfortable. And the advantage is that there will be no veil flapping around as it does when it's on your hat."

"Is the color all right? I wanted the tan one, but Mum's always buying me blue things."

Alice observed the blue of the jacket and could find nothing to criticize. Violet checked her reflection in the mirror again. Alice opened her closet and focused on finding her own jacket to wear to the pier. It would no doubt be windy.

"I need to help Dad see to a corpse this afternoon," she said over her shoulder. "We like to have the bodies completely ready the day before the service, to save us from any last-minute panic. You could come to the embalming room with me, if you wish, or just wait here. I'll only be a few minutes."

When Alice turned around, shaking out her green winter jacket, Violet was staring at her with round eyes. "I'll wait here."

Alice went to find Thaddeus. Patty was in the office, using a steamer to remove the wrinkles from a purple dress.

"That's a fine frock," said Alice.

"Covered in animal hair," Patty grumbled. "Apparently the deceased had a pet ferret. A ferret, of all things!" She raised her eyes to the ceiling.

"People keep odd pets, don't they?" said Alice. "Iguanas, for example. I prefer cats, personally. Is Dad in the embalming room?"

Patty nodded and Alice went through. The odor hanging in the air indicated he had only recently finished hosing fluids down the drain set in the floor. No other aesthetic services had been started.

"Is this a rush funeral, Dad?"

"I'm afraid it is," he said, stretching his back. "The deceased only passed away yesterday. But the brother is returning home to Ireland tomorrow evening and the family wanted to have the funeral before he goes."

"That *is* a rush." Alice examined the body. "They look quite young."

"Yes."

"Is this a she or a he?" Alice inquired, looking at the body again. At first glance, she would have said it was a young man, but on closer inspection she realized the corpse was wearing stockings and a lilac petticoat.

"The preferred pronoun was *she*."

"Well, what do you need me to do for her?"

"We're not ready for you, I'm afraid. Once she's dressed, I'll do the makeup and Patty will do the hair, then you can do the jewelry—there's quite a few pieces. But you have to get to your *soiree* now, don't you, Alice?" Thaddeus rubbed his chin with a gloved hand. "Would you mind doing the accessories when you get back?"

"Not at all," said Alice. "I can come in after dinner. Will you still be able to pick Violet and me up at sunset?"

"Yes. Pier 20, I think you said?"

"That's right." She kissed his cheek. "I'll see you then, Dad."

Alice fetched Violet and they set off, the brisk wind buffeting their faces from the moment they crested the hill leading down to the cove. Violet said she hadn't been to Pier 20 before, but Alice was familiar with most of the piers lining the cove. Pier 20 was all but abandoned, used only by a handful of aged fishing boats. It was unpatrolled and looked run-down, with an empty sea container in the parking lot. Its open door creaked gently in the wind.

It was easy to find Cal and the others once Alice and Violet made it through the broken gate. Music was coming from beneath the old wooden jetty. Alice hoped that this would reassure Violet that their invitation was not a prank after all. They went down a sandy trail to the beach and Cal's group came into view. They were standing around a rusty metal barrel, out of which thin smoke rose.

Cal spotted them and waved eagerly. "Alice! Violet!"

Tess turned to stare, the corners of her mouth tugged downward in that perpetual grim line by her two lip rings. Cal jogged up the beach to greet them.

"You came!" He hooked his arms through theirs and tugged them back down toward the other kids. "There's only a few of us here at the moment, but lots are coming later."

"We won't be staying after dark," Alice told him.

"Yeah, that's cool. I get it. I'm just glad you came. Check it out, we collected driftwood and we've got a fire going, see? Took us, like, a million matches because the wood's soggy, and it's not burning too great, but at least we got it lit. Hey, look who's here!" he called to his friends.

"Hi," said Tess, jutting her chin, and Gav and Amy chimed in with their greetings.

Alice said hello, but Violet had gone quiet. She stood by the fire with her eyes fixed on the sea.

"Want some corn chips?" said Cal. "Is the music okay? It's Gav's choice."

"It's fine," Alice said, but Tess broke in scornfully.

"No one asked me what *I* think of the music. It sucks." She narrowed her eyes at Cal and jerked her head at Alice and Violet. "You into one of them, Cal?"

"Give it a rest, Tess," said Amy. "He was just asking."

"I don't mind what you play," said Alice. "Violet, what about you? Violet has a favorite band, only I can't remember what they're called."

Violet nudged her, but the other kids looked over at her expectantly. "The music's fine," she said.

"Who's your favorite band?" Cal asked her.

Violet seemed to be reddening, although it was hard to tell with the veil over her face and the dim light under the dock. She mumbled something and Amy's eyes lit up.

"Oh, I *love* Moon Squad! Are you a K-pop stan, too?"

Violet murmured assent and Amy started an animated conversation with her about their shared music taste, which seemed to ease Violet's tension. Alice was pleased. She had been getting quite worried about Violet.

"How many people do you expect to your *soiree*?" Alice asked Cal.

"Soiree!" he choked. "You kill me, Zombie Queen. I've only ever heard my nan use that word. Could be a big one tonight. A couple of dozen, maybe? I've invited a bunch of people, and some of Gav's friends from work are coming, and Tess said she's asked people from school, too. Should be fun."

Alice thought to herself that it was probably for the best that she and Violet would be leaving early. She wasn't at all sure she would enjoy such a large party.

Tess still had her dark eyes trained fiercely on Alice's face. "Cal says you work at a funeral parlor," she said. "Is that true?"

"Yes."

"Your parents own it, right?" said Cal.

"My father, yes."

"Cool after-school job." Tess was still eyeing Alice. "Can you show us around, sometime?"

"There's not much to see," Alice said. "There's the service room, the reception area, the embalming room, the office, and the rest is just our house."

"Holy..." Tess trailed off, staring. "You *live* there?"

"Not in the funeral section."

Tess glanced around at the others. "Can we see the bodies?"

Alice frowned but stayed polite. "No, that won't be possible."

"C'mon," Tess pressed her. "You live there. What's the problem?"

"Her dad probably wouldn't want a bunch of ghouls at his place," Amy told Tess.

"I think my father would let me bring you to the house if I wanted to."

"*Yes!*" Tess exclaimed. "I've always wanted to see a dead body."

Alice was quick to clarify. "No, that doesn't mean I will show you a body. The bodies are not there to be looked at by strangers. That would be deeply disrespectful."

Awkward silence followed this statement. At last, Tess sniffed.

"Bundle of fun, aren't you?" She turned away to change the music.

The conversation moved on, and under the cover of the others' chatter, Cal started to explain that Tess had a hobby of being rude. However, Alice wasn't really listening because she had just noticed something extremely interesting on a rock beside the speaker.

It was a miniature disco-light projector, a hexagonal prism of plastic panels in green, yellow, red, and purple. It was switched off, but attached by a cable to a familiar silver portable charger.

Colored lights.

"We'll turn that on when it gets dark," he said, following her gaze.

"Hey, let's play a game!" Amy cried suddenly. "Hide-and-seek!"

"What are you—six?" Tess drawled.

"Tess is fifteen," Cal said to Alice and Violet. "So she's *way* more mature than the rest of us." Tess tried to shove him and Cal ducked out of her way. "Amy and I will be *it*," he said, grinning. "Everyone else go hide. We'll give you till one hundred."

He plonked himself down on the sand and closed his eyes, counting out loud. Amy joined him, giggling, and Gav ran off to hide without a moment's hesitation.

"Lame," Tess said over the top of Cal's counting. She perched herself on one of the concrete ledges and examined her nails.

Alice thought Tess's heeled boots didn't look suitable for games anyway. She headed for the trail up to the pier.

"What are you doing?" Violet hissed, dashing after her.

"Going to find a hiding spot," she said.

"We're *playing*?"

"Of course. I don't particularly like party games, but you must play if you're at a party where there are games being played."

"What?"

"That's what my father taught me." Alice surveyed the pier. "There's the sea container over there. Why don't we hide behind that?"

"Seventy!" Cal shouted below them.

"Fine," said Violet, pulling her jacket more tightly around her.

They headed for the sea container, but when they got there Alice realized it was so close to the fence that there was no room to hide behind it. They would be clearly visible from the dock when Cal and Amy came searching for them.

"Ninety!" came the faint shout from below the dock.

"It's open," Alice said, nodding at the container. "Let's hide inside the door."

"Coming, ready or not!" Cal hollered.

They scuttled inside, and Violet shook her head. "I can't believe we're playing hide-and-seek."

"Shh." Alice kept her own voice low. "Did you see that lighting device Cal had down under the dock?"

"What, the disco light?" said Violet.

"Yes." Alice was about to remind Violet of how George had seen colored lights on the morning he'd died. Then she remembered that she only knew this fact through the resonance of his toy boat.

"Disco lights aren't dangerous to my skin, I don't think," said Violet.

"Oh—yes. Good. But it runs on a portable charger, did you notice? And we found the portable charger under the dock."

"Oh!" Violet said it as a gasp. "Oh yeah!" She seemed to be thinking about that, but suddenly spun around and peered past Alice at the darkened rear of the container. "Alice! Something just moved back there!"

Alice turned to look, and at the same moment, the container's great door groaned shut and the outer bolt shot home. Violet screamed so long and loud that Alice had to cover her ears. When it ended, she felt around until she located Violet's arm in the darkness.

"Please don't scream again," she said earnestly. "It appears the door has closed, perhaps in the wind. Let's open it."

"It wasn't the wind." Violet clutched her so tightly it hurt. "Someone shut us in!"

In the dark, Alice found and lifted the door latch and pushed, but nothing happened. "It appears the door is locked."

"I knew it!" Violet was panting with fear. "We're shut in and there's a rat or a serial killer or something in here with us!"

"Stay calm, Violet." Alice rattled the door but that made no difference. She thumped on it instead. "Cal! Amy!"

Violet joined in, much more loudly. After a minute, Alice was obliged to grope around until she could take Violet's arm again.

"Please, Violet. Be quiet."

It took a few moments for Violet to obey, then things went very quiet, except for the faint vibratory ring of the container's metal walls. Alice listened.

"What is it?" Violet whispered.

Alice listened for a while longer. "Nothing, I'm afraid," she said. "I don't hear anything or anyone at all. Violet, I think we may be stuck in here."

Violet lost no time. She screamed and banged so loudly that Alice started to feel quite unwell. She didn't like loud noises at the best of times, and this was most certainly not the best of times.

"Let us out!" Violet's voice had gone from a shriek to a holler, and she was sounding truly furious by now. "Let us out, you dumb jerks!"

"Who are you talking to?" Alice asked during a lull in the shouting.

"Cal, of course," snapped Violet. "They've locked us in here. I told you, didn't I? I told you they'd do something to us."

Alice frowned. "I don't think Cal would do this."

Violet made a noise that sounded like a small explosive had detonated in her mouth. "He just *did* it, Alice!"

Alice was about to argue that Cal had not once shown any hint of evil intention, when a scuttling movement sounded behind them and Violet let loose with another earsplitting shriek. Even Alice was alarmed this time. She didn't mind rodents, as a general rule, but the thought of being closed in a sea container with a cornered rat was disturbing. How big was it? Dockside rats could be large. Was it defensive? Angry?

"Shh, Violet," she whispered. "We don't want to frighten it even more."

A loud scrape and clunk made Violet grab Alice, which in turn made Alice gasp. She was trying to remember if there was anything on the floor she could snatch up to defend them against a potentially aggressive, oversized rat, when the big door creaked open.

Alice and Violet blinked into the afternoon light. "Violet! And you—Alice England!" Gina Prince swung the door wider. "What on earth are you doing in here? Oh my—" She blew her breath out in a sharp puff. "I'm so sick of kids messing around with the pier equipment!"

"We weren't messing around, Aunty Gina," Violet stammered. "Someone shut us in!"

Gina frowned, then softened and pulled Violet in for a quick hug. "Are you all right?" She scanned the pier. "There's no one else around."

Violet looked around the vacant pier as well.

"Why would you girls want to hang around *here*?" Gina was saying. "There's a perfectly good shopping mall in Damocles Cove, you know. It's silly to come to the pier."

"You're not the manager of Pier 20, too—are you?" Alice asked, stepping out after Violet.

Gina shot her an exasperated look. "No. I was heading home for the night, actually, but I saw kids running around Pier 20 as I drove past and thought I'd better come and clear them out." She sighed and ran a hand through her long hair. "Violet, do you want a lift home?"

Violet looked like she might accept, so Alice interjected. "No, thank you," she said. "We appreciate you letting us out of the sea container, but our lift is already organized and will be here soon."

Gina ushered them to the broken gate and crossed to her car, parked on the side of the road.

"Wait here for your lift," she instructed them. "And make sure you stay away from the pier in the future." She gave Alice a long, stern look. "I've heard about kids who lock themselves in sea containers or go into limestone caves or damaged boats and pretend they're trapped. For attention. To be on the news or get famous on social media. That's an extremely foolish thing to do. Imagine if no one found you."

Violet's mouth fell open. "We didn't lock *ourselves* in that container, Aunty Gina!"

Gina glanced at Alice again, her expression dubious. "Well, make sure you stay out of trouble." She got into her car, giving the girls a nod as she pulled away.

Violet glared after the white car. "I can't believe she would think that. Why would we lock ourselves up?"

"Why would anyone else lock us up?" Alice remarked.

"Why don't you ask Cal?" Violet shot at her.

"I will." Alice made for the beach.

"Wait! You can't go back down there!"

"I want to ask Cal if he saw anyone around the container."

"Why won't you believe me?" Violet demanded, coming after Alice. "It was Cal—or at least one of his sketchy—" She stopped abruptly because Cal and Amy appeared with Gav, coming along the dock.

"Where did you guys go?" Cal called, waving. Violet made a derisive noise.

"Gav thought he had the best hiding spot!" Amy was laughing, her bright hair blowing in the sea breeze. "He was down at the end of the dock, standing behind the PRIVATE MOORINGS sign. I mean, you're skinny, Gav, but not that skinny!"

"We got locked in the sea container," Alice said as the three came to a halt in front of them.

This caused a stir. "*Locked in?*" Gav's eyebrows shot skyward.

"What d'you mean?" Amy was still giggling a little. She glanced at the sea container. "You got stuck in there?"

"Someone locked us in," Violet said, glaring at Cal.

"What?" He gazed around the pier. "Who?"

"That's what we'd like to know." It was clear even to Alice what Violet was implying.

Cal lifted his hands. "Hey, we didn't do it!" He sounded quite hurt, and Alice was convinced he knew nothing of their brief imprisonment—well, almost convinced.

Violet turned her glare on Amy and Gav, but they seemed similarly bemused. "Where's Tess?" she asked.

The other three exchanged glances. "Still down on the beach, I think," said Amy.

"What's going on?" It was Tess, and she was coming from the wrong direction—from beyond the sea container, rather than from the beach. Violet shot a look at Alice. "What was all the screaming about?" Tess asked, her mouth in a wry smirk.

"Like you don't know," Violet muttered.

"Did you lock them in the container?" Cal asked Tess.

He sounded angry.

"What? No. As if." She stalked away toward the trail. "This pier sucks, Cal," she threw back over her shoulder. "There's not even a proper bathroom."

"Come on." Cal nudged Alice and Violet. "Let's go have some chips."

eighteen
A LITTLE ADVICE

ALICE finished applying fuchsia pigment to the corpse's lips and switched brushes to make a start on the eyeliner. She was mostly focused on the makeup, but couldn't help going back over the events at Pier 20 earlier that evening.

Cal's party had grown larger over the next hour, before Thaddeus came to pick them up. It was quite noisy and crowded under the dock by the time they left. Violet had simply brooded after the sea container incident, barely responding when anyone tried to include her. She seemed convinced that one of them had done it—and Tess was obviously Violet's chief suspect. When Thaddeus had dropped her home afterward, Violet still looked bitter over the whole thing.

Alice finished the first eyelid, the black line perfect. She thought again about the disco-light projector. She had asked whose it was during the soiree, and honest Gav had told her it belonged to Cal.

Cal owned a disco-light projector that he ran off a portable charger.

The portable charger they had found at Pier 19.

George Devenish had seen colored lights on the morning of his death.

Alice tried to focus on the task at hand. She referred to the photo of the deceased during life to compare the eyeliner. In the picture, the dead woman was wearing a glamorous dress and a necklace with the name TIA written in gold. Tia seemed to have had a penchant for eyeliner wings and highlights to the cheekbones. Alice bent over again and painted the left eye wing with her steady hand. She had been doing corpse makeup for more than a year now, and believed she had a genuine talent for it. Alice had initially learned from watching her father and Patty, but later improved her skills by studying a course of online makeup tutorials. Her father now claimed the student had surpassed the master. They had a tool kit of face paints and theatrical makeup, because everyday cosmetics were not always suitable when dealing with the dead. Alice had talked her father into the purchase of an airbrushing kit, and he had since declared it was worth its weight in gold.

She completed the right eye wing and selected a sponge for the highlighter.

The disco light. So, it seemed Cal had been lying to her. He—and possibly his friends—had almost certainly been at Pier 19 on the morning George died. And yet, Cal had denied it when she'd asked him outright if he was there. Why? And if the CCTV cameras didn't reach under the dock, the police probably didn't know the teenagers had been there, either.

Tia's cheeks now had a beautiful sheen, her cheekbones sharp and dramatic. Alice moved on to the final touches: combing the eyebrows and using a cotton swab dipped in cleaner to remove the makeup that had found its way onto Tia's tiny diamond nose-piercing. She clipped on giant oval earrings—*cubic zirconia,* Alice thought—and pinned a cameo brooch onto the breast of Tia's purple dress.

Perhaps the presence of Cal and his friends at Pier 19 that night wasn't even important. Perhaps it had nothing at all to do with George's death.

Or perhaps she and Violet had been locked in the sea container as a warning. Were they getting too close to the truth?

She picked up a heavy crystal necklace and unlatched the brass clasp. It was resonant. This had belonged to Tia's grandmother. When Tia was younger and had a different name, she would climb up in front of Grandma's mirror and try on her jewelry. This necklace was Tia's favorite. Her grandma caught her once and Tia thought she would get into trouble, but she was indulgent and even let Tia try on her clip-on earring collection. When she changed her name, Tia still enjoyed the love of her kind grandma, who promised that the jewelry collection would eventually come to her. Sadly, Grandma had outlived Tia. The grieving grandmother had spent several hours that morning choosing jewelry pieces as a parting gift for her dear granddaughter.

Alice stood back and inspected Tia's body from head to toe. Her father had done a good job with the hair, she was pleased to see. She checked the photo again, then took off her glove and used a little hair cream on two fingers to create curls in the ends of Tia's long hair. Last, Alice fluffed the dress sleeves, which were flattened from when she'd leaned over to apply Tia's makeup.

Perfect.

Alice covered the casket with a sheet, taking care not to let the material droop onto the face. She went to find her father.

⚜

Tia's funeral was a touching affair. Alice watched the elderly grandmother weeping during the service and hoped she knew how much Tia had loved her.

There was no funeral scheduled for the afternoon, so Alice sat down at the table to do some homework, but was interrupted by a knock at the door. Her father went to answer, and a minute later, came back into the kitchen with Gina Prince.

"Alice, this is Ms. Prince. She says she knows you."

"Yes." Alice closed her book and stood up to greet the woman. "Hello again, Ms. Prince."

Gina smiled as though amused that Alice was offering her hand. She shook it anyway. "Call me Gina—both of you. I'm sorry to turn up uninvited like this. I know you're a busy man, Mr. England, so I won't waste your time. I simply wanted to have a quick chat."

"Please—it's Thaddeus," he said. "Would you like a cup of tea?"

"That would be delightful—what's the time?" She tapped her phone screen to check, and Alice caught a lock-screen photo of a child holding an animal—perhaps a possum at a petting zoo? "It's just past two o'clock, so I've got half an hour before I pick Lily up from ballet. I'm not delaying you?"

"Not at all," said Thaddeus. "We're finished for the day. Alice, would you get the cups?"

While Thaddeus and Alice prepared tea, Gina spoke about her busy Saturday, the sudden coolness of the weather, and the convenience of living at your place of business. Then they all sat at the kitchen table, Alice having moved her books to the side. Gina gave a sigh.

"I don't really know where to begin, so I'll jump straight in." She looked at Alice. "I'm worried about you."

"Worried about *me*?" Alice glanced at her father.

"You and Violet."

He was frowning. "Why would you say that, Gina?"

"It's those kids you've been hanging around with. That boy—Cal, is it? And the girl with bright-red hair and that other boy, the skinny one."

"What about them?" said Alice.

"They've been hanging around my pier for years, causing issues for my security guys." She clasped her hands around her teacup, her dark eyes earnest. "It's not that I think they're bad kids. Not really. Yes, they get into trouble—it could be because of their home lives or something. But I don't think they're *really* bad kids." She grimaced. "It's just, I can see you're a *good* girl—you and Violet—and I can't help but worry. I'm a parent, too," she said to Thaddeus. "I can't bear to see a nice kid like Alice get herself wrapped up in that crowd. I mean, that business with the sea container yesterday…"

"Sea container?" Alice's father repeated.

"Violet and I were shut in a sea container while we were socializing with Cal and his friends at Pier 20," Alice explained.

Thaddeus considered this information, a concerned line appearing on his forehead.

"We're not sure how it happened," Alice added. "We're still investigating."

This didn't appear to completely alleviate his worries. "This is what I'm talking about," said Gina. "We can't pin anything on these kids, but things seem to go wrong when they're around. Do you know what I'm saying? They're always *there* when there's trouble."

"And you think Alice and Violet might be influenced?" Thaddeus asked.

Gina wasn't quite sure how to reply. "Well, I don't think the girls are likely to misbehave—not by a long shot. But it would make sense for them to stay away from kids like that. Wouldn't you agree?"

Alice and her father exchanged a brief, silent conversation, then Thaddeus turned back to Gina. "I do appreciate your concern," he said. "However, Alice is a responsible young person with a lot of insight. I don't believe she'd involve herself with people who might harm her."

"Oh, gosh, no!" Gina shook her head energetically, curls bouncing.

Alice pictured a lime-green satin-lined casket for her—jasmine and honeysuckle on top. "If I'm honest with you, Thaddeus, I haven't seen these kids doing anything *too* awful, not personally. But Higgo—he's my security officer—he says they attract trouble. He's adamant they're getting up to no good—that they're a disaster waiting to happen. And he'd know, I suppose. Higgo's on-site almost every day." She joined her hands under her chin, almost as if she were praying. "I've argued with myself since I saw Alice with Calvin, trying to decide whether I should say something. I don't dare speak to Luanne about Violet—she's so overprotective, and poor Violet would be the one getting into trouble. But after I found the girls locked in that sea container yesterday, I was worried. I have a daughter, Thaddeus, and I would want someone to let me know if she was at risk in any way whatsoever."

"Of course," he said.

"Lily's only nine, but I'm already dreading the teenage years." She sighed. "It's such a minefield. I don't know how you manage on your own, and run a business, too. Are you a member of the Commerce Club here in Damocles Cove?"

"I've heard of it," he said. "But I'm not a member."

"Oh gosh!" A smile broke on her face. "You should join. We all support and recommend one another's businesses. It's a great community. Can I send you an invitation to our next event? We'd love to have Tranquility Funerals join."

"By all means," Thaddeus said. "Please do."

"What did George think of Cal and his friends?" Alice asked.

Gina blinked at her a couple of times. "George? Well, let's see. He never took much notice of those kids, now that I come to think of it. He didn't seem to have any complaints about them, anyway. But George could be a little too relaxed about trespassers at the pier at times. He didn't always pay much attention when something smelled like trouble. I suppose you could say he was a risk-taker."

"Really?" Alice leaned forward, gripping her teacup. "George was a risk-taker?"

Gina nodded, almost reluctantly. "Poor George. His allergy held him back so dreadfully, and all he wanted was to be free of it. I felt like I almost had to protect him from himself sometimes." Her eyes had started glistening and she dug in her handbag for a tissue. "Sorry. It's so hard to believe he went like he did. At my pier. He'd told me he'd be ready for daylight shifts soon—can you believe it? He said his allergy was going to be completely under control within months."

"Within months!" Alice exclaimed. "Due to his treatment?"

"Oh, you know about that, do you?" Gina nodded. "George was seeing that Port Cormorant doctor and claimed things were moving very quickly—the treatment, the changes in dosage, the improvements in his condition. He—well, he almost *bragged* about it sometimes. I couldn't help but wonder whether it was the truth or wishful thinking. George was a pure optimist. He had this unshakable faith that there must be a way for him to live normally. And Higgo was just as bad," she added, pocketing her tissue. "He encouraged George, always telling him he could beat his condition. He used to say that George'd be taking the day shifts before he knew it. I don't know, though—I thought it was irresponsible for Higgo to egg him on like that. But they were good friends, and George thought the world of Higgo. If Higgo thought he could do it, as far as George knew, he could." She smiled sadly at Alice and Thaddeus.

"I wonder what made George so confident he would be safe in the sunlight," Alice mused.

"If you ask me," said Gina, leaning forward, "it was that doctor.

Philip Grampian. Violet's mother told me all about him at the funeral. It sounds like he leads people on—vulnerable people who are desperate for a treatment for their allergies. Have you seen what he charges for consultations and treatment?" Her neat eyebrows lifted and she gave Thaddeus a significant look. "It would make your eyes water." Gina checked her phone. "Well, I'd better get off—I don't want to be late for Lily. She hates having to wait." She chuckled indulgently. "I'm sorry if I've overstepped by coming to see you about those kids. I don't want to stir up trouble, but after what Higgo said about them, and that carry-on at Pier 20 yesterday, I thought it would be remiss of me not to intervene." She stood up and collected her bag.

"May I ask you something, Gina?" Alice said quickly.

"Of course, honey."

"I understand that Higgo was at the pier on the morning George was found dead." Gina's eyebrows drew downward, and Alice hurried on. "I was wondering if you know why he was there?"

Gina stood in silence for a few moments. "Who's been saying Higgo was there?"

Alice thought about telling Gina it was Gav who had said that. Knowing the woman's prejudice against Cal's friends, she decided against it.

"Wasn't he?" she said.

Gina looked down. "He was, actually. Higgo started to feel better and rushed in to finish his shift, worried that no one would be on duty. He's the one who found George—dead. It was extremely upsetting for him."

"Very sad," murmured Thaddeus.

"Yes. His best friend." Alice was struck by the pathos of this. *Pathos*, her father had explained as they'd once tucked a letter to a dead man from his elderly mother into his cold hands, was a Greek word meaning anything that caused you to feel pity. "Very sad."

"Heartbreaking," Gina agreed.

"And you?" Alice added. "Were you there?"

"Me?" Gina stared. "What on earth would I be doing there?"

"You work there," Alice pointed out.

"Yes, but not at six on a Sunday morning. I work school hours, generally. About eight thirty to three every weekday. I do the rest from home."

"I imagine you must have had to go in early that day, though," Alice said. "Once you found out your employee had passed away."

"Yes, of course—I got called in once George was found. It would've been about…let's see. Seven, perhaps? It was quite early."

"How did *you* find out about George?" Alice asked. She wished she had her notebook. Gina was proving a fruitful source of information.

"Well, my phone volume was down so I didn't hear any of the calls. The police turned up on my doorstep. I got the fright of my life, I can tell you. Police on my doorstep first thing in the morning, and me in my robe, still dripping from being in the shower!" She managed a small smile.

"And you must have rushed straight to the pier," said Alice. "Did you bring your daughter?"

"Gosh, no! I left her with her father."

Alice nodded. She was finished.

Gina stepped forward and touched Alice on the arm. "Please do take care. I wouldn't want those kids to get you or Violet into trouble."

They came out to see Gina off. When Thaddeus opened the front door, the neighbor's cat was on the lawn in their front yard. It took one look at them and raced for the wall, leaping over in an agile blur of black and orange.

"Oh, what a shame," Alice said to her father. "I've been hoping it would come out of the shrubbery."

Gina smiled. "You like animals?"

"I like cats very much."

"Do you have any pets?" Gina asked.

"No." For a few moments, Alice enjoyed the thought of a funeral parlor cat. Then she recalled that cats liked sitting in inappropriate spots, and envisioned a cat sitting on top of a freshly accessorized corpse. Perhaps pet cats were not suitable for a funeral home.

"It was nice to meet you," Thaddeus told Gina, shaking her hand. "Please do send me some information about the Commerce Club. I'm very interested in joining."

Gina smiled and swished away in her long, flowy skirt.

nineteen
A DECLINE IN GENIALITY

AUNTY Gina came to see you?" Violet's eyes were wide. "*Why?*"

"To warn me about Cal and his friends." Alice contemplated her morning snack: fruit salad in a small container. "She thinks we ought to stay away from them."

Violet munched her iced biscuit. "I knew they were trouble."

"They're harmless. We had a perfectly nice time at Cal's soiree."

"Alice, we got locked in a sea container!"

"Yes, but we have no conclusive evidence to decide who did it, at this stage."

"It was *Tess*. Do you realize she called me a ghost slug?"

"A ghost slug!"

Violet looked glum. "I searched it up on the Internet. It's this horrible white slug that preys on and eats earthworms."

"Yes, I know," said Alice. "Ms. Littlejohn told me about it. Why would Tess call you that?"

"Because it lives deep under the ground and I can't go out in the sun. But Cal's friends are *nice*, right? They don't cause any trouble, right?" Violet gave Alice a sharp look. "Still think she's harmless?"

"I think it's extraordinary that Tess knows about the ghost slug," Alice replied. "It was only discovered as a species a few years ago, and Tess doesn't strike me as the kind of person who takes a keen interest in taxonomy or natural science."

"She takes an interest in insulting people," Violet said. "I guess that inspires her to look for creative names to call people."

Alice nodded. "Yes, that makes sense."

"So, what did you say to Aunty Gina?" Violet asked. "What did your *dad* say?"

"Nothing really. He was concerned to hear about the sea container incident, but he knows I'm a good judge of character. I doubt Gina would have believed me if I'd tried to convince her Cal and the others aren't as troublesome as she claims."

"Wow." Violet brushed crumbs out from under her veil. "Your dad's chill, isn't he? I hope Aunty Gina doesn't talk to Mum, too. She'll have an absolute *fit*. She'll ground me, call the police, *and* go around to visit all their parents to tell them to stay away from her little girl."

Alice was aghast at the thought of this overreaction. "I'm joking," said Violet. "Although she would have a meltdown."

"To me, the important part of Gina's visit was what she told me about Higgo," said Alice. "Apparently Higgo is the one who thinks Cal and his friends are troublemakers. And here's the really intriguing thing: Higgo *was* at the pier that morning, just like Gav said. In fact, he's the one who found your uncle's body."

Violet's forehead creased. "Poor guy."

"Yes, it must have been a shock—if he arrived after George's death."

Violet lifted her eyes slowly to Alice's face. "You think Higgo was there *while* Uncle George died?"

"I don't know. All I know is that he was the one who reported the death."

"The bell's about to go," said Violet, checking her watch. "So, what are we going to do?"

"Are you free after school on Wednesday?" said Alice. "I think we ought to pay Higgo a visit."

⚜

The pier was particularly windy on Wednesday afternoon, and it was a wind that blew right through them, chilling Violet and Alice to the bone. Pier 19 seemed abandoned. There were no workers in sight, and the dock machinery stood idle. The only movement was the dark waves slapping against the sides of moored boats, and the pendulous swing of a hook and cable hanging from one of the cranes.

"There's no one here," said Violet. "We'll have to come back another time."

"The gate's unlocked," Alice pointed out. "It's the same time and day as the last time we came here when we saw Higgo, so I imagine it's the correct shift. Gina and her team wouldn't leave the pier unattended."

Violet sighed quietly. "Fine."

They went down to the dock, but even Ernie the lone fisherman was nowhere to be seen. Alice led the way to the end of the jetty, examining the teddy bear strapped to the post. It was substantially worse for wear after several weeks in the weather. Its fur was crusted with salt and mold, and the eyes were gone, leaving it to watch them with its stitched, sun-bleached face. Violet shuddered to look at it.

"Let's try the manager's hut," said Alice.

She urged Violet, who seemed to be moving more reluctantly by the second, down to the brick cabin tucked into the edge of the pier. Alice knocked, and Higgo answered the door. He looked dreadful, Alice thought—distracted and unkempt. His graying, ginger hair was thin and stood on end, as if he'd been repeatedly rubbing at it.

"You!" he snarled when he saw her. "What are *you* doing here? And Violet!" He dragged a hand through his hair, confirming Alice's theory. "I told you girls to stay away!"

"May we come in?" Alice used an extra-polite manner, so as not to exacerbate his mood. "It's rather wild and windy out here, and we'd just like to have a brief conversation, if we may."

He stared for a moment, then went to shut the door on them. Almost reflexively, Alice jammed her shoe between the door and the frame. Higgo drew a sharp breath.

"Just a moment of your time." She sounded calm, although she was as surprised by her actions as he was.

He drew himself up to his full height. "Go on, get away from here," he said, his voice hard.

Violet clutched at Alice's arm and tried to drag her away, but Alice stood firm.

"Wait, Violet," she said. "Why can't we speak to you?" she asked Higgo.

"I'm busy," he said.

"No, I don't think you are. It appears you've been drinking a hot coffee—I can see it steaming on the bench over there in a World's Best Dad cup—and reading the sports pages of the *Coastal Chronicle*. Well, that's where you've got it open, so I presume that's what you were reading."

"Alice!" Violet hissed.

"Get out of here." His voice became lower, more threatening.

"I simply want to ask you something, sir."

"Alice!" Violet whispered again, tugging at her arm.

"Hold on, Violet. There's no reason for us to scurry away simply because Mr. Higginson appears to be in a bad mood."

Higgo's mouth opened in surprise, then after a moment, he

closed it and shook his head. "Fine. If I answer your *question*, then you will leave and not come back. Deal?"

"Not come back?" Alice considered it. "I don't think so. I like it at the pier, and it's open for the public to visit during business hours. We're not doing anything illegal. We understand that we're not allowed to board the boats or interfere with the machinery. We only want to admire the view, walk the beach, or in this instance, speak to you."

His lip lifted in a hint of a sneer. "Well, if I answer this question, will you at least leave *me* alone?"

"Yes," said Alice. "For today."

Leaving the door ajar, Higgo turned away and slumped back into his chair, taking a slurp of his coffee. Alice came into the hut after him. Violet edged in and stood against the wall. There was a set of keys on the desk and Alice saw a photo of a little red-headed boy on a key ring. On the whiteboard over Higgo's shoulder, the names Higgo, Pauly, and Ashok were scattered across the roster. There was an *Ashok* that had been crossed out for the following Thursday's graveyard shift, and Higgo's name was written in red as replacement.

"All right," Higgo said, lifting his gaze wearily to Alice's face. "What's this hugely important question you've got for me?"

Alice clasped her hands behind her back. "I want to know why you came to the pier the morning George died. You were ill. Someone else had taken your shift. So, why did you come down so early?"

She saw Higgo hastily conceal his shock. "What's this fascination with George's death?"

Alice was unable to think of a reply that he would believe or understand.

Higgo sat straighter in his chair. "Look here. I don't know what you two think you're doing, playing at being detectives or something, but a man died. It's not a joke—not a game. He was my friend—Violet's uncle. He was a devoted godfather to my toddler, who's got a disability. George was a good man—better than most. Going around pretending he was murdered or whatever, that's not funny. It's—it's wrong. It's a horrible thing to do to his friends and family. How d'you think Helen would feel if she knew?"

Alice drew herself up tall. "We're not playing a *game*, Higgo. I was raised in a funeral home. I don't consider death silly or funny."

He seemed speechless and drank his coffee again, as though that counted as a reply.

"I'm sorry," Violet ventured. "It's true, though. We're not playing a game. We really want to know why no one was able to help Uncle George. There were people around—"

"People around?" Higgo's face came up smartly. "What makes you think that?"

Violet looked at Alice.

"Well, *you* were here," Alice said. "And I think there were teenagers hanging around, too. Perhaps partying under the dock…"

"Teenagers! I always move them on as soon as I see them. There was no one around that morning." He studied Alice. "Who's been talking to you, telling you stories? You been talking to those kids?"

"Do you mean Cal, Tess, Amy, and Gav?" Alice asked.

"Yeah." He muttered a few unkind words about Cal and his friends.

Alice replied carefully. "They don't say very much at all about that morning, although one of them mentioned that you were here."

Higgo snorted. "I wouldn't listen to what Cal says. Lying, thieving little creep—and they're all the same."

"Gina already told me what you think of them." Alice noted his look of surprise. "Why *do* you think so badly of them, Higgo?"

"They've been hanging around for years, getting up to no good," he said.

"But what specifically have they done?" she persisted.

"That's between them and us," he snapped back at her. "All you've gotta know is that it's best to stay away from those little creeps, or you'll find yourselves in a world of trouble." He switched his gaze to Violet. "Do you need me to speak to your parents about it, or are you going to do what I suggest?"

"No, it's okay—we'll stay away from them." Violet opened the hut door and stood there, giving Alice a look.

"Gina's already spoken to my father," Alice told Higgo. "There's no need for you to press the matter any further." She went out the door after Violet. "I do hope you start to feel better soon," she called before Higgo shut the door.

He hesitated. "Huh?"

"Grief is a very individual journey," she added.

A darkness came over Higgo's face again. He glowered and pulled the door sharply shut.

The two headed for the gate. "He's scary," Violet said quietly.

"Yes. He seemed much kinder and gentler just a few weeks ago. Something has changed him—and I'm not sure it's simply the grief of losing a friend," Alice said.

"Mum was telling me about Higgo's little boy, Harry. He's got a disease—I can't remember what it's called. He needs all these expensive therapies, and Higgo's wife can't work because someone has to drive him around to different doctors all the time. They might have to sell their house so they can afford to live. Uncle George even ran a fundraiser for them at the community center last year—a quiz night."

"It sounds like Higgo is under quite a bit of strain," said Alice.

They walked up the hill in silence. Alice lagged a little due to her weak leg and the steepness of the incline, but Violet seemed consumed with her thoughts. At the top, Alice paused to catch her breath. Violet gave her a pensive look.

"What are you thinking about, Violet?" Alice panted.

"I think—I think maybe we should stop."

"Stop?"

"Stop doing this. Trying to find out more about Uncle George's death."

Alice stared. "Why?"

"Higgo. He's scary. He's big, too. I mean, what if he gets really mad at us and comes after us?" Violet's gaze was locked on Alice. "If he could do something to harm Uncle George, why couldn't he do something to hurt *us*?"

"Violet." Alice resumed walking. "You mustn't let yourself be intimidated by Higgo's size or manner. If he *is* our culprit, then that's precisely what he wants!"

"Well, duh. That's why we should do the smart thing. Why not tell my dad what's been going on and let him talk to the cops?"

Alice suspected this would be a disastrous move. Violet's parents were unlikely to believe them—not everyone was as fortunate as she was when it came to parental trust. And even if they did, and the matter was referred to the authorities, the police would probably tell them, very condescendingly, that they were two children with vivid imaginations who ought to be worrying about their schoolwork. She was surprised Violet didn't understand these things.

Alice changed her approach. If she couldn't reason with Violet, maybe she could distract her.

"Listen, Violet, I have an idea."

"What now?"

"Well, I believe we've investigated your uncle's death extremely thoroughly so far. However, there are a few suspects who have escaped our questioning. I would like to speak to your aunt."

"Aunty Helen?"

"Yes. We have given her some space to recover from the initial shock of her loss, but the time has come for us to subject her to an interview. Can you arrange it, do you think?"

"I suppose we could go see her after school one afternoon this week," said Violet. She still looked dubious but brightened a little. "She makes chocolate fudge brownies whenever I visit."

"Even better. And then there's your mother."

"What?" Violet stopped dead. "You want to question my mother? No. *No way.* She'll freak out."

"In what way?" Alice asked, pausing to let Violet catch up.

"*Ugh.*" Violet rolled her eyes. "The usual. She'll say some topics are 'not for children' and start ranting about that *monster*, Dr. Grampian. Seriously, Alice. We *can't* talk to my mum about this. She'll probably say we can't be friends anymore if she thinks you're being a bad influence, talking about Uncle George's death, or whatever."

"I wouldn't want to discombobulate your mother," Alice said with some regret.

"Discom—who?" said Violet.

"Discombobulate. It's when you feel like your insides are a big bag of apples bobbing in a barrel of water." She thought for a moment. "If I give you a few questions, do you think you could try to find out the information from your mother?"

Violet shrugged. "Maybe. Depends what I'm asking."

"I'll think about it and give you a list."

Violet broke into laughter, shaking her head. "Anyone else, Alice?"

"Yes, Violet." Alice smiled, pleased that Violet appeared to have rallied her spirits. "I was saving the best for last. It's school break next week, and you and I are going to take a day trip."

"Where to?"

"To Port Cormorant. We're going to pay a visit to Dr. Grampian."

twenty
DARK TREATS

HELEN Devenish's home was adapted for her dead husband's allergies, but not at all in the same way as Violet's house was. There were no window shutters or latches on the front door, but inside it was dim, with thick tapestry curtains that radiated a daylight glow around the edges. There were lamps everywhere, old-fashioned yellow tungsten bulbs struggling to illuminate the gloom.

The kitchen and living room contained a profusion of knick-knacks, from ceramic terriers to green glass vases, from model vintage cars to china statuettes of waltzing couples. There were also a vast number of dried wildflower arrangements and scented candles. Alice's nose tickled.

Altogether, Helen's place had the homey but rather fragile feel of a secondhand store, except for the warm smell of baked chocolate treats. There was a strong scent of tea tree oil in the air, too, which was not quite as pleasant. Alice noted a tray covered in a tea towel on the kitchen counter between a box of cocoa and an essential oil burner: the brownies, she hoped.

Violet left her veil and gloves in place.

"It's lovely to see you, Violet." Helen moved around like a confused honeybee, pulling chairs in and out, touching a side table, and shifting the fruit basket. She moved a floor rug with her foot just before Alice stepped on it, which almost made Alice trip. "And your friend! I'm so happy you have a friend, nowadays."

Violet seemed embarrassed. She cleared her throat. "Where's Ollie?"

"At the groomer's, today. Poor little thing was covered in mats. I have to admit, I haven't been brushing him since George—" She stopped herself at the word. "But George would be horrified if he saw Ollie in that state, so I finally did something about it today."

"Ollie's Aunty Helen's dog," Violet explained for Alice's benefit.

"A Highland terrier," Helen added, nodding.

"I see. I must congratulate you on getting your dog back into its grooming schedule, Mrs. Devenish. It's a sign of your fortitude that you've been able to recommence that routine." Alice thought she saw resentment in Helen's quick glance. Then it was gone, and Helen was all smiles and nods, indicating a horsehair chair where Alice could sit.

"Do call me Helen, my sweet." She sighed, not noticing that Alice had almost sat upon a pair of rusted garden shears on the horsehair chair. Alice relocated them to a side table. "I couldn't do anything at first. I was *paralyzed* with grief. Then Gayle, my old friend from the patchwork club, she came over and dragged me to aqua aerobics. Literally *dragged* me." She gave a little chuckle. "I'm lucky, really. I've got good friends."

"That's important," said Alice. She had heard her father say these things so often when comforting mourning relatives, and they came out of her mouth quite naturally. "Friends and easing back into a routine."

Helen nodded vehemently. "I said that to Luanne. Luanne wanted me to clear out the house. She thought it would be thera- peutic for me. You know, like a spring clean—getting rid of George's things and making the house more—more normal, I suppose. Less of a haven for someone with a sunlight allergy." She directed a self-conscious glance at Violet. "I argued, saying I wanted it to be a safe place for Violet and Lucas to visit. But Luanne said it didn't matter because the children aren't allowed to remove their protective gear anywhere except home, anyway."

That startled Alice. "But George lived here safely…"

"Yes! Yes, oh, Alice sweetie—if only you knew how many times I've said those exact words to Luanne. But she's so rigid on the matter. She refuses to trust anyone, not even me."

She laughed again as if this were somehow amusing, although it clearly wasn't. Violet looked at the floor, and Helen's laugh ended in a sigh.

"Anyway, I can't bear to get rid of George's things yet. And even opening the curtains to let the light in feels strange. I suppose it will have to happen eventually, but there's no need to rush into it."

Violet lifted her face and smiled at her aunt. "I kind of like it. It makes me feel like Uncle George is still around."

"That's it exactly." Helen beamed. "Now, I hope you girls are hungry because I've baked a great, big batch of brownies. Milk? Or tea?"

"Tea, please," said Violet, and Alice echoed the request.

"I won't be a minute." Helen went to the kitchen.

Violet looked at Alice. "I wonder if that funeral card is here somewhere," she whispered. "The one you saw that said sorry to Uncle George."

Alice looked around and saw a stack of mail on the table. "It could be in there."

Violet jumped up and scurried over to look, rummaging quickly through the stack of letters. Before she finished, Alice spied a familiar envelope sitting on a low velvet footstool by the window. It looked like the one she'd posted to Helen—in fact, she could see the corner of a condolence card sticking out of the opening.

"Oh, wait, Violet—it's over here." She crossed to the footstool and slid the cards out into her hands. Violet joined her.

"Do either of you take sugar?" Helen called, making them both jump.

They called their answers and Alice handed Violet a stack of cards to sort through, shuffling through the rest herself.

"It's not in this lot," said Alice. "It must be in yours."

But Violet was having no luck, either. She reached the last card and looked at Alice helplessly. "It's not here."

"Has she got rid of it, I wonder?" said Alice.

"What are you girls up to?" Helen spoke so close behind them that Violet gave a little shriek and dropped the cards she was holding in her hands, creating a shower of white cardboard decorated with flowers and doves.

"Oh!" said Helen. She stood there with the two cups of tea in her hands and stared first at the cards all over the carpet, then at the remainder of the cards in Alice's hands.

"Sorry," said Violet. "We're sorry, Aunty Helen."

Helen turned and put down the teacups. Violet scrambled to pick up the dropped cards and Alice helped her put them all back in the envelope.

"Some very nice messages," said Helen. "People said very kind things."

"They did," said Alice. "George was clearly a respected and well-liked man."

Violet mumbled something, pink-cheeked, that sounded like, "Just wanted...see all the...good things...Uncle George..."

"It's all right, Violet," said her aunt. "I miss him too."

Helen went back into the kitchen, and Alice and Violet sat down again, Violet attempting to compose herself with a few deep breaths.

Helen brought a plate of warm brownies to the coffee table, and once again the smell of chocolate filled the room—laced with that powerful tea tree oil scent. "I won't have one myself," said Helen. "I've eaten too many already. But you girls can help yourselves to as many as you want."

They were as good as Violet had promised, but the sharp odor of the oil was becoming more dominant, infiltrating Alice's sinuses. By her second brownie, it rather affected the taste. She stopped at two. Her father wouldn't want her to ingest this much sugar, anyway. Violet had a third, but even she sneezed once or twice from the tea tree smell.

Alice gathered her thoughts. "Helen, forgive my curiosity, but may I ask you about the night your husband passed away?"

Helen stared, her mouth hanging open slightly. "Oh! Yes, I suppose…"

"Thank you. What time was it when he was called into work to replace Higgo?"

"Golly, it's like being in the police station all over again. Let me think." Helen rested her hand on her chest. "It was about two thirty, I think. Petra—that's Higgo's wife—called him. She was in a flap because she couldn't get hold of Gina. Poor Higgo was in bed, feverish and awfully unwell, and Petra didn't know what else to do. She knows how important it is that someone's always at the pier, checking the boats that come in. It might not sound like much of a job, being a wharf security officer, but it's a position of national importance."

Alice hesitated. "It is? How so?"

Helen's eyes widened. "Border control! You never know what's coming in across the ocean. George saw it all, you know. People trying to get into the country illegally, smuggling, prohibited foods and plants, even criminals. And overfishing. People with huge numbers of protected fish. You can't leave a pier unattended."

Alice was impressed, although Violet gave her a minuscule eye roll as if this was something she'd heard many times before and was skeptical about.

"George must have been a very responsible man," Alice said.

"He took his job extremely seriously, thank goodness." Helen looked up at the wedding photo on the living room wall: a much younger George in a top hat and tails, and herself in a puffy white gown, smiling in front of a fake background of a flower-strewn hillside. " 'Cherry-Bomb,' he'd say to me—that was what he called me! *'Cherry-Bomb, it's just me and my flashlight between the security of the nation, some nights.'*" She laughed and sighed again.

Alice drew the woman back to her question. "So, Petra Higginson called at two thirty a.m. and George went into work?"

"Yes, George tried to get hold of Gina as well, but her phone kept ringing. He didn't really have a choice. He threw his uniform back on and rushed out. I don't have much memory of it, to be honest. I was woken up by Petra's phone call, but I went straight back to sleep. I only vaguely knew he was going out. If I'd known it would be the last time I'd see him, I would have..." Tears came to her eyes and she rubbed them away. "I don't know. Next thing I was aware of, the police were knocking at the door in the morning. I knew. As soon as I saw the uniforms, I knew."

She covered her eyes. Alice waited while Helen recomposed herself.

Unexpectedly, Violet spoke. "Aunty Helen, did Dr. Grampian bully you into donating Uncle George to medical research?"

Helen looked so stunned that Alice thought she had better clarify. "Violet means George's remains."

This didn't seem to help. Helen continued to stare at her niece. She shot a look at Alice and it appeared to hold rather a lot of dislike. But once again, it vanished before Alice could be sure.

"I found out," Violet was saying to her aunt.

Helen could barely form a word. "But how...?"

"It's okay—no one else knows," Violet said. "Not Mum or Dad. Only me."

Helen covered her face and burst into tears. "George wanted it! He told me! I promised him!"

"To donate his body?" Alice asked.

"He said he would gladly donate his body to science if it would help even one person with a life-threatening allergy! Kids like Violet and Lucas." She sobbed for a few moments. "Dr. Grampian helped me arrange it. It didn't happen the way your mother said, Violet. It was my decision. George would have wanted it."

"I didn't know Uncle George was that obsessed with fixing our allergy," Violet said, staring up at the photo on the wall.

"It was *all* about you and Lucas." Helen drew a shaky breath. "He adored you kids and all he wanted was to make your lives better."

"Wow," Violet said softly, dropping her gaze to her hands.

"He was crazy about you two. And Higgo's boy, too. When little Harry came along a couple of years ago and Higgo asked him to be godfather, George was as pleased as punch. Of course, Harry's got medical issues as well, which made George feel even more connected to him. He did so much for that family, the poor devils. They're up to their armpits in debt and your uncle was always trying to help."

Alice was attempting to demonstrate her sympathy with a grave facial expression, but she had abruptly started to feel unwell. A sharp ache had begun in her stomach and nausea was rising in her esophagus. Helen was talking about how George loved children and how, when Violet and Lucas came along, his search for a treatment for his allergy became even more urgent. Alice waited for as long as she dared, then stood up.

"May I use the bathroom?"

"Of course, sweetie." Helen blinked up at her with wet eyes and, this time, Alice thought she saw suspicion. "It's at the end of the hall."

Alice only just made it there when the vomiting commenced. Within minutes, there was nothing remaining of the brownies in her stomach. Alice sat back and put a hand to her clammy forehead. She would have to borrow the phone to ask her father to come and pick her up. She hoped the afternoon funeral service was over so she wouldn't have to wait. The way she was feeling, a wait would be highly unpleasant. Alice only wanted her bed and perhaps a toothbrush.

A frantic thumping sounded on the door. "Alice? Are you done? I need to use…" There was a gulping noise.

It was Violet. Alice emerged, weak and coughing, and Violet shoved past her, ripping off her hat and veil so she could take her own turn crouched before the bowl. Helen appeared in the hall and observed her niece in mid-heave, and Alice standing shakily by the bathroom door.

"Oh dear," she said, peculiarly bright in manner. "Are you girls sick?"

⚜

"Is tea tree oil poisonous, Dad?" Alice asked her father the next day.

"Not if used as per the directions."

"What about if it's eaten?"

He raised his eyebrows. "Eaten! It shouldn't be eaten. Why do you ask?"

The illness had been officially declared a twenty-four-hour stomach virus, but Luanne Devenish had muttered about the inappropriately stored eggs in Helen's kitchen, and Thaddeus had remarked on the fact that no one else in either family had caught the bug. Alice thought it very odd that she and Violet had fallen ill at the exact same moment.

"I just wondered if it was possible Helen put tea tree oil in the brownies she cooked for me and Violet."

"I don't imagine so," Thaddeus said. "I think it would have a strong, unpleasant taste, even baked into a food like that."

"Yes, it would, wouldn't it?" Alice sighed.

"Do you have reason to think it was in the brownies?"

She thought of the strong smell in Helen's house. "Only that there was tea tree oil in the kitchen and Violet and I became suddenly ill after eating the brownies."

"Did Helen seem in a scatterbrained mood? The kind of mood in which one might make that kind of mistake?"

Alice recalled those odd flashes of hostility and mistrust she'd seen in Helen's face from time to time. "Not scatterbrained, no. Not particularly."

"Well, then I think we must assume it was a stomach bug or, as Luanne suggested, some bad eggs."

"Hmm," said Alice.

"Bad eggs are no yolk, that's for sure," Thaddeus said with a smile, but Alice wasn't inclined to laugh at his play on words. She considered the matter quite serious and extremely unpleasant.

On her day off school, Alice did not spend her time idly. She prepared a list of questions for Violet to ask her mother. Soon, she would have spoken to everyone on the periphery of George Devenish's death, and while not all those people had necessarily been honest, the process had been enlightening. She had an intriguing list of facts—and some guesses.

The other thing she worked on was studying the list of people who might have sent the missing card—the card that said *George, I'm sorry.* Luanne Devenish, Lucas Devenish, Leonard Higginson, Philip Grampian, Gina Prince, Cal, or Gav. She wished she had the card in her hand again, so she could attempt to narrow down the initial even further. Something nagged at her, as if she'd missed someone off the list, but Alice couldn't think of anyone she hadn't already considered: Helen, Tess, Amy, and Eric were the only other suspects, and none of their initials fit.

The next morning, Alice felt like herself again. She dressed for school and joined her father at breakfast.

"Helen Devenish dropped by while you were in the shower," he said.

"Really?" Alice sat up straight. "What did she want?"

He pointed to a plastic container on the bench. "She felt sorry for you, being so sick, and she brought you some of her homemade brownies."

Alice regarded the container with horror.

"Don't eat them all at once," Thaddeus said. "They're full of sugar. Perhaps half of one per day."

Alice shuddered. Even half would be too much; in fact, she would never eat a crumb of Helen's brownies again. Or possibly any brownies at all. They would be sniffed for the presence of tea tree oil and then go straight in the trash can.

At recess, Alice discovered that Violet was still away. She took a seat on the bench near the principal's office and ate her almonds in solitude, a little vexed by Violet's absence. Even more aggravatingly, she could only eat half her almonds. Her stomach must have shrunk from not eating much over the past twenty-four hours. Alice sat looking at the nuts that remained, discontented.

"Hey, Zombie Queen."

She looked up. Cal had arrived, his bag hitched over his shoulder.

"Cal! What are you doing here?"

"Here at school, or here near Mr. Prince's office?"

"Both."

Cal grinned. "You're a crack-up, Zombie Queen. Where's Ultra?"

"She's still unwell. We both had a stomach virus, or possibly food poisoning. It was dreadful. I'm better, but Violet must still be sick."

"Ugh, stomach bugs are the worst. I heard there's something going around. Hey, listen." He sat down beside her on the bench. She offered him her remaining almonds and he accepted them gladly. "Can you hang out this afternoon? I've got something I want to show you."

"What is it?" she asked.

"A surprise." His eyes were sparkling.

"I'm not fond of surprises," she said.

Cal burst into laughter. "You'll like this one. Meet me after school at Pier 20."

"Wait, Cal." Alice hesitated, unsure whether to tell him what was on her mind, but she decided he had the right to know. "Gina Prince came to see my father. She and Higgo think you are a bad influence and they don't want me or Violet to fraternize with you."

"To *what*?"

"Fraternize. Mix. Mingle. Socialize."

Cal stopped tossing almonds into his mouth. "Gina said that?"

"Yes, she came to visit my father and me. She said that I might be influenced by the unruly ways of you and your friends."

Cal shook his head. "You talk weird." He seemed deflated—even hurt.

"Have you been doing illegal things?" Alice asked. "You or your friends?"

Cal stared at the ground and shook his head. "Nah."

"Are you sure, Cal?" she asked gently.

"Yeah." He checked her face as if hoping he had convinced her. "Seriously, I haven't done anything illegal, Alice. Gav's been in trouble a few times but he hasn't done anything wrong at the pier. He's got family problems. The rest of us, we just hang out. We're not breaking any laws."

"It's odd that Gina and her staff would make that allegation against you, then. Don't you agree?"

"Gina probably gets her info from Mr. Prince. He hates me." Cal tossed another almond.

"I'm not so sure," said Alice. "She didn't mention Mr. Prince or your school habits. She just seemed convinced you were a troublemaker."

"You believe her," he said flatly.

"On the contrary," said Alice. "I decided not to take their advice, and to continue to associate with you, because I disagree that you are a scoundrel. And I don't know your friends as well as I know you, but I also doubt they're the kind of people Higgo or Gina seem to think they are."

Cal's face lit up. "Cool. You're cool, Zombie Queen."

Alice was startled. She knew she wasn't cool, but it was rather pleasant to be thought of as such.

"So, will you come down to the pier later and see my surprise?" he asked.

"I can't say a definite yes, but I'd like to," she said. "If I don't have too much homework and my father allows it, I'll be there."

"Good one."

"Calvin Lee!" came a distant yet familiar shout from the direction of the office.

Cal's shoulders shot up into a fearful hunch. He sighed, stood up, and shouldered his bag. "Mr. Prince wants to see me."

Alice checked the principal's office window, hoping he hadn't overheard their discussion about his wife. The window was closed, thankfully—but she could see the vast outline of Mr. Prince gesticulating at Cal from inside.

"Hope I'll see you after school," said Cal as he loped away.

twenty-one
A SERPENTINE REVELATION

ALICE had homework, but she was extremely curious about Cal's surprise and decided it could wait. Her father had already told her he didn't need her assistance with the corpse for tomorrow's funeral, so Alice embarked on the walk to Pier 20. She was weaker than usual, and still had a nagging ache in her stomach from the bug—or—poisoning, so she walked slowly.

When she reached Wharf Road and turned right to get to Pier 20, a white car was emerging from the gates of Pier 19. It was Gina Prince. Her daughter, Lily, was in the back seat. The vehicle came to a halt beside Alice, and Gina wound down the window.

"Alice, how lovely to see you! What are you doing down here?"

Alice was unsure how to reply. She was on her way to see a boy Gina had expressly advised Alice not to see. Was it even Gina's business what she was doing? Alice sighed. Gina was a responsible adult and possibly a business associate of her father; she had to answer.

"I'm—"

She was interrupted by Lily, who had wound down her window and was holding a pet carrier up to show Alice her kitten. "Look! This is Demerara. Do you like her?"

Alice squinted into the afternoon light, trying to see into the carrier. Demerara was a very young-looking kitten, gray-furred and pink-nosed, with a stripe down her forehead between two round, dark eyes.

"She's lovely," said Alice. "Very unique. What breed is she?"

"She's—"

"Lily, *I* was talking to Alice," said Gina.

"Sorry, Mummy."

Gina smiled at Alice. "Are you going to the beach?"

"Yes. Pier 20."

Worry crossed Gina's face. "Please be careful, Alice. That's a rough place."

"I will."

Gina didn't seem completely satisfied, but she waved and rolled onward. Alice thought that the woman appeared to be watching her in the rearview mirror as she drove away. Before Alice even reached the jetty at Pier 20, she could hear Cal and his friends there. They had their music playing, and there was movement beneath the dock. She made her way down the sandy trail to join them. In the shadow of the dock, Cal, Tess, and Gav were in a circle, seemingly deep in conversation. Cal looked up and saw her, beckoning frantically.

"Come here, Alice! Check it out!"

As she drew nearer, Alice realized Cal had a small live snake draped around his neck. She stopped and stared.

"You have a snake. Is it venomous?"

Gav and Tess seemed to think that was hilarious. Tess laughed especially loudly, although Alice thought it was a reasonable question to ask of someone holding a reptile.

Cal ignored his friends. "No, it's a Stimson's python, totally harmless. Isn't he beautiful?"

Alice came closer and examined the snake. It was rather lovely, with a little oblong head and giraffe-spots, and a tiny squiggle of a tail.

"You can pat him," Cal said. "He's really gentle and sweet."

She shook her head. "I think I'll just look at him for a while. When did you get it?"

"Yesterday afternoon. His name's Ziggy." Cal lifted his pet's head and admired its slitted eyes, golden in color. "It's a caramel-albino morph—check out the color." He looked mesmerized.

"It's certainly a fine-looking snake," Alice said.

"Where're you keeping it, Cal?" Gav asked.

Cal fished in his pocket and pulled out his phone. "I've got a tank with lights and stuff." He showed them a photo of a big glass tank. It looked wildly out of place in a small, untidy bedroom. The tank had a sliding front panel and was lit up with a purple-white light. Inside was an elaborate habitat of desert sand, rocks, ferns, wood, and a little pond, presumably for the snake to play in. There was a wire mesh cover and something that looked like a thermometer stuck to the side. Even Tess looked impressed.

"Wow, that would've cost a fortune," said Gav.

"State of the art," said Cal. "It's got a heat mat and everything." He pocketed the phone and watched his snake adoringly.

"Snakes are quite expensive, aren't they?" Alice ventured.

Cal didn't seem to hear. "Look at his tail, Alice. It's like a little worm! So cute."

Alice looked dutifully at the tail. "How much?" she asked.

"Huh?"

"How much was the snake?" she said. "You said last week that you've wanted a pet snake for years. I imagine you saved up, is that right? The reptile habitat must have been costly, too. I suppose you were saving for a long time."

Cal wouldn't meet her eyes and his cheeks were becoming redder by the moment.

"Hey, how about you quit with the questions?" said Tess, stepping closer to Cal and giving Alice a hostile stare. Alice wondered if she had been impolite. Perhaps it was not tactful to ask people about money they had spent.

"I'm sorry. I'm simply curious. I'm very impressed that Cal has managed to save enough for this lovely pet. Do you have an after-school job, Cal? I didn't realize you'd been working so hard to save up."

"It was a present," Cal said, turning away.

"Oh, I see. A birthday present?"

"Shut up," Tess snapped at Alice.

Shocked, Alice shut up. Cal turned and frowned at Tess, then swung back around to Alice.

"It's something I've wanted for a long time. I got it as a present yesterday, that's all. It's no biggie. Nothing major."

Tess glared at Alice, then nudged Gav. They wandered out from under the dock and down to the water's edge.

"I thought it might have been your birthday," Alice said to Cal, her voice low with discomfort.

"Nah, but thanks. It was just a nice surprise. I only asked you to come down because I thought you might like to see Ziggy. I know you like nature-y stuff. I've seen you collecting stuff on the beach."

"I don't collect stuff," Alice said, feeling a little better.

"Oh, okay. I thought you did. Anyway, he's pretty amazing, huh?"

She agreed that the snake was amazing. At Cal's suggestion, they followed Tess and Gav down to the waterline and took a stroll along the shore.

"Are you hungry, friend?" Cal asked his snake. "He hasn't eaten yet. Probably a bit scared, living in a new environment."

"What do you feed him?" Gav wanted to know.

"Pinkies. Baby mice. When he gets bigger he'll eat adult mice and rats."

"Told you," Gav said to Tess.

"Dead or alive?" she asked Cal.

Cal made a disgusted face. "Dead. I wouldn't feed him live animals."

"I wouldn't be able to resist watching him eat live food," Tess said with a smile that Alice thought might be false bravado.

"You're a psycho, Tess," said Gav.

"Where do you get the mice from?" Alice asked Cal.

"The pet shop," he told her. "They cost a bit. I've arranged with Mum that if I do the dishes every night, she'll pay me enough to cover Ziggy's food."

Alice thought about his lack of funds and the expensive snake and tank, and had more questions, but didn't want to ask them in case Tess became aggressive again. She noticed a small piece of coral on the sand and picked it up, studying it. She placed it in her pocket.

"See?" said Cal. "You collect beach stuff."

"Oh, I can see how you might think it's a collection," said Alice. "But it's not."

❧

Violet was back at school the next day. Alice passed her on the walkway as she went to science class and they exchanged a brief wave. Alice was too engrossed by the classwork—a diagram of the phylum Cnidaria, which included jellyfish, corals, and anemones—some of her favorite creatures. Ms. Littlejohn was just as keen on sea animals and told Alice how, despite their often incredibly long and numerous tentacles, there was no evidence that a jellyfish had ever become entangled in itself.

The only problem with Alice's science lesson was that Kimberly Larsson was in her class, and Kimberly always felt the need to remind Alice that she was weird, smelled like dead people, had a possessed leg, and was actually a reanimated corpse. Alice had grown rather bored with these taunts over the years. She almost wished Kimberly would come up with something new. She toyed with the idea of telling Kimberly that she and her father feasted on the organs of the bodies, or that they kept jars of human souls on the shelves in the embalming room. She decided it was best not to do so—she didn't want to damage the reputation of Tranquility Funerals.

At recess, Alice met Violet at the good bench and inquired after her health. Violet screwed up her face.

"I've been fine since yesterday morning, but Mum was paranoid. She thought I might have to pull off my veil if I spewed at school and I'd end up having an allergic reaction. So of course, that meant I wasn't allowed to come. It was a bonus in a way. I didn't have to go to health class, and we're studying puberty, so I was happy to skip that."

Alice caught Violet up on the latest developments, including Cal's expensive pet snake.

"Do you think he might have stolen it?" Violet asked, sounding awed.

"No. I don't believe Cal would steal, but even if he did have that propensity, how could he steal a pet python, complete with a large tank and all that equipment? I doubt he would have the knowledge or tools required to break into a pet store. I looked it up, and there's nowhere in Damocles Cove that even sells snakes. He would have had to go to Port Cormorant."

Violet had to admit that such a theft would be quite a feat. "His friends might have helped him."

"His friends didn't seem to know very much about how to keep a snake. If they'd helped him steal it, they would probably know more. And I read the newspaper every day and haven't seen anything about the theft of a snake and its tank from a pet store or a private home."

"Okay, he must be telling the truth, then," said Violet. "It would have been a present."

Alice still had her doubts but there was no other explanation. "Are you able to come with me to Port Cormorant during the school break next week?" she asked.

Violet chewed a thumbnail through her veil. "To see Dr. Grampian?"

"Yes."

"I don't know, Alice. It's weird. Kids aren't even *allowed* to see doctors without their parents, I don't think. I mean, who would pay the bill?"

"That's true," said Alice. "But we aren't seeing him for a medical reason."

"Maybe he'll be too busy to see us." Violet seemed oddly hopeful. "Or he might not want to."

"No, he's quite happy to see us," Alice replied.

Violet stopped chewing her nail. "How do you know?"

"Because when I called him to make the appointment, he said he could meet us in his consulting room on Monday at eleven a.m., and I made it very clear that this would not be a medical consultation and therefore we would not be paying a fee. He said he understood."

"You've already made the appointment?" Violet shook her head slowly. "I can't believe he agreed to it! Especially for free. Mum reckons he charges a fortune."

"I told him we would like to ask some questions about George, and when he asked who 'we' were, I told him it was you and me. Then he seemed quite comfortable about seeing us."

"Bizarre," said Violet. "You know, Mum reckons he'd love to get his hands on me and Lucas for his research. Maybe that's why he said yes."

Alice considered this idea. "It seems highly unprofessional for a doctor to behave that way, but I suppose it's possible. If you're not comfortable with going, I understand. I can go on my own."

"No," Violet said. "I'm coming. This is about *my* uncle George, remember?"

"Of course."

"And there's a really good K-pop and anime shop in Port Cormorant." Violet's eyes gleamed. "I've been dying to check it out."

Alice consented reluctantly. She couldn't quite grasp why Violet insisted on adding frivolous activities to their serious investigations. However, it would make it much easier to speak to the doctor about George if Violet was there, so Alice would just have to tolerate it.

twenty-two
A CURATIVE APPOINTMENT

ALICE had to ask to be excused from helping at a funeral service on the morning of their visit to Port Cormorant. Luckily, her father could spare her, although it did mean Patty's loud friend Ellen had to come in and take her place. Alice assured Thaddeus that she would not make a habit of taking days off, but the appointment was both important and difficult to rearrange. She was honest about the purpose of their day trip, even down to Violet wanting to visit her K-pop store.

For the first time in as long as she could remember, Thaddeus didn't seem terribly happy with her. "You appear to be asking a lot of questions about George Devenish's death," he said.

"Yes, I am. Violet and I are investigating it together."

"*Investigating* it?"

"Yes. I think there's more to it than meets the eye."

Her father seemed speechless, so she explained further. "I think there were people around when he died, and I don't understand why no one helped. The facts I know don't match up with the story we've been told."

Thaddeus was quiet for a long time. "And how do *you* know the facts?" he asked at last.

This was it. This was the moment she finally told her father the truth about the resonance. Alice's heart bumped fast. She opened her mouth to tell him how certain treasured objects held stories about the bodies that came through their funeral home.

The framed photo of baby Alice and her twin in Thaddeus's arms fell off the wall onto the floor again. This time, the glass broke.

Her father went over and bent down to retrieve the frame. He picked up the shards of glass and gazed down at the picture, then lifted his head slowly to look at Alice. Something large and quiet passed between them.

"She tells me things about them," Alice said in a small voice.

Afterward, when she thought about it, Alice realized that her words could have meant a variety of things. She wasn't even sure what they meant herself. However, the tears in her father's eyes and the way his hand shook when he looked down at the photograph of his twin daughters—the live and the dead twin—told her he understood exactly what the words meant.

"May I go?" she asked into the still air. Thaddeus nodded.

⚜

Violet was already at the train station, looking around anxiously. When Alice reached her, Violet waved at a car in the parking lot. Alice realized Luanne Devenish had been waiting so that Violet wouldn't be alone. The car rolled slowly away and Violet seemed to relax.

"Did you have any problems convincing your parents to let you come today?" Alice asked, the thought occurring to her for the first time.

"Not really. It took a couple of nights, but Dad talked Mum into it. But if anyone asks, we're just going to the Temple Mall for clothes shopping and Momo, okay?"

"Momo?" echoed Alice.

Violet rolled her eyes. "The K-pop shop. Do you like bubble tea?"

"I've never tried it."

"I'll get you one. They're the best."

They both had transport passes, thanks to the school's insistence that every student had one in order to streamline excursions. Alice had always liked trains. This one ran along the line with a soft hum, making perfectly timed stops at the stations while a robotic voice announced the name of the station. There was a train-line map printed up high on the wall of the car, and Alice read it at each stop so she knew which was coming next. Violet talked about Momo and bubble tea and the last trip she'd taken to Port Cormorant with her uncle George and aunty Helen, but Alice forgot to listen because she was so focused on the train map.

It took forty-five minutes to reach Port Cormorant, which Alice found impressive. She'd gone in the car with her father in the past and it always took at least an hour. The doctor's clinic was near the university, which meant another train trip from Central Station.

"Look, there's a bookshop," said Violet, pointing at an upper level of the station. "Let's go and—"

"Violet, we don't want to be late for our appointment. We can look at the bookshop when we get back to Central Station after we've seen the doctor."

Violet checked her phone for the time. "But we've got ages. You said the train ride to the university only takes ten minutes, which means we'll be half an hour early. That's crazy."

"I don't think it's crazy. You must account for things going wrong and delaying us, Violet. What if the train encounters mechanical problems? What if we can't find Dr. Grampian's office and have to ask for directions?"

Violet frowned. "You've got a map. You've spent ages working out how to get there. We're not going to be late. Even if one of those things happened, we'll still be on time." Alice couldn't think of an argument quickly enough, and Violet grabbed her arm and dragged her up an escalator toward the bookshop. Violet headed for the graphic novel and manga shelves, leaving Alice hovering anxiously at the front of the store. She checked her watch repeatedly, looking longingly at the platform. A train left for the university and another one pulled in.

Alice crossed to Violet, who was immersed in a book with big-eyed girls in sailor suits on the cover. "We need to go. There are only two more trains we can catch and one of them is waiting here already."

"Let's take the next one," said Violet, barely looking up.

"Violet, please." Alice heard the panic in her own voice.

Violet studied Alice's face, then sighed, replacing the book on the shelf.

"Fine."

Alice rushed Violet down the escalator to the platform and they hurried onto the train. They found seats as the doors closed and Alice breathed an inward sigh of relief. Violet had her lips pressed together as though irritated.

The train arrived at their station ten minutes later. They walked along the sidewalk, past the old gates of the university. Violet stared into the grounds at a gigantic, shady Moreton Bay fig tree, and the great sandstone library beyond it.

"Maybe we'll study here one day," she said.

"I'll be working in the funeral home," said Alice.

"But you could get a degree in something, so you've got another option."

"I don't want another option," said Alice. "I like working in the funeral home. I will go to embalming school so I can get my certificate, but that will be just a formality, because my father will teach me embalming in the next couple of years."

"You wouldn't want to do anything else?" asked Violet. "Like, history? Environmental science?" Alice was shaking her head. "Nursing? Engineering? Archaeology?" Alice hesitated on that one and Violet pounced. "You want to study archaeology?"

"I have an interest in it. But I want to work in the funeral home."

Violet adjusted her hat. "There's nothing to stop you doing an archaeology degree, *then* going to work in the funeral home."

Alice was silent, turning this idea over in her mind. She remembered she was supposed to be navigating and checked her map.

"Down here," she said, pointing to a leafy street on their left.

Within minutes, they had arrived and stood surveying Dr. Grampian's clinic. It had obviously once been an elegant home. It was designed in the Tudor style: white walls crisscrossed with dark wooden beams and a shingled roof.

"It looks like a witch's cottage," said Violet.

Alice had never seen a witch's cottage so she couldn't give an opinion. She read the shiny steel plaque that said Dr. Grampian shared his clinic with two other doctors—Dr. Reinholdt, cosmetic surgeon, and Dr. Hasluck, gastroenterologist.

"Oh good," she said. "It's useful to know a gastroenterologist in case of future poisonings, whether deliberate or from bad eggs."

Violet was looking at her phone. "I told you, Alice. We're fifteen minutes early."

"There's absolutely no harm in being early for an appointment," said Alice.

She pushed through the door into a hushed waiting room with thick white carpet. Alice couldn't help but wonder about the practicality of white carpet in a doctor's clinic. After all, gastroenterologists presumably saw chronically vomiting patients on a regular basis.

A receptionist was seated behind the counter, across the spotless room. She had a perfect blond chignon and looked like she had used the services of Dr. Reinholdt, perhaps more than once. She ran her eyes up and down the two girls, from their jeans and shirts to Alice's bumpy ponytail and Violet's hat and veil.

"We have an appointment with Dr. Grampian," said Alice.

The receptionist looked at her computer screen and made a couple of clicks.

"England and Devenish?"

"Yes."

"Take a seat, please."

Alice and Violet sat down and were made to wait for twenty minutes. At last a mother and child came out of a door and went to see the receptionist, who smiled tightly and reached for the credit card machine. Dr. Grampian stepped out of the door. His dark hair was parted and neatly combed, and he wore a pale pink shirt with pinstriped gray trousers.

He observed them with a steady gaze through black-rimmed glasses. "Miss England and Miss Devenish?"

"Yes." Alice stood up and Violet followed suit.

He indicated for them to go into his office and followed them in, closing the door.

"I'm Alice," she said to the doctor, extending her hand. He shook it gravely and turned to Violet.

"And you must be Violet." He peered at her. "You two have come quite a distance, today—all the way from Damocles Cove, is that right?"

"Yes. The train was very convenient," said Alice.

"That's good to hear. Now, I understand you have questions about allergy treatment. As you know, I can't say anything specific about George Devenish as it would be a breach of medical law. But I can answer general questions." His gaze returned to Violet. "You and your father attended my seminar in Damocles Cove a couple of weeks ago."

"How did you know that?" she said, her voice wobbling.

"There was an attendance list," he said. "And I noticed you."

Even Alice thought this sounded unnerving.

"Have you had an epiphany?" he asked, smiling.

"A what?" said Alice when Violet didn't answer.

The doctor chuckled. "*Epiphany* means a moment of enlightenment. A breakthrough. I thought Violet might have decided to seek treatment for her allergy."

Violet shrugged. "I'm not sure." She twitched her veil lower.

"We've had the overhead lighting in our offices modified," he added. "No UVB. You're welcome to remove your protective headwear if you wish."

"I'm fine," she mumbled.

He watched her for a moment longer and Violet squirmed under his gaze. Alice was put in mind of a cat watching a small lizard.

"Dr. Grampian," she said, trying to draw his attention from Violet. "If someone with a sunlight allergy comes to you, how would you treat them?"

"Well, that really depends on the severity of the case," he said, bringing his eyes back to Alice—although in some strange way he still seemed to be watching Violet. "My treatment involves identifying what causes an allergy, then helping your body tolerate the allergen—the thing you're allergic to—better. Usually that means we alter the allergen in some way to make it less dangerous."

"I remember you saying in your seminar that, for a nut allergy, you boil the nuts for a very long time to make the proteins safe."

Dr. Grampian nodded, his hair not moving a millimeter. "Correct. That way we can expose the person to a safer version of the nut in very small doses, allowing them to build up natural resistance."

Violet nudged Alice. She was staring at a lamp that sat on a bench along the wall. It had a kind of black fabric sock pulled over the shade.

"Is that the light you use to treat sunlight allergies?" Alice asked Dr. Grampian.

He got up and brought the lamp over, handing it to Violet. Violet looked at it as if it were a live venomous animal, holding it gingerly as she turned it over to inspect the head of the lamp. It appeared to be a fairly normal lamp except for the black fabric stretched over the shade.

"The fabric blocks out most of the UVB rays," he explained. "It makes the light less dangerous."

"How fast does it start to work?" Violet asked, mesmerized by the lamp. Her hand wandered toward the on/off button.

Alice leaned over and removed the lamp from Violet's hands. Something like disappointment flickered across the doctor's face.

"The patient might expect to notice some improvement after around six months," he said.

"How long before they can go out in daylight without getting sick?" Alice asked.

He clasped his hands beneath his chin. Dr. Grampian's hands were the smoothest Alice had ever seen on a man. "Well, we couldn't just send them out into the sunlight without doing some testing first."

Violet shot a look at Alice. "What about if they thought they could handle it? Like, if they'd been having the treatment for a few months and they felt like they could handle some daylight. Maybe low light…like at dawn."

The doctor's expression changed and he sat back in his chair, studying both of the girls intently. "You're talking about George?"

Violet and Alice said nothing.

Dr. Grampian answered anyway. "It would take longer than a few months of treatment to get to the point where the patient would be safe in full daylight. Low light—dawn light, is a different matter. With the treatment he'd had, I would have thought George would be safe in dawn light."

Alice stiffened and Violet's mouth dropped open. They exchanged an astonished look.

"Hang on," Violet choked out. "Are you saying he was way less allergic already? That the morning light shouldn't have killed him?"

The doctor didn't nod or shake his head. "I said precisely the same thing to the coroner, which is why I don't mind saying it to you now. It's impossible to know for sure, as we never got to do the testing, but I believed George was at the point where he would have survived exposure to low UVB light."

"Did you say that to him?" asked Alice.

It was as though he was trying to see inside her brain, his gaze was so piercing. "Are you two *looking into* George's death?"

"Yes," said Alice, knowing instinctively that he would see straight through a half truth. "Yes, we are. So, did you tell George that he would be all right if he was exposed to sunlight?"

Faint anger flickered on Dr. Grampian's tranquil face like the distant threat of a storm. "I don't recollect exactly what was said in the last few consultations with Mr. Devenish, and even if I did, our conversations were private."

Alice leaned forward. "This is important, though—don't you think? George's boss told us he was optimistic. Almost foolhardy. If you'd told him he'd be fine in daylight, maybe George decided to try it. Maybe he took your comments as permission to try it out."

"Alice," Violet whispered.

The doctor's smooth expression was replaced by a deep frown. He got to his feet.

"Firstly," he said, and his voice had turned grim, like the low rumble of approaching thunder. "George Devenish was an optimist, but certainly not foolhardy. And secondly, you ought to be very careful—very careful indeed—about what you go around saying to people. About what you *suggest* and what you *ask people*."

Not many things frightened Alice, but this shift in the mood unsettled her. Violet's gloved hand had found hers and curled around it tightly. Alice stood so that she didn't have to look up at Dr. Grampian, and Violet hastened to stand, too.

"I don't want to intrude too much on your time," Alice said to hurry the appointment toward a close.

"Then perhaps it would be a good idea if you left." His voice had become calm and pleasant again, but his eyes remained steely.

"Yes," said Alice. "Thank you for seeing us."

He nodded and held the office door for them. Violet and Alice left, heading for the clinic exit, Violet already whispering about how creepy the doctor was and no wonder her mum hated him so much. When Alice turned to close the front door properly, she risked a glance back through the clinic and saw the doctor was still standing in his office doorway, watching them leave, his expression grim and calculating.

twenty-three
A DIFFERENCE OF OPINION

THAT guy was hands down the creepiest creep I've ever met," Violet declared when they were on the train. It wasn't the first time she'd said as much.

"He was a little sinister, wasn't he?" Alice agreed.

"You shouldn't have said he caused Uncle George's death, though."

Alice whipped her head around to stare at Violet. "I didn't say that!"

"Yes, you did. You said Uncle George went out in the sun because the doctor said he could."

Alice frowned, thinking back over the conversation. "I suppose I did say that, but in no way does that suggest it was the doctor's fault."

Violet rolled her eyes. "Yes, it does. That's why he got offended."

Alice sat and thought about that for the remainder of the train ride. It made her feel uncomfortable to think she'd been so deplorably tactless—although she wasn't totally convinced she'd implied the doctor was at fault like Violet said.

They arrived in central Port Cormorant, and Violet became much brighter, talking about bubble tea and Momo again. The city was bright, crowded, and busy, with a brisk breeze blowing people's hair into their faces and making them shout to be heard. Alice rather wished they could go home. She followed Violet from the train station to a garishly colored kiosk with a great number of people lined up, and loud music pumping from a speaker. Staff in cherry-red aprons zipped from the counter to multiple drink dispensers, mixing potions in large plastic cups with straws that seemed as wide as bamboo stalks.

"What flavor do you want?" Violet asked. "I always get lychee."

"Um, lychee sounds all right."

They eventually reached the front of the line and Violet hollered their order through the noise. Alice found herself holding an enormous cup of pale-pink liquid with a layer of squishy transparent balls at the bottom. Violet ushered her away from the kiosk, maneuvering her onto the sidewalk, and leading the way, sucking concertedly on her straw.

"Do you like it?" she asked Alice.

Alice sucked on the straw, but nothing happened. She sucked harder and almost choked when a squishy sphere shot right into the back of her throat.

"I swallowed one! Are they edible?"

Violet roared with laughter. "Of course!"

"It's *very* sweet," said Alice.

"Yeah, lychee is sweet. Yummy, though. Lychee is JS's favorite flavor."

"Who?"

Violet launched into an explanation of how JS fit into Moon Squad. Alice tried to follow the story. People were walking straight at them and Violet seemed to be able to weave in and out as if she had been born and raised in a big city. A car honked right next to them, making Alice jump. Crosswalk lights flashed and clocks chimed, people spoke loudly into mobile phones and music blared from shop entrances. Alice longed for the peace of home, or even the train car.

"There it is!" Violet's eyes were shining as she gestured toward a neon-pink sign that read MOMO.

She hurried Alice up a steep set of stairs and they emerged into a shop so brightly lit that Alice couldn't help but wonder if Violet was safe, even with the veil in place. There were figurines and dolls and posters and stickers and merchandise of every description. Pop music blared through the sound system. Violet gave a little squeal and rushed over to a bench, where she immediately began flicking through a large plastic sleeve display book labeled FAN ART PRINTS. Alice sipped her sickening drink and tried to take an interest in the items in the store. However, she neither understood nor recognized anything she saw—from the resin models of anime characters to row upon row of the same CD, offered in different *editions*, which seemed to simply mean different colors.

Alice attempted to be patient, but after half an hour she had only become more agitated and desperate to go.

"Violet, do you think you'll be finished soon?"

Violet barely looked up. "Yeah, I won't be long. I just want to check out the stickers. I've got eighteen dollars and I've spent thirteen, but I can't decide between this drawing of JS as a llama or these earrings."

She looked at Alice as though for assistance with the decision. Alice looked at the llama-boy picture and the earrings, which depicted the Moon Squad logo in silver plating.

"The earrings can be worn," she said. "Or the picture could go on your wall."

Even Alice knew her advice had been next to useless, but Violet *hmm*'ed in agreement, looking from one object to the other. Alice steeled herself for another interminable wait and passed the time by sorting the store's sticker collection, which must have become disorganized after other fans like Violet had riffled through.

Another quarter of an hour passed. "Violet, do you think we could leave?"

"Already?" Violet looked a little annoyed.

"It's been forty-five minutes."

Violet sighed. "Should we take a lunch break, then come back?"

"I'd rather not come back here," said Alice. "Do you think you could finish up so we can start for home?"

"What about lunch?"

"I have sandwiches for us. We can eat at the station. Why don't you come to my place and we can go over what we learned today?" Alice watched Violet hopefully.

"Uh, no thanks." Violet seemed disgruntled. She put back the earrings and went to pay for the llama artwork and her other selections. "Come on, then," she said, heading for the stairs.

Alice followed gratefully, but Violet's mood did not improve. They came out onto the street and made their way through the crowds back to the train station. There, they stood on the platform to wait for the next train to Damocles Cove. Alice offered Violet a sandwich, but the girl just shook her head and stared down the railway line.

"Have you asked your mother the questions yet?" Alice asked.

"What?"

"The questions I gave you."

Violet seemed irritated. "No. They were weird questions. I kind of tried asking her one but she just got really mad and, like, completely interrogated me about why I wanted to know."

"Which question?" said Alice, her interest piqued.

"The one about why she thinks Dr. Grampian's treatment is so dangerous. I get the feeling Dad and her have had a lot of arguments about it."

"I see." Alice spied the train coming into the station and stepped forward to wait at the yellow line. "I wonder why she took such umbrage at that. I think we need to create a mind map," she said. "My father has some butcher's paper. I might fetch us a piece and we can create a detailed diagram of every fact and supposition we have. I expect that will help us see things more clearly."

"*You* can do a mind map," said Violet. "I'll decorate my file with my new stickers."

Alice couldn't help a vexed sideways glance as they stepped onto the train. "Violet, you really must take our efforts more seriously. How are we ever going to find out what really happened if you don't focus?"

"Focus?" Violet snapped the word. "Alice, you're *obsessed*. We only ever do stuff related to Uncle George. All I wanted was an hour in my favorite shop, but you wouldn't even let me have that! And now you want to get back and practically do schoolwork about how my uncle died." They found a seat in the car. "It's weird. And it's not fair. Sometimes I should be allowed to choose what we do. That's how friendships work."

"This isn't about friendship. This is about solving a mystery—possibly a crime. It's important, Violet."

Violet drew a sharp breath. "That's how you see it? We're just solving a mystery?"

"*Just* solving a mystery?" Alice shook her head. "It's so much more than a *just*. It's important. Vitally important. Why else would we have been spending so much time together, interviewing people and gathering information?"

"And when you solve this *mystery*," said Violet, her voice tight and strange, "then we'll just go back to how things were before? You'll have lunch on your bench near Mr. Prince's office, and we won't hang out anymore?"

Alice was puzzled. "We can if you like, but we won't need to anymore. If we find out what really happened to your uncle, there won't be any need to discuss anything. The mystery will be solved."

Violet became very quiet. Alice thought that, at last, the gravity of what they were trying to achieve had gotten through. She entertained herself for the rest of the ride by studying the railway line map and thinking about the doctor's response to her questions about George Devenish. Did the doctor have a guilty conscience? What exactly had he told George about his condition? Was Grampian the reason George had stayed out in the daylight beyond his capacity—and if so, was the doctor now trying to cover it up? Perhaps the doctor had sent that card, signed with what might be a letter G.

George, I'm sorry.

If he had given George bad advice, which had led to George making a terrible decision about his safety, then Dr. Grampian would almost certainly be feeling sorry. And worried about his reputation.

Would he sign a card with his last initial, though? People didn't really do that. His first name was Philip, and the letter certainly hadn't been a P. Alice ran through the suspects again and decided with some regret that the initial couldn't be an H, either—which put Helen out of the running. A pity, since she had already shown that she might be a poisoner. Then Alice gasped as a thought hit her. Violet looked up, startled.

"Violet!" whispered Alice. "I've just had an epiphany! *Cherry-Bomb!* That was your uncle's endearment for Helen. The letter on the card—it could have been a C."

"Why would Aunty Helen murder her own husband?" Violet replied, sounding cross. "She was crazy about him." Alice perceived that she had offended Violet with the suggestion and didn't say anything else about it. But privately she moved Helen higher up her list of possible culprits. Had she made George sick with her cooking, which had weakened him to the point where he couldn't get out of the sunlight at the pier that morning? Alice knew from experience that when being so violently ill, there was little someone could do but to surrender to the heaving and retching.

Violet had her phone in her hands and Alice noticed she was sending a text message to her mother, requesting a pickup from the train station. Alice assumed Violet didn't want to walk back to the funeral parlor after all their tramping around Port Cormorant. She was glad Violet had thought of it. Her leg was hurting a little.

However, when they got off the train and came out into the parking lot, Violet mumbled a goodbye and dashed to her mother's car where it stood in the waiting zone. She climbed in and shut the door, not looking at Alice. In the back seat, Lucas wound down his window and waved.

"Violet, are you going home now?" Alice asked through the open rear window.

"Yeah."

"I thought we were going back to my house?"

"I've got homework."

"On the school break?" Alice was astonished. What had gotten into Violet? "Can it wait? We have things to do."

"What have you got to do?" Lucas asked.

Alice hesitated, seeing Luanne listening. "We were going to, uh, see a friend's pet. He has a snake."

Lucas brightened. "Cool! I know a girl who has a pet sugar glider."

"A sugar glider!" Alice was shocked. "That's a native marsupial. Surely it's not being kept as a pet?"

"I need Violet at home, I'm sorry, Alice," Luanne broke in. "Perhaps you two can catch up later during the school break."

"I see," said Alice, crestfallen. "All right. I'll give you a call tomorrow, Violet."

Violet didn't even seem to have heard her speak. Luanne pressed a button that wound up Lucas's window and the car pulled away.

Alice started the walk home, her weak leg aching.

twenty-four
A FURRY EPIPHANY

WHAT are your plans for this fine Wednesday?" Thaddeus asked, cracking the top off his hard-boiled egg—a weekly treat.

"Don't you need me to see to a body?" Alice said, putting down the *Port Cormorant Mail*.

"Yes, but she won't be ready for you until later," he said. "I still have a bit of work to do on Miss Heffner." He sighed. "Leaky corpse."

"Oh dear," said Alice. "Is it bad?"

"Nothing that a bit of wadding and some extra plugs won't fix," he said. "But she won't be ready for you until the afternoon. Are you seeing Violet today?"

Alice shook her head, experiencing a pang. She hadn't heard from Violet for a couple of days now. Alice had called her mobile three times, and each time, it went to voice mail. She had even tried the Devenish landline. Luanne had answered and told her Violet was not at home. Alice was beginning to suspect Violet was avoiding her.

"I will probably spend a little time outside, perhaps a walk, and then do some reading," she told Thaddeus.

"There are some brass vases that need polishing," he hinted.

"I can do that," she said, although it wasn't a job she enjoyed. *Give me a corpse and an eyeliner pen over a polishing rag any day of the week*, she thought. But her father was a hard worker who did plenty of the less enjoyable tasks in the business, so Alice would do her share.

She went back to the newspaper. There was an interesting article about plans for a new aquarium to be constructed in Damocles Cove. Apparently it would allow people to stand in a transparent cave under the sea to view the amazing marine life in the area, including the protected sea dragon. It showed a photo of a scuba diver shining a special underwater lamp over a coral reef.

A few pages in, another article caught her interest. It was about Dr. Philip Grampian. His research had won a large sum of money from the government, allowing him to run a medical trial. It would give people who had serious allergies the chance to be treated for free. She would have missed this small article, wedged as it was between two much bigger stories; one about the manager of the Quay playing panpipe music to keep juvenile delinquents from hanging around—and the other, a plea for people to come forward if they knew anything about the sale of illegal pets in the coastal area. Whistleblowers would be protected, the police promised.

"I wonder if green iguanas are legal pets?" Alice said to her father. "I saw a boy with one a couple of weeks ago. Have you seen anyone with an illegal pet recently, Dad?"

"I can't say that I have," he said. "And I think iguanas *are* legal pets, as long as the owner has a special license."

She looked back at the article. "What's a whistleblower?"

"Someone who tells the truth about—or gives information regarding—crimes taking place," he said.

"Like a medical receptionist who tells on a doctor for giving bad advice to patients with serious allergies?" she suggested.

Thaddeus blinked. "Er, yes, just like that."

Alice finished her breakfast and went to tidy her room. She

found her new autunite stone in its Perspex box under the bed as she cleaned, and thought again about Violet. It made her quite despondent. Sinking onto her bed, Alice went over their conversation on the train trip home from Port Cormorant. Violet had seemed almost offended by Alice's desire to solve the puzzle of George's death. She'd never seemed bothered by it before, but now she wasn't even taking Alice's calls.

This was a vast problem, because without Violet, the truth was beyond Alice's reach. Violet was the key to Alice being able to investigate the people involved: George Devenish's loved ones and workmates—and even Dr. Grampian. Now that Alice had annoyed him, there was little chance he would speak to her again.

How could Alice solve the mystery without Violet? She tried to see a way around the problem and failed abjectly, her heart sinking even further. This was a disaster. Would she honestly be obliged to go about her day—her year—even her *life*, without ever knowing what happened to George Devenish? Without putting together the puzzle of the poor man on the end of the jetty, the loud music coming from beneath the dock, the purple light, and the rising sun?

It was almost too much to contemplate. Alice pocketed the autunite and opened the wooden box with Victoria's pendant in it. She unlatched her necklace and slipped her twin's saint charm onto it, letting it drop down to clink against her own charm. They nestled up against each other as if magnetic. She put the necklace back on, wondering why she'd never thought to do this before.

Perhaps because she'd never felt quite this lonely before. Alice abandoned tidying and went outside to get some air. The cat from next door was sitting on the fence but jumped down on the neighbor's side as soon as Alice stepped through the front door. She sighed inwardly.

Another mystery she couldn't solve: the name of the neighbor's cat.

Alice sat on the step with a defeated thud and allowed the morning sunshine to warm her skin. This was too bad. Too, too bad. She missed Violet's company. It had been pleasant to have someone to discuss things with, and to have a companion on the best bench at lunchtime. To go to a beach soiree with, or on unauthorized midnight adventures into the funeral home's filing system. Or even to go on the train to the city and spend an uncomfortable hour drinking lumpy tea and staring at incomprehensible objects in Momo. Suddenly, Alice saw the depressing truth—a double truth.

She was never going to find out what happened to George Devenish.

And she was all alone.

Tears came to her eyes and she dabbed at them wonderingly. *Crying?* She never cried. She must be having a hay-fever attack, or could it be an infection in her eyes?

A sound like *mrrp* came at her shoulder, along with gentle, warm pressure. Alice turned her head to find the cat from next door pushing itself against her. She caught her breath and blinked furiously to clear her tears. As gently and slowly as possible, she held out her hand. The cat rubbed its head on her fingers, giving another of those chirps. Alice moved her hand carefully under its chin and turned over the name tag so she could read it.

Maya.

A sense of deep comfort came over her. *Maya.* It was perfect.

"Hello, Maya," she whispered, making her hand available for the violent ear rubbing the cat now wanted.

What an excellent pet this cat would make: careful with strangers, yet affectionate with those she had come to trust. And cats were legal pets, unlike iguanas. She felt sorry for that poor iguana suddenly—being paraded along the beach on a leash when it belonged on a tropical island somewhere, foraging for hibiscus flowers. Why couldn't people be content with domesticated pets like cats and dogs?

Lily Prince's pink-nosed kitten in the pet carrier slid into her mind. She studied Maya's small black nose and thought how different this cat looked from Lily's kitten. Lily's kitten almost didn't look like a cat at all.

Alice sat up straight, which made Maya mew in disapproval, but Alice paid no attention because she was having an epiphany. She stared unseeingly at the front gate for several minutes. At the end of those few minutes, an idea had formed itself. It consisted of a pink-nosed kitten, a name written in red marker on a whiteboard, and George Devenish meeting a boat at the end of Pier 19.

Alice stood up, pausing only to give Maya a final ear rub. "Thank you, Maya. Thank you for befriending me and for your inspirational nose."

She dashed inside and ran all the way to the office, bursting through the door to the embalming room. Patty and her father turned their surprised faces her way, Patty holding a pile of cotton wadding and Thaddeus with the metal suction trocar in hand.

"Alice, we're rather in the middle of...," he began.

"Dad, do you know what *demerara* means?"

He stared. "Alice—"

"Demerara?" said Patty. "Like the sugar?"

Alice held in a gasp. "Pardon?"

Patty nodded. "Demerara's a type of sugar for baking."

"Thank you!" Alice said to Patty.

She slammed the embalming room door behind her.

Alice called Cal. His phone kept ringing so she tried Violet's mobile instead, but got the voice mail service again. She left a message to tell Violet what she was planning, then borrowed her father's mobile to send a text message to Cal. Neither of them called back.

Alice spent the afternoon doing research and fine-tuning her plan. She decided against telling her father what she wanted to do. She was fairly sure he would forbid it, and while she hated to do anything he didn't approve of, this needed to be done. She needed proof.

Alice ate her dinner and said good night as usual, but at one a.m., she crept out of bed and got dressed. She wore dark clothing and tucked her red hair into a navy-blue beanie. She collected her bag, in which she had packed a flashlight, a water bottle, and a notepad and pencil to write down anything important, such as serial numbers or license plates. Then she set off for the pier.

The night was deeply cold and dark, without any moon. She walked quickly, her breathing loud in her own ears. There were unexpected rustles in shrubs at her feet, and movements above her head in tree branches, and Alice had to reassure herself several times that these were just nocturnal creatures. Like her and Cal and Violet: different but harmless.

Closer to the pier, she switched off her flashlight in case she drew attention to herself. Pier 19 looked dark and abandoned. The gate was pulled shut, but not locked, so Alice slipped through, making as small a clanking noise as possible. She scanned the parking lot. One car. Probably the security officer on duty. There was a light on in the manager's hut farther along the wharf, and a dim red light glowed at the end of the jetty. The wind was strong and battered against her jacket and face, making her ears ache even under the beanie. Alice contemplated the area, trying to work out the best hiding spot.

Under the jetty.

She felt her way down the stone steps. At the bottom, she could smell a strong fishy odor and stepped on something that made her shoe slide. This was extremely disconcerting, but she didn't dare use the flashlight to see what she'd put her foot into. She ducked under the dock. The tide was high and there was only a little sand remaining between the waves and the first beams of the jetty. Alice crouched next to one of the pylons. From here, she had a view of the manager's hut and could see a little of what was happening overhead. Or at least hear it.

Then the waiting began.

She didn't have to wait long for movement from the manager's hut. It was only about fifteen minutes before someone came out of the door—the big, round shape of a man she hadn't seen before. He lumbered along the wharf, shining his flashlight around casually. She lost sight of him as he reached the section of the wharf that joined the jetty, but she could hear his heavy footsteps making the boards creak overhead. Through the wind, Alice thought she heard a car. She peered out toward the parking lot, where a vehicle was coming to a stop. The headlights and engine switched off.

A door slammed. Footsteps crunched across the gravel, then hit the wooden planks of the jetty over her head. Alice strained her eyes but she couldn't see anything through the boards—not in the dark.

"Top of the morning to you, Higgo," came a rumbling voice.

"Morning, Pauly."

"Cold one."

Higgo grunted agreement. "Any action?"

"Nothing. No one's crazy enough to be out in this cold." Pauly wheezed a chuckle.

"Head off, if you like," said Higgo. "I'll cover your last five minutes."

"Thanks, buddy. What are you doing on shift tonight, anyway? I thought Ashok was supposed to be doing Thursday graveyard, these days."

There was a pause. "Ashok must be sick."

"Nah, the boss switched your shifts a couple of weeks ago—I saw it on the roster."

Another pause. Higgo was trying to think of an excuse, Alice realized. "I've gotta help Petra with Harry tomorrow, so Gina switched my shifts around to give me the afternoon off."

"Right." Pauly sounded dubious.

"I'm going to get a coffee. See you around." Higgo's footsteps retreated.

Pauly lumbered off in the direction of the parking lot, and a minute later, his car started and he drove away. Alice watched Higgo go inside the manager's hut.

More waiting—this time for much longer. Higgo came out of the hut every half hour and did a patrol of the wharf and dock. Alice was horribly cold, even in her puffy jacket. The damp of the rock had seeped into the seat of her pants and her legs were icy, her sweatpants doing nothing to protect her from the wet and cold. She rubbed them to try to warm up. Her weak leg ached.

At last, when hours must have passed, she heard a distant chugging. Higgo had only just finished a patrol, so Alice ventured out from under the dock and crept up the stone steps. There were lights out on the water: green and red. A boat was coming in. Alice felt a surge of triumph that turned to panic when the manager's hut door swung open, light beaming out and illuminating the wharf. She scuttled back down the steps, half falling down the last couple—straight into a warm, black shadow.

twenty-five
THE UNRAVELING OF SECRETS

HEY, careful!" said the shadow.

"Cal!" Alice whispered. "Quick, get under the dock."

They dashed underneath and tumbled onto the sand just as Higgo reached the jetty and passed over the top of their heads. He hesitated, shining his flashlight into the cracks of the boards as if he'd heard something, and Alice caught her breath, clutching Cal's arm.

Then the flashlight beam swung away and Higgo's footsteps echoed along the timbers toward the end of the dock. A shout came from the boat, which was close against the jetty by now.

"Yeah, bring her around," Higgo shouted back.

"I got your message. What's going on?" Cal asked Alice. She was trying to hear the shouts from the boat crew and Higgo, but she paused to give Cal a pointed look.

Unfortunately the look was wasted because it was too dark for him to see it.

"I could ask *you* that question," she said. "I think you've seen something like this before. Am I right?"

Cal said nothing, but she could almost hear him reddening. It told Alice she was right. A moment of quiet peace stole over her. It was truth, she realized. The clean, perfect shape of truth.

"There, it's secure," Higgo called. "Stand clear!" There was a loud bang.

"What was that?" Cal whispered.

"A gangplank, I'd say," she said. "So they can get the cargo off the boat."

"Cargo?"

"Yes. Illegal cargo."

Alice moved closer to the action, which meant stepping into cold seawater in her sneakers—extremely unpleasant. But necessary. Through the pylons, out at the farthest part of the jetty where the boat was moored, a dull glow of mauve light had spread out on the water's surface. Alice waded in deeper until she reached the old iron ladder leading up to the jetty. She began to climb. Cal appeared at her side, hitching his long coat up out of the water.

"Alice!" he said. "Don't go up there!"

Unluckily, the moment he spoke was the exact same moment there was a lull in the noise from above.

"What was that?" came a sharp voice from above them. "Is there someone else here, Higgo?"

Alice stopped.

"Of course not," snapped Higgo. "It's four o'clock in the morning. Do you *see* anyone else?"

"I hope there's no kids under the dock again." A pause. "I'd better go take a look. We don't need a repeat of last time."

"I'll check," said Higgo, his tone impatient.

Alice dropped off the ladder with a soft *splish* and ushered Cal back under the jetty. They found a mussel-crusted pylon each to hide behind and stood mid-thigh in the freezing seawater.

For a minute or so, no one appeared and all they could hear

were the sounds from above the dock: human grunts, heavy boxes being pushed across the gangplank, the slap of water on the sides of the boat, and—occasionally—a weird snorting squeak. Then the flashlight shone from the bottom of the stone steps, bouncing over the dark water and across the wooden beams and pylons. For an agonizing moment, the light hit the pylon right in front of her, and Alice believed she was discovered. Then it jumped away and she heard Higgo crunching across the sand and back up the steps.

"All clear," he said to the man on the jetty.

"Help me with this, would you? Careful, that one's awake and it bites."

"I know that voice," Cal said softly, sounding puzzled.

There were more noises of moving things around and a peculiar high-pitched bark. Alice moved back to the ladder.

"Wait!" Cal whispered, grabbing the arm of her jacket. "Don't! They'll see you."

"I need to see what's happening," she told him firmly, and resumed climbing. Her leg felt weaker than usual, and Alice wondered what would happen if the men spotted her and gave chase. She couldn't exactly run. The two pendants chose that moment to clink together against her chest. It was as if Victoria was urging her to have courage, so she pushed herself harder to get to the top.

Once she was high enough, Alice peeped over the edge of the dock. A broad-shouldered man was heaving a large wooden crate off the boat and adding it to a stack of boxes of various shapes and sizes. Higgo was watching.

"Give me a hand, would you?" the man said roughly.

His voice *was* familiar.

Higgo shifted in the dim light. "I told you before. I don't want anything to do with this."

The man grumbled in reply but at that moment, Alice forgot to listen anymore because she had spotted something that answered all her questions.

Clipped onto the side of the boat, illuminating the dock, hung a purplish lamp. Alice fumbled in her pocket for the little Perspex box of autunite and drew it out, holding it up to the light. It immediately glowed a vivid, fluorescent green.

"Alice," Cal hissed from below her. "It's ultraviolet!"

"Yes, I see that."

"No—down here!"

Alice looked down. Gazing up at her with complete astonishment—without her veil on—was Violet.

Alice hurried down the ladder, her leg trembling. "Violet, where's your veil?"

"I couldn't see a thing in this dark—I took it off."

"Put it back on, straightaway!"

Startled, Violet sloshed backward through the water and dug in her pocket. "Why?"

"Because there's a powerful UVB light on that boat and I'm almost sure it killed your uncle."

Violet made a sound of panic and dug harder in her pocket, then gasped. "It's not in here! I must have dropped it."

"Take cover under the dock," Alice ordered. "Cal, help her find her veil. Here, take my flashlight."

Violet vanished under the dock and Cal jumped into action, wading through the dark water and shining Alice's flashlight around. Alice scrambled down, her leg aching right to the bone.

"Why is there a UV light on the boat?" Violet hissed, holding her hands up to shield her face from the purple light filtering through the cracks in the jetty.

"They use them in deep-sea diving," said Alice. "And it probably makes it harder for passersby to see what's going on."

"Found it!" Cal splashed across to them and passed a sopping hat to Violet.

She wrung it out and pulled it onto her head, squeaking as cold water dripped onto her shoulders.

"Well done, Cal," said Alice, then fell silent because another set of lights and noises had lit up the parking lot. It was a truck. It came to a halt and the headlights blinked out.

"That will be the land transport," she said, craning her neck to see.

"What is she talking about?" Violet asked Cal, who shrugged.

"Shh," said Alice. "I'll explain in a minute."

The next few minutes were a flurry of activity up above. People came onto the dock with hand trucks and rolled the crates efficiently to the vehicle. Alice, Cal, and Violet waded out of the water. They waited under the dock until the truck finally started up again and rumbled out of the parking lot gates, the headlights low. The boat was already chugging away across the cove, its purple light switched off. Now there was only silence all around and above them.

"Has everyone gone?" Violet whispered.

"I think so," said Alice.

"What about Higgo?" said Cal. "Did you see him go back to the manager's hut?"

Neither Alice nor Violet had. They waited a couple more minutes, shivering in their damp clothing. The sky had turned a metallic gray, promising the sunrise. At last they heard heavy footsteps over their heads: Higgo returning to the manager's hut. But when he was directly above them, he stopped.

Yellow light flashed through the cracks in the beams. "All right, you lot. It's safe to come out now. I think we'd better have a conversation."

twenty-six
THE TRUTH

THE manager's hut grew rapidly warm and steamy from the water evaporating off three pairs of wet pants. Higgo made them all a hot chocolate and sat down, watching them with tired, red eyes.

"All right. What are we going to do about this?" he said.

"We're going to inform the authorities," Alice said promptly.

He gave a sigh so long, it seemed to come from the bottom of his feet. "I'd prefer it if you wouldn't do that."

"Really?" Alice fixed her gaze on Higgo's miserable face. "You see, I don't think that's true. I think you'd prefer for me to tell."

He raised his eyebrows.

"I don't think you want to be doing this anymore," she went on. "I think you never liked it, but you came to feel trapped, like you couldn't get yourself out of the situation."

"You don't know a thing," he growled, making Violet sink back against Alice a little.

Alice shook her head. "You don't need to play this role of a gruff, unkind man, Higgo. I know you're a good person, deep down."

Something in Higgo's face crumbled a little, like rocks shifting.

Alice took a breath and glanced around at Higgo, Violet, and Cal. "I've recently become aware of a secret trade in exotic pets in Damocles Cove. Green iguanas, snakes, sugar gliders, monkeys, that sort of thing. Some legal, some illegal." She paused to observe Higgo's reaction, but he said nothing. "It occurred to me that a boat would be a good way to smuggle exotic animals into the area. Some of the animals are coming from overseas, you see, and others are caught by divers in the ocean. But of course, there are pier security officers checking all the boats to make sure that the species and number of fish being caught is correct, or to make sure any imported animals are permitted. And if the security officers were doing their job, exotic pets wouldn't be getting through the wharf." She paused. "But I also remembered that people can be bribed."

She checked Higgo's face again. His gaze had dropped to his coffee, and his hand was clutching the cup so hard she was a little concerned he might tip it onto himself.

Alice turned to Cal. "Like you."

He jumped slightly. "Huh?"

"You were bribed, weren't you? You saw something and you were bribed to stay quiet about it."

Cal went red, then white. He dropped his eyes to his damp jeans.

"Cal?" she said gently. "Cal, please think about the greater good. Think about a man who died here, trying to do the right thing."

Cal was casting his eyes around the tiny office as if he could find the answer there. "Fine!" he burst out. "Okay, *yes*, I was bribed!"

He turned his face away. That odd stillness settled upon Alice again: *the truth.*

"Thank you, Cal. That proves to me what a good person you are, no matter what anyone else says. Now, will you tell me what it was you saw that you were supposed to keep quiet about?"

"They'll take Ziggy away," he mumbled.

"Yes, but this is bigger than Ziggy. You know that."

Cal heaved a sigh, but nodded and turned back to face them.

"I didn't actually see anyone do anything wrong, okay? I mean, if I saw someone doing something illegal, I would've said. What I saw seemed kinda unimportant, but she said *we* would be the ones who got into trouble if I told anyone. Me and Tess and Gav and Amy. She said we'd all be in big trouble if the cops thought we were around that morning."

"Who said?" Alice asked.

"Gina Prince," Cal said miserably. "She came by my place the next day, when Mum was at work, and gave me a new charger for the one I lost. She said I shouldn't say anything that might get me into trouble—that if anyone knew I was there that morning when George died, the cops'd think I was involved somehow. Then she said her daughter had a pet sugar glider and she could get me one if I wanted, since I was mature enough not to go talking to anyone about what I saw. I said no thanks, I was more into snakes and reptiles, and she said she could get me a python. And I said okay because, y'know, I've wanted a snake forever. And like I told you, I didn't see anyone doing anything wrong. I swear, I wouldn't have accepted the snake if I'd seen, you know—a murder or something. But I looked it up in the news, and George died of natural causes, so I knew it was okay, and I took the snake." He looked at Alice and Violet pleadingly.

"I understand," said Alice, and Cal sagged with relief.

"Aunty Gina," Violet said wonderingly. "Why would she bribe you? What was it you saw?"

Cal tipped his head toward Higgo. "Him. I saw him."

Violet's mouth hung ajar. "Aunty Gina was keeping you quiet about seeing Higgo? Why?"

"Yes, why, Higgo?" said Alice. "Explain your presence at the pier that morning."

Violet was gazing hard at him. "Hang on—did you leave a card at Uncle George's funeral that said 'I'm sorry,' and was signed only with an *L*? Was that you, *Leonard*? Why did you apologize? Did you have something to do with his death?"

"No! I mean, yes, I left the card, but I had nothing to do with…"

"I thought it was Helen for a while," said Alice. "I wasn't sure if the card had been signed with a *C* or an *L*. I thought she'd written the card and signed it *C* for *Cherry-Bomb*—George's nickname for her. And I thought she'd poisoned me and Violet with tea tree oil in some brownies because we were getting too close to the truth. But now I realize we simply had a virus—or Helen needs to store her eggs at a colder temperature."

"I sent the card to say I was sorry he died, that's all," said Higgo.

"Or were you sorry that it had happened when you should have been on duty?" Alice watched him carefully. "It was the purple light on the boat, wasn't it? It set off George's allergic reaction when the boat came in. He didn't wear protective gear at night and he didn't realize they had a powerful UVB light for underwater diving hooked up on the boat. When they switched it on, he had an allergic reaction."

Violet gasped and spun back to Higgo. "And you just let him die?"

Higgo shook his head wildly. "No! I wouldn't do that. No one realized he was having an allergic reaction until it was too late. By the time I got there it was all over. He was—gone."

"Then Aunty Gina bribed Cal to keep quiet about you being there," Violet said slowly.

"But Gina wasn't trying to protect *Higgo*, I don't think," Alice told Violet. "She was trying to protect herself and the illegal pet business running out of Pier 19."

Violet sat up straight. "Uncle George couldn't have known about the illegal animals. There's no way he would have been part of it."

"No, he wouldn't, would he?" said Alice. "George believed it was his duty to stand between his country and any illegal fishing or smuggling at the pier. There was no amount of money he could have been paid to pretend not to see such crimes."

A tear had formed in Higgo's left eye and it broke the bank of his eyelid, dribbling down his cheek. One from the other eye soon followed, then he wiped both away with a hasty hand.

"He was simply in the wrong place at the wrong time, wasn't he, Higgo?" said Alice. "He wasn't supposed to be working that night, when one of the boats full of illegal animals was coming into port. *You* were."

Higgo's gaze remained locked on his coffee.

"It wasn't your regular night," Alice went on. "Ashok or one of the others normally took the graveyard shift on Monday mornings. But Gina had rostered you on, because a *special* cargo was coming in, wasn't it? Just like this morning. A live cargo of exotic animals—and Gina needed to be sure the *right* security officer was there to let them through. Only, you got sick—so sick you could barely think or move. I suspect you had eaten some of Helen Devenish's baking—but that's another matter. You were so sick you weren't even able to get out of bed to let Gina know you couldn't go to work. Your wife arranged for George to cover your shift." Alice dipped her head to try to catch Higgo's eye. "Your wife didn't know what was going on. And George didn't know either, did he? They didn't know you were being paid sums of cash to let the boats through with their crates of illegal pets."

Higgo glanced at Alice's face and she saw all his desperation and despair.

"But you started to feel better, didn't you?" she went on, her voice quiet and steady. "You recovered from your sickness and realized you had missed most of your shift. You wife told you George was covering for you, and you panicked. You knew there was a boatload of animals coming in and if George found out what was on board, the whole operation would be exposed. So you rushed down to Pier 19—only when you got there, it was too late. The boat had arrived and George was dead."

Higgo's chin trembled.

"What was on board?" she asked softly.

He wouldn't reply. His jaw was working, and he steadfastly refused to meet Alice's gaze. He licked his lips and opened his mouth, then closed it again.

"Was it a marine species?" Alice was almost whispering. "A protected species they had caught to sell as pets? Was it starfish? Octopuses?"

His shoulders had been gradually dropping. Higgo looked like a much smaller man.

"Listen," said Alice. "You're not going to get away with this. There are witnesses. Cal has told me the truth—he saw you there at the dock, well before the police came that morning. And then Gina tried to bribe him." She paused. "But I also know about your son, Harry, and his condition. I know it must take a lot of money to give him what he needs."

"Don't talk about my son," Higgo managed, but it lacked fight.

"Listen to me," she said. "I still think you're a good man. You've made mistakes, but I suspect you were in a desperate position. So I want to make a suggestion. I think you should be a whistleblower."

Violet and Cal stared blankly, so Alice explained.

"I believe Higgo should speak to the police about what Gina's been doing here—Gina and whoever she's working with. It's called whistleblowing. It means he won't get into as much trouble as if the police caught him."

"I'll still get into trouble," Higgo said, his voice flat.

"Yes," said Alice. "But not as much. And more importantly, you will be doing the right thing. By the animals. By your country. And by George."

⚜

The three walked through the rising daylight without speaking for a long time.

"I know who Gina's working with," Cal said suddenly. "I recognized his voice before when he was unloading the boat. It was Mr. Prince."

"Oh yes," said Alice.

"Our principal?" Violet squeaked.

"Yep. They're in it together—old Prince and his wife."

Violet shook her head. "I can't believe Aunty Gina has been doing this." She paused. "Well, actually, maybe I can. She's always been kind of obsessed with money and presents. And Lily's got that sugar glider. But I can't believe she'd cover up Uncle George dying. She's going to be in big trouble, isn't she?"

Alice nodded. "She may go to jail."

"I guess I'm going to lose Ziggy over all this," Cal said with a sigh.

"Are Stimson's pythons legal pets?" Alice asked.

Cal gave a weak laugh. "Yeah. They sell them in pet shops all over."

"Well, that's something. Perhaps one day you'll save up enough to get another."

"What were you doing under the dock that night?" Violet asked Cal. "What exactly did you see?"

Cal explained how they'd been having a party for Amy's birthday. They had music and Cal's disco light and balloons. George had been working earlier in the night. He gave Cal and his friends a couple of warnings, but they'd ignored him, knowing he never did anything serious about it. Cal knew Ashok did the graveyard shift on Mondays, so he was surprised to see George again in the early morning. When it got to about five thirty a.m., George yelled at them through the jetty boards, ordering them to leave. This time they could tell he meant it.

They gathered their gear and left, but when they'd walked a way along the beach, Cal looked back and saw his disco light still flashing under the dock. No one wanted to walk back with him, so Cal went to get it by himself. The sun was coming up, and as he drew closer, Cal could hear an argument up on the jetty. He also heard an engine chugging and chains clanking, as if a fishing boat were being unloaded.

Cal collected his disco light but the charger was positioned high on top of a post and the cable had slipped out. Cal had to climb up to reach it, then a bright flashlight was suddenly shining down into his face.

"I couldn't see for a second," he said. "Then the light switched off and I realized it was Higgo. He kind of growled, *'Get out of here!'* Like he was super mad at me, and I just grabbed my disco light and ran for it! I didn't even worry about the charger, I was just out of there. I went home and got into bed and slept all day."

"And Gina came to see you the next day?" said Alice.

"Yeah, she brought me a new charger and offered me the snake to stay quiet." He looked glum. "I didn't get it, not gonna lie. I mean, I knew I might get into trouble if I said I was at the pier that morning, with George dying and everything. And I knew she was being nice to me and giving me stuff, but it didn't really click until she came around to my place with the tank and the gear and Ziggy. She said I could keep him if I kept my mouth shut. And then I got to know Zig and he's such a cool little dude. I didn't wanna give him up after that. So I had to keep the secret."

"I'm sorry you had to go through this, Cal," said Alice.

"Yeah." Cal shoved his hands into his pockets. "I know I should never have accepted Ziggy. I'm gonna miss him, that's all."

❧

Alice got home, took off her wet clothes, and took a warm shower. When she finished, her father was awake and fetching the newspapers off the front doorstep. Alice made them both a cup of tea and explained what she and Violet and Cal had discovered during the night. She left out some of the more perilous moments, knowing her father would find them worrying.

As it was, he found the whole thing extremely worrying anyway. He wasn't at all pleased to discover that Alice had crept out of the house and gone to seek evidence of serious crimes being committed at the pier. Alice was obliged to promise that she would never deliberately put herself in such danger again.

When he'd calmed down—Alice made him a second cup of tea, this time with chamomile—he went back over the story again.

"Well, Alice," he said with an exhalation of breath. "How will you prove any of this?"

"I very much hope that Higgo will become a whistleblower on the illegal pet trade. He might not get a conviction if he speaks out against the animal smugglers."

"And is he likely to blow the whistle?"

Alice shrugged. "If he doesn't, I'll have to turn him in—although I don't like the idea of it. Higgo has a little boy who has a disease and needs expensive treatment. He seems like a nice man who's been led astray by temptation—and possibly threatened by his boss. But the law's the law, and if I must hand him over to the authorities, I will."

Thaddeus sipped his tea thoughtfully. "This is all very intriguing. How did you work it out?"

"Well, there have been various news articles over the past few weeks about exotic pets and invasive species. A woman who saw a monkey in her garden. The discovery of an introduced frog species."

"Yes, that's right. And you were asking whether it was legal to keep iguanas as pets."

"I saw, with my own eyes, a boy walking his iguana at the beach. But what clinched it was Violet's little brother mentioning that his friend had a pet sugar glider. I'd seen Gina's daughter with an odd-looking kitten on more than one occasion, and she and Lucas are friends. When Patty said the animal's name, Demerara, was a type of sugar, I realized it must be a sugar glider. Then I thought about Cal getting that python, even though he couldn't afford to buy such a pet. It seemed there were exotic pets popping up all around us. It made me wonder if this underground pet trade might be very close—even right under our noses."

"How long are you going to give Higgo?" Thaddeus said. "He might decide not to blow the whistle and try to get rid of any evidence."

"There's only so much he can get rid of," she answered. "The evidence is everywhere in Damocles Cove—there are already a number of exotic pets around. And there are witnesses now, remember? Violet and Cal and I witnessed a boat bringing the cargo in this morning. I've told Higgo he has a day to step forward as a whistleblower before I speak to the police myself." Alice smiled at her father. "I think I've taken the right approach."

Thaddeus couldn't quite smile in return just yet, but he nodded. "I think, Alice, that you probably have."

✤

When her father went to meet a client, Alice sat out on the front step, hoping the cat would visit her again. From her vantage point, she could see Maya perched on the neighbor's mailbox. She made a smacking sound with her lips to get the cat's attention. Maya turned her head and made the *mrrp* noise back, then stood up and stretched. She began the languorous walk along the top of the fence toward Alice, but the thud of a car door startled her, causing her to leap down and dash under the camellia bush. Alice looked up at the culprit. There was a white car parked outside their house and Gina Prince was standing beside it.

Alice got to her feet as Gina came through the front gate, her eyes fixed on Alice the whole time.

"Hello, Ms. Prince."

"Hello, Alice." Gina's smile was bright and friendly, but her eyes didn't match. "I thought I'd better check in with you. I'm a little concerned you haven't taken my advice."

Alice watched her cautiously. "Your advice?"

"To stay away from those dock kids, remember?"

"Ah yes. But I'm not sure your advice was given in the spirit of genuine concern for me." Alice raised a hand to halt Gina's protest. "And I should point out that invasive species can cause major ecological issues."

Gina's brow creased. "What did you say?"

"Green iguanas. They don't belong here. They'll prey on our native wildlife and compete with our own reptiles. They may even carry diseases. And native animals like sugar gliders don't belong in kitty carriers or houses. They're wild creatures and they deserve to live in their natural habitats. They're pollinators, not pets."

"Sugar gliders are sold as pets all over the world," said Gina.

"That doesn't make it right," said Alice. "And they're not legal pets in this state. And what about monkeys? Someone's pet monkey has escaped, you know. A local woman spotted it in her garden."

"I don't know what you're talking about, child."

"I think you do. The laws are there for a reason, Ms. Prince. The selling and importing of animals is controlled for a *reason*. Those laws protect animals, and they protect our natural ecosystems. You know about cane toads, don't you? Rabbits? Red deer? Japanese sea stars?"

"That's enough," Gina barked. "I haven't imported anything *illegal*. All my pets are perfectly legal. As long as the owner has the correct license, they can buy any pet they like."

"I'm sorry, but I don't think that's true," Alice replied. "I don't see how it *can* be true. The only legal pet I know you've handled is a Stimson's python—the one you gave to Cal to keep him quiet about seeing Higgo at the wharf." Alice straightened her shoulders and gave Gina a stern look. "And it was unkind of you to spread those rumors, saying George was reckless about his allergy. Very unfair. He was careful. Yes, he was optimistic, but not irresponsible. You wanted everyone to think George was taking risks with his allergy, but you only said it to throw us off the scent of your illegal activities." The last few pieces clicked together in Alice's mind. "You knew Violet and I were starting to work it out, didn't you? That's why you said mean things about Cal and tried to get our parents to keep us away from the pier. And you were probably the one who locked us into that sea container, too—weren't you? To scare us away from the pier? That was also extremely unkind. There was a rat in there with us, you know—possibly large and aggressive. Violet was terrified."

Gina's eyes had narrowed. She observed Alice for a long moment.

"All right," she said at last. "What is it you want?"

"Pardon?"

"What do you *want*?" Gina hissed, taking a step closer. "Money?" Alice shook her head.

"What, then? Vouchers? A new phone?" Gina moved nearer again. "A pet of your own? You should try adopting one of our little sugar gliders—then you'll find out how lovely they are. Lily adores hers." When Alice shook her head again, Gina sneered as though she found Alice disgusting, as though Alice was the one doing something underhanded and ruthless. "What, then?" she snarled. "*What do you want?*"

Alice's heart was thudding. "Only the truth," she said.

Gina froze. "The truth?"

"I just wanted to know the truth. And now that I know it, I want others to know it too."

Gina closed in on Alice and seized her arm. "I have a lot of connections." Her voice was low and barbed. "Business connections." She glanced at the old England's Funeral Parlor plaque on the wall behind Alice. "There are a lot of people who would support me if I were to start saying how *substandard* your dad's business is. I could make it so that, in hardly any time at all, no one in Damocles Cove would even dream of using this funeral home."

Alice stared. Was this true? Did Gina have the connections to ruin Tranquility Funerals?

The woman's grip grew tighter. "I've got an idea," Gina whispered into Alice's face, so close that Alice could smell her mouthwash. "How about you stop making your ridiculous accusations and pretending to be a little eco warrior, and shut up? How about you shut up *now* before I make sure your father is ruined?" Gina shook her by the arm. "Well?"

"Aunty Gina—let her go."

It was Violet's voice. Gina dropped Alice's arm so quickly that Alice wobbled, and thought for a moment she might slide to the ground. She peered around Gina and saw Violet and Cal there beside her mailbox. Violet began to open the gate, but Cal didn't wait for that—he swung himself over the low fence and was at Alice's side in an instant. Violet joined them, glaring at Gina.

"Are you okay, Alice?" she asked.

"Of course she is!" Gina's voice had become jolly. "She's fine, aren't you, sweetie?" She laughed, but neither Cal nor Violet smiled.

"Are you okay?" Violet asked Alice again.

"I'd like her to leave," said Alice.

Violet and Cal both looked at Gina, whose smile fell away.

"Goodness, I can take a hint!" She turned and swished down the path in her long skirt, leaving the gate open in her hurry. The three watched in silence until Gina had climbed into her car and pulled away.

"Let's go inside," said Alice. "I think I might benefit from a strong cup of tea."

⚜

Alice took some sweet things from the Tranquility Funerals refreshment cupboard. Patty arrived to prepare the funeral spread and protested when she saw them snacking on the business supplies, but Alice explained that the circumstances called for it.

"I'm glad you two arrived when you did," she told Violet and Cal as soon as Patty had left them alone. "Your timing was impeccable."

"Was Gina going to kidnap you, do you think?" Cal's eyes were wide.

"I don't think so. But I didn't like being grabbed like that."

"Aunty Gina was smuggling in sea dragons the day Uncle George died." Violet selected a chocolate chip cookie. "Higgo went to see Aunty Helen and told her everything."

"Sea dragons!" Alice repeated, and a little knell of triumph resounded inside her head. "I thought it must be a marine species of some sort. That's why they had that UV diving lamp."

"Tell her how much sea dragons sell for, Ultra," Cal urged Violet, his mouth full of cookie. He hadn't stopped eating from the moment they'd opened the first packet.

"Guess," Violet said to Alice.

Alice had little patience for guessing games but knew it must be a significant sum. "It must be more than a thousand," she said. "Perhaps even several thousand. They're protected, after all, and why else would the Princes go to such an effort to smuggle them in?"

"Ten to twenty *thousand* dollars per sea dragon," Violet said solemnly, and Alice blinked in shock. "That explains Aunty Gina's awesome birthday presents, huh?"

"Does she know about Higgo blowing the whistle on their illegal pet business?" asked Alice.

"Yeah, that's why she came here. She's running around trying to shut everyone up, offering people things to stay quiet."

"She said she could ruin Tranquility Funerals," Alice said, the fear of that moment hitting her again. "That she could say bad things about us and people would stop using our business."

Cal snorted. "Who's going to listen to a criminal?" This was true. Alice felt better.

"I just feel sorry for her kid," added Cal.

"Yeah," said Violet, her face softening. "Poor Lily."

Alice contemplated another cookie. Surely her father would

understand, under the circumstances. "Has Higgo already been to the police?" she asked.

"Yes, he went to the cops after he saw Aunty Helen this morning. He wanted her to hear it from him before he turned himself in. She came straight over to our place and told us. When Higgo found Uncle George that morning, he panicked and called Gina. She came down and swapped the CCTV footage for a different night's, then went back home to pretend she was nowhere near the pier. Uncle George had been sitting there, dead for about an *hour* before they called the ambulance." Violet sounded quite upset, and Alice wasn't surprised. She lay a sympathetic hand on Violet's arm, who gave her a wobbly smile.

"What'll happen now?" Cal asked.

Recovering, Violet shrugged. "Higgo's getting an immunity deal from the cops. He told them what he knows and they're going to raid Aunty Gina's place and a few other houses."

"I suspect he'll have to find a new job, but at least he won't get convicted of a crime," said Alice.

"I don't know if he should get off scot-free," said Violet, picking a chocolate chip out of her cookie and nibbling it. "He betrayed Uncle George."

"He did," said Alice, and left it at that. Inwardly, she was rather glad Higgo would not be prosecuted alongside Gina. She thought he had suffered enough. "You might be called as a witness, Cal," she added.

Cal brightened. "You reckon? That'd be cool. I almost can't believe this really happened. Nothing interesting ever happens in Damocles Cove, and now I find out there were bad guys selling illegal animals right in front of us at Pier 19. The number of times we had parties under that dock!" He puffed out a long, expressive breath.

"How did you know, Alice?" Violet asked. "You *knew* there were other people around when Uncle George died. How did you—how *could* you know that?"

Cal turned to watch her as well, and she found herself the object of significant unwanted attention. She automatically touched the pendants on her necklace.

"I—I have strong intuitions about dead people sometimes," she said.

They were silent, digesting her words.

"Maybe that's because you spend so much time around them." Cal's voice was hushed with awe.

"I wonder if Uncle George *needed* someone to know how he really died," Violet said, her tone soft. Cal gave a visible shudder. "Somehow he got you to investigate and find out the truth."

The silence went on even longer, and Alice was beginning to think she would have to create a diversion, when Cal suddenly smiled and gave Violet a knowing look.

"Hey, don't forget—she's the Zombie Queen," he said.

twenty-seven
AN UNVEILING

ALICE and her father took their time perusing the newspapers the next morning. There was a feature in the *Coastal Chronicle* about the exposure of the illegal pet industry. It ran over two pages and included a large photograph of Mr. Prince and Gina, with the headline EXOTIC PET EMPIRE, which Alice thought gave them a pomp and circumstance that was quite undeserved. The photo was taken outside the Prince home, where Gina and their principal were being led away by police.

There were other photos, too: marmosets, iguanas, parrots, hedgehogs, and a tank full of sea dragons. An environmental scientist had given his opinion that it would only take a couple of people to accidentally let their exotic pets go and "These sorts of species could breed rapidly, and soon we would see huge populations forcing our native animals into extinction." Another scientist, a specialist in sea dragons, had added that if people like the Princes regularly took that number from the sea, the species would become extinct within a couple of years.

Alice's cornflakes had gone soggy while she read. She tipped them out and made herself a piece of toast with peanut butter, sneaking a little honey onto it while her father was busy reading.

"Are you still on good terms with Violet?" Thaddeus asked

suddenly. "I've heard you leaving messages for her over the past few days and wondered if something had gone awry."

"Yes, we had a bit of a falling out," said Alice. "But it's resolved itself."

"I like to see you having a friend."

"Thanks," said Alice. "She's a good friend—loyal and trustworthy. So is Cal."

"Are you going to see them again soon?" Thaddeus asked, sipping his tea.

"Actually, I was going to ask you if I can go to the Quay with them tonight. Would that be all right?"

"It's school break, so I have no objection," he said. "I'll give you a ride, if you like." Thaddeus assumed the look that meant a major pun was coming. "I'd like to make a *toast* to good friends," he said, lifting his grainy toast high. "They are indeed the *quay* to our happiness."

Alice spent much of her day designing a logo for the time in the distant future when she would change the name of Tranquility Funerals back to England's Funeral Parlor. She wondered if it would be too macabre to include a skull in the new logo. Skulls represented death, and she saw no reason why anyone would try to argue that death was an inappropriate theme for a funeral home. The other local funeral businesses all used flowers or birds in their logos, and Alice found that rather predictable. Yes, a skull would be fitting—and memorable. She applied colored pencil and held her design up for a critical look. It was tastefully done, she decided, and it looked so venerable in that sepia tone.

At the Quay, the first surprise was that Cal still had his python. He was wearing the snake over his arm, and a grin as wide as his face.

"The cops said I'd probably be allowed to keep him," he said.

"Stimson's are legal and you don't need a license. There's still a chance I'll have to give him up, if they need him for evidence or whatever, but they'll most likely give him back at the end. Isn't that right, Zig?" he asked the python, who flicked its tongue in answer.

"That is wonderful news," Alice said. "They probably recognized what a good snake owner you are and knew they needn't rehome him."

Cal looked highly flattered by this remark. He unraveled the snake and moved it onto his other arm. "Not so tight, Zig," he said. "He squeezes hard, sometimes, for such a small guy!"

"They're strong," Alice confirmed. "They have more than ten thousand muscles, did you know? Even tiny snakes."

"Wow, really?" He stared at Ziggy with renewed admiration. "Mum's struck a deal with me. She'll cover the cost of his food if I get myself to school on time at least four days out of five." He grinned at Alice. "At least Mr. Prince will be gone. Did you hear that Ms. Goodwill's taking his job until they get a replacement? She always goes easy on me—although she keeps asking me to join the Board Games club." He gave a slight eye roll.

"Should we get some chips and fish?" Violet asked.

"I'm broke," said Cal.

"We'll get some extra for you," said Alice.

The second surprise was when they sat on the little beach with their chips and Violet removed her hat and veil.

"Violet!" Alice exclaimed. "What about the lights?"

Violet looked unconcerned, although she went a little pink in the cheeks. It couldn't be an allergic reaction, though, because it faded almost straightaway.

"I called the Quay management office before we came and asked them what sort of light bulbs they use to light the beach. The facilities manager knew. They don't contain UVB so they should be fine. I have my EpiPen, just in case."

"This seems like a big change," said Alice. Cal was already tearing paper away to get at the chips. "Won't your mother overreact?"

"Mum and I sorted a few things out," said Violet.

She ate some chips. Alice thought Violet didn't want to say anymore and she was still trying to decide whether it was tactless to ask when Violet rushed to speak.

"Aunty Helen came over last night and told Mum and Dad the truth about donating Uncle George's body to the university. She and Mum had a huge fight about it. I heard the whole thing. But Dad took Aunty Helen's side. He said Mum was suffocating us by protecting us too much, and she needed to let us *own* our allergies. He wants to start treatment with Dr. Grampian, and reckons she should let me and Lucas make up our minds if we want to get treatment, too. He said that we're like prisoners, and the precautions she makes us take are over-the-top." Violet paused and caught Alice's eye. "You know what else? Dad told me that when I started at Damocles Cove High, the school actually arranged to change all the light bulbs to the safe kind—but Mum never told me. So, in some of the classrooms—like the drama room and cooking room, and some of the science labs, the ones without windows, I don't even need to wear my gear. But Mum hid it from me because she didn't want me to do it."

"That's crossing a line," said Cal, his mouth full of chips.

She nodded. "I've told her *I'm* in charge of what I wear and how I manage my allergy from now on."

Alice was quite astonished by this change in Violet. "What did she say?"

"She walked out," said Violet. "Dropped everything and walked out. We were worried for a while, but she came back a few hours later and agreed we could make more decisions for ourselves. She and Dad have been all huggy and kissy ever since. It's disgusting."

"So, will *you* see Dr. Grampian for treatment?" asked Alice, rescuing herself a few chips before Cal finished them all. "Will you try to get into that medical trial he's running?"

"Dad told me about that, but I don't know," said Violet. "Grampian's a bit creepy. But I'll think about it. It would be nice to be free—free to walk in the sunlight, or whatever. But it's also nice just to be free to make my own decisions for a change. You know?"

Alice did know. Violet had such fortitude, to tolerate a life in shadow, hampered by sleeves and veils and trouser legs and long socks; to face her mortality every time the sun came up. Alice was deeply proud that Violet had chosen her as a companion. Her heart swelled with admiration for a few moments, and she didn't know how to express what she was feeling. She leaned down and picked up a perfectly round, smooth mauve pebble, and placed it in her pocket.

Violet shot her a grin. "For your collection?"

"I don't have a collection."

"Do you two do this mystery-solving thing much?" said Cal.

"Pardon?" said Alice.

"You know. Going around as Zombie Queen and Ultraviolet. Discovering something weird about a death and teaming up to go on adventures and solve crimes."

Alice and Violet smiled at each other. "Maybe," said Violet. "Why?"

He stared at the water, twisting his mouth shyly. "I just thought, y'know, you might need a third team member."

"The Dark Gamer?" Violet suggested with a smirk. "Nocturnio?"

"Shut up." Cal was grinning.

"I, for one, would very much like to do this again," said Alice.

Violet glanced at her sharply. "You would?"

"Yes, I like solving puzzles."

Violet fidgeted with the chip paper. "And what about teaming up—with me and Cal?"

Alice didn't hesitate. "Yes," she said. "That, too."